Dear Reader,

Home, family, community and love. These are the values we cherish most in our lives—the ideals that ground us, comfort us, move us. They certainly provide the perfect inspiration around which to build a romance collection that will touch the heart.

And so we are thrilled to offer you the Harlequin Heartwarming series. Each of these special stories is a wholesome, heartfelt romance imbued with the traditional values so important to you. They are books you can share proudly with friends and family. And the authors featured in this collection are some of the most talented storytellers writing today, including favorites such as Roz Denny Fox, Amy Knupp and Mary Anne Wilson. We've selected these stories especially for you based on their overriding qualities of emotion and tenderness, and they center around your favorite themes—children, weddings, second chances, the reunion of families, the quest to find a true home and, of course, sweet romance.

So curl up in your favorite chair, relax and prepare for a heartwarming reading experience!

Sincerely,

The Editors

ROZ DENNY FOX

Roz saw her first book, *Red Hot Pepper*, published by
Harlequin Books in February 1990. She's written for
several Harlequin series, as well as online serials and
special projects. Besides being a writer, Roz has worked
as a medical secretary and as an administrative assistant
in both an elementary school and a community college.
Part of her love for writing came from moving around with
her husband during his tenure in the Marine Corps and
as a telephone engineer. The richness of settings and the
diversity of friendships she experienced continue to make
their way into her stories. Roz enjoys corresponding with
readers either via email, rdfox@cox.net, or by mail
(7739 E. Broadway Blvd #101, Tucson, AZ 85710-3941). You
can also check her website, www.Korynna.com/RozFox.

HARLEQUIN HEARTWARMING

Roz Denny Fox

The Boss Next Door

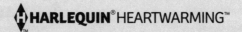

Recycling programs
for this product may
not exist in your area.

ISBN-13: 978-0-373-36616-3

THE BOSS NEXT DOOR

Copyright © 2013 by Rosaline Fox

Originally published as HAVING IT ALL
Copyright © 1998 by Rosaline Fox

Printed in U.S.A.

The Boss Next Door

CHAPTER ONE

SHERRY CAMPBELL pirouetted in front of her sleepy roommate, seeking an opinion on her new appearance. She'd undergone a total makeover since returning home from a summer spent trekking on the historic Santa Fe Trail. The pioneer-wagon-train reenactment had left her tanned and trim—a plus, but not her main objective. She'd battled heat, flood and tornadoes to prove a point to male colleagues at her Columbia, Missouri, college. Namely, that modern women were as tough and capable as their pioneer sisters. With help from a few well-chosen friends, she'd fulfilled that mission.

For all the good it had done. Women still had to validate their worth on her campus. Which was why she'd metamorphosed into this stranger—to convince a board of stuffy regents and an administrative interview team that she was capable of replacing the current dean of Human Services. The dean was in charge of Women's Studies, student counseling and the Hub, the women's crisis center that was Sherry's pet project. All the deans at Wellmont College were men. Always had been and, according to some, always would be.

She had a chance to change that.

Allowing herself a small determined smile, Sherry smoothed the navy pin-striped power suit over her flat stomach. "I look so…so buttoned down, Yvette, they'll *have* to sit up and take notice. This is the image they court. I'm not giving them one reason to pass me over for some Ivy Leaguer."

Yvette Miller, the person who'd engineered Sherry's recent transformation, yawned. "I don't pretend to understand what's going on inside your head. You look nothing like your old self."

She and Yvette rarely saw eye to eye anymore, Sherry realized. "I thought I explained that my goal is to blend in with the good old boys," she said, tugging at her short, short hair. Gone were her shoulder-length brunette locks, replaced by a sleek, gold-tipped cap barely two inches long, except for a slight dip over her forehead, where Yvette's beautician friend had left a bit of a wave.

Sherry fingered the discreet gold stud embedded in one earlobe. Already she missed the art-deco earrings that were practically her trademark around campus. Those, and her favorite Mickey Mouse watch. "These suit sleeves would have hidden Mickey. I feel positively naked without him."

"Mickey is funky. That Ironman Timex is what a man would wear."

"You're right." Sherry sighed. "I really hope I'm not a token woman being trotted out to show the community that our administration's open-minded. Rumor has it that of the three final candidates, only one's a woman. *Moi!* And there's a man of color. All very politically correct," she said.

"Still no poop on number three?"

"Nothing, other than that candidate three is also a man. Surprise, surprise."

"Have you asked Nolan? Maybe your business is like mine. In the clothing industry men always have a better pipeline to the top than women do."

"My brother is so mired in his and Emily's wedding plans his pipeline isn't even attached."

"How can you not applaud his wholehearted commitment to Emily and her two kids?" Yvette asked dreamily. "I'd like for some good-looking guy to pay off my debts and whisk me away on a white charger."

"Nolan doesn't have a white charger. He drives a compact. When did you hop on the marital bandwagon? I distinctly remember you saying, 'Another good woman bites the dust,' when you heard their joyous news."

"Well, it's just so romantic. He asked me to find Emily a designer wedding gown regardless of price, because she got shortchanged in her first marriage to that shyster land developer. Nolan wants Emily's wedding at Thanksgiving to be perfect. All women dream of having a perfect wedding. A perfect marriage."

"Mm." Sherry didn't say the obvious—that a perfect wedding wasn't any guarantee of a perfect marriage. Not only that, she didn't want to admit that she still wasn't sure how she felt about her only sibling marrying her best friend. She wanted to be happy for them, she really did. But what would happen when their bubble popped? And it would. Didn't she work every day with the grim statistics? One in three marriages broke up.

"In college, Sherry, who wore out the bride magazines every month planning our storybook weddings?"

"Back then we were naive enough to think marriage was the be-all and end-all in a woman's life, Yvette. The reality is that few marriages have storybook endings."

"Wait and see. I'll find Mr. Right. You don't even appreciate handsome men anymore. It'd do you good to go with us girls and sigh over some good-looking guys."

"I see what happens to cast-off wives who are totally dependent on your hunks. Marriage isn't the answer, Yvette. Women are still led down a primrose path. You ought to see how many needy women we turn away from our displaced-house-wives program for lack of funding. As dean, I'd have more control over the budget. So, yes, men, or should I say a man in my life, are at the bottom of my priority list."

"Maybe you need to find a new job. Our friends think you've dealt with battered women too long. You've gotten cynical. Rumors are, you hate men. Since your summer trip, even people I know who work with you at the college joke about you being the female Davy Crockett." Yvette moved to inspect her long curly hair in Sherry's mirror. "Trying to prove you're better than a man is not healthy."

"Equal, not better. Terms like 'female Davy Crockett' are meant to put women down. That stuff goes on all the time on campus. Speaking of which, I should leave now. I'd like to get to the boardroom early so I can assess the other two candidates."

She stepped into navy pumps. "So far, Yvette, you and my department secretary are the only ones who know I've tossed my hat in the ring. By tonight candidates' names and faces will be splashed all over the local news."

"If *I* wanted the job, I'd shout it from the rooftops."

"I never thought I'd make final cut. When I learned I had, the family was caught up hiding

Emily and her kids from her rotten in-laws. Now they're deep in wedding plans." She shrugged to show it didn't matter. Yet on a purely emotional level it did.

Yvette followed Sherry to the door. "Well, I'm on the road for the next week."

"By the time you get back, maybe they'll be calling me Dean Campbell." Sherry's high spirits lasted until she hit campus and couldn't find a parking place. She'd forgotten this was the last day of registration and the day the faculty returned full force. According to the reader board, it was also new-student orientation. "Rats." Rather than showing up early as planned, she was lucky to dash through the double doors that led to the boardroom on the dot of nine. Almost the last to arrive for the coffee hour.

Talk stopped while all eyes skimmed the latecomer. Sherry's stomach balled as she weathered microscopic inspection by administrators, board members and their perfectly groomed wives. All appeared baffled.

Dr. Harlan Westerbrook, the courtly white-haired college president, left a huddle of men and moseyed toward Sherry. Moseying was his way. A common joke around campus was that he'd be late for his own funeral. Sherry waited to be properly greeted in accordance with the pecking order.

"Sherilyn?" One bushy eyebrow met the president's cottony shock of hair. "I'm so used to seeing you dashing about campus, hair flying like a hippie, that I must confess I didn't recognize you."

Smugly satisfied, Sherry wanted to laugh, but said, instead, "Isn't adaptability one of the criteria for this job? As a teacher and counselor at the Hub, I have to blend in with the women we serve. Trust plays a major role in keeping disadvantaged students attending classes. Don't you agree, Doctor?"

"Um, yes... Well, come and meet the other finalists." Taking Sherry's elbow, the president steered her toward a short man with olive skin and thinning black hair. "This is Dr. Eli Aguilar. He's currently department chairman for minority programs at a prestigious California college." Westerbrook named the institution and let it impress before he introduced Sherry. "Dr. Sherilyn Campbell, Eli. Department chairperson of Women's Studies. This little lady has kept our departing dean on his toes." Westerbrook patted Sherry's hand. "Reginald insists she's not responsible for his seeking early retirement, though."

The two men laughed heartily. Sherry didn't smile. This was typical behavior, intended to keep women outside the select circles. She offered her hand first. "I won't apologize for going to the mat with the dean to retain services vital to troubled women. I'd be interested in hearing your views on whole-life training for displaced housewives, Dr. Aguilar. It ranks high with me. Counseling in areas like nutrition and grooming may be costly, but academic studies alone don't provide an automatic key to success in today's workplace."

Aguilar adjusted his tie a few times before Westerbrook rescued him. "Now Sherilyn," the president chided, "it's our job to put you three candidates on the spot—not for you to interrogate one another. Speaking of candidates, here comes Dr. Lock."

As their chief gazed over her shoulder, Sherry turned expectantly, one hand extended, a cool smile on her lips. Her outstretched fingers went limp and her smile died as she cannoned headlong into the startling punch of candidate number three's azure blue eyes.

Westerbrook's voice continued to drone in the background, but for the life of her, Sherry couldn't grasp a word he said. Oh, but she *had* to pay attention. *Lock. Dr. Garrett Lock, Assistant Dean of Collaborative programs...somewhere. His background, sociology.* Tongue frozen to the roof of her mouth, Sherry latched on to the newcomer's name and imprinted it in her mind. *Texas.* Westerbrook said Lock had driven to Columbia from Texas. Of course. As he collected her slack hand, he acknowledged her with a honeyed drawl that glued Sherry's toes to the soles of her sensible new pumps.

"Dr. Campbell." Bending slightly, he clasped her hand warmly and kicked up the wattage of his smile. "Any relation to Nolan Campbell? If I recall, his field is history."

Sherry registered the heat sliding up her arm… and little else. Except that Lock's rakish grin exploded like a sunbeam in this dreary walnut-paneled room. He had the most gorgeous sun-streaked blond hair, a good inch longer than her new do. Evenly tanned skin. And teeth so white Sherry thought they must surely be capped.

She tried to respond to his question about Nolan, but the most awful noise wheezed from her throat as if nothing could get past the balloon expanding in her chest. *Hypoglycemia. It sometimes hit when she skipped breakfast. She needed food, fast.*

"Sherilyn is Nolan's sister," Westerbrook answered for her. "Fine man, Nolan. Dedicated professor. I didn't realize you knew a member of our staff."

Garrett extracted his hand from the woman's clammy palm. Something looked familiar about those great cat eyes of hers. Definitely not your normal shade of brown. More like aged amber. He stepped back for a second assessment. Garrett was gifted with a keen memory. He'd hardly forget a woman with such classic bone structure—especially one with hair shorter than his son Keith's latest hatchet job, which came courtesy of Carla's new husband. *The banker* was how Garrett thought of Keith's stepfather. That or *the jerk.* Although he shouldn't place total blame for being uprooted from a job he loved on the man his ex-wife had married. Carla was the one who'd suddenly demanded maternal rights, and as a result Garrett's life had been turned inside out. He might not want this job, but if he didn't get it…well, with him in Huntsville and Carla in St. Louis, Keith would spend half his growing-up years on a plane. An eight-year-old didn't deserve to be zapped around like a yo-yo.

It took Garrett a moment to realize that his sudden fierce frown must be the reason everyone was staring at him so oddly. "Forgive me." He flashed a wide smile. "I was trying to decide if Dr. Campbell resembles her brother. Don't tell him I said so, but when they handed out looks he must've thought they said *books,* and passed because his shelves were full." His joke sparked rollicking laughter from the men. Women gazed at him adoringly.

Sherry did neither. In fact, she'd begun to see that being this close to candidate number three played havoc with her equilibrium and made absolute mush of her brain. "Excuse me," she said abruptly. "The coffee calls. I believe I'll get a cup and then mingle. Dr. Lock…Dr. Aguilar, we'll meet again, I'm sure."

Phew! A flood of relief eased the spasm in her chest as Sherry escaped Lock's presence. What was there about him that so unnerved her? Even now she felt his laser gaze tracking her progress across the room, and her feet tangled. *Stop it!* She consciously erased the frown from between her brows. Filling a cup to the brim with coffee, she gravitated toward the cluster of women Lock had just left. Regents' wives chorused hello, then returned to the topic they'd been discussing.

"Doesn't that handsome Dr. Lock just shiver your timbers?" The speaker was a plump impeccably dressed matron—a power on campus in her own right. Sherry knew of several instances in which this lady had influenced staff hiring.

The matron's bony companion fit the expression that a woman could never be too thin or too rich. She cast her voice in a regal whisper to entice listeners. "Sheldon told me—in confidence, mind you," she murmured, referring to her husband, the current board president, "that Dr. Lock is divorced." She said the word one breathless syllable at a time. "Can you imagine *any* woman foolish enough to let him leave her?"

Sherry sympathized with Lock as every last woman stared at him. In spite of her own efforts not to turn, her gaze automatically strayed toward him. She recalled her earlier chat with Yvette on the subject of admiring handsome men. Her response now seemed hypocritical in view of the way she was gawking at Lock.

Sherry spun back. Normally she wasn't the least bit impressed by broad shoulders. In Lock's case, though, she was forced to admit that he wore his dark green suit to perfection. Not a single crease where other men's suits were wrinkled. Obviously tailored to fit. His usual attire? Or an indication of how badly he wanted the job. Without appearing obvious, Sherry gave closer scrutiny to the loose way Lock stood, hands on hips, every so often pausing to gesture with a well-manicured hand. Well-manicured but not soft, she noted, remembering how it had felt during the brief meeting of their palms.

He broke off in midsentence, glanced around and caught Sherry giving him the once-over.

Annoyed at the heat suffusing her neck, Sherry deliberately steadied her coffee cup, took a sip, and transferred her inspection to Aguilar. His suit fit well enough. But of her two opponents, she judged Lock the man to beat in this race.

"Sherilyn, dear." A thin voice broke into Sherry's assessment of her competitors. "I understand you piloted a Conestoga across the prairie this summer. Frankly, I never understood why anyone would wish to reenact the old days. Notice I didn't call them the *good* old days. I belong to the historical society for philanthropic reasons. You must come and address our group, dear heart. Lyle Roberts, from the History department is our professional adviser. He said you even had a run-in with an escaped convict and that you beaned the man. If it'd been me, I would have fainted dead away. You must have nerves of steel. Weren't you frightened at all?"

Sherry, who'd practically forgotten the incident as she prepared for these interviews, drew a fleeting mental image of those blue, blue eyes. No wonder her heart had flip-flopped a moment ago. Lock's eyes were similar in intensity and color to the eyes of…that man. The man who'd loomed out of the fog the night she'd fallen behind the other wagons. But eye color was where the similarity ended. Although… She shivered. Both men hailed from Texas.

Lock exuded city polish. Dallas or Austin would be Sherry's guess. The bearded ragged stranger claimed to be from Huntsville—home of a maximum security prison. Sherry still suspected he'd been an escapee. Gooseflesh peppered her skin.

"Sometimes," she said, wetting a dry bottom lip, "adrenaline drives us to acts of courage. As a rule, I'm not given to violence. Thank goodness I didn't accidentally kill the man. I wish Lyle would stop talking about it. He's miffed because a handful of women made mockery of his archaic beliefs. Professor Roberts thinks women belong in the kitchen, not in the workforce."

The wife of the board president raised a silver brow. "I've been more than happy to let my husband be the breadwinner during our married life."

Sherry took a big gulp of coffee. She wouldn't touch that statement for love or money. Scratch a vote. But then, she'd already decided these women were biased in Lock's favor. Question—how much influence did they have on their husbands?

She noticed the chill in the air. Now she was almost sorry she'd left the men.

"Sherilyn, do you have immediate plans for starting a family?" the wife of the board president asked next.

"By immaculate conception, you mean?" Sherry murmured, hating herself for giving in to the impulse to make a sharp reply. Relenting somewhat, she offered a thin smile. "You obviously have me confused with my brother. He's the Professor Campbell who's getting married in November."

Sherry was spared more grilling when Dr. Westerbrook rapped on one of the tables.

"Delightful as this coffee hour has been," he boomed, "we're here for business. If the candidates would step forward and the guests would be seated, we'll have time for a few informal questions before we take a tour of the campus. I trust the selection team has had a chance to peruse all applications, supplements and curriculum vitae," he said, employing the academic term for résumé.

Heads bobbed. Sherry took a deep calming breath and detached herself from the group of women.

A hush fell over the room as the three finalists set coffee cups aside and made their way to the teak podium that bore the college seal. Or rather, two of the candidates left their cups behind. Sherry realized that Garrett Lock had ditched his saucer and kept his cup. Smart man. It not only made him appear more relaxed than the other two, but he had no worries about what to do with his hands.

Sherry tried thrusting hers into the pockets of her suit jacket, only to discover that she hadn't removed the stitching put in at the factory to keep the pockets from sagging. *Rats*. Why was she so tense? She had the home-court advantage, so to speak. After all, she knew the foibles of the people asking the questions. *And their strengths,* mocked that little voice. Indeed, they wielded all the power. No wonder her palms were sweating. And poor Dr. Aguilar. If he smoothed his hand through his thinning hair many more times, he'd leave these interviews bald.

Garrett, who fell in beside Sherry, raised his cup in salute. "Let the roasting begin," he muttered near her ear.

She was surprised—and impressed—that he dared to joke. But when his clean citrusy scent engulfed her and his solid shoulder brushed her arm, sending shafts of heat to her icy fingertips, Sherry wished she'd stood elsewhere. She edged a step closer to Dr. Aguilar, determined to ignore Lock's presence and make a good showing.

"I have a question." The board president leaned back in his chair, hooking his thumbs in his vest. "This is for all three candidates, starting with you, Dr. Aguilar. Suppose we asked you to cut twenty percent from the Human Services budget?"

Aguilar thought a moment. "I, ah, would have to see the budget and study it very carefully before making any determination. I'm a very thorough man."

The president rocked back on two chair legs. "Dr. Campbell?"

Sherry's heart plummeted. Naturally he'd smirk. They'd gone through this exercise last year. As department chair she'd been very vocal in her opposition to cuts. She was still opposed. Looking him in the eye, she said, "Enrollment is up. Operating costs, too. We have a staff member on sabbatical and one on paid leave. Cutting anywhere would be disastrous." *There, let Lock try to top her knowledge of the operation.*

All eyes in the room shifted to him. He gestured with his cup and said in a maddeningly slow drawl, "Well, y'all, I've never seen a budget that didn't hide some pork. If you say cut, I'd trim the fat. It's as simple as that."

Sherry's response to the undercurrent of approval manifested itself in the form of a keen desire to kick Garrett Lock right in his skinny behind. *Trim the fat, indeed!* She was so royally ticked off she almost missed the next question. For fifteen minutes thereafter, the candidates fielded rapid-fire questions. Just when she thought they were winding down, she was blindsided by a challenge aimed strictly at her.

"Professor Campbell," demanded the dean of Science, "as current department chair, do you feel you'd be able to work effectively with either of the other two candidates should they be awarded the position?"

"I—I—I…" she stammered. Clearly it was a question intended to undermine her candidacy. One that took a potshot at women by intimating they were too "emotional" to accept defeat. Anger bubbled, yet Sherry sensed it was crucial that she give calm, rational answers.

Surprisingly, help came from Garrett Lock.

"Excuse me, but isn't that question somewhat

premature? I don't know about Dr. Aguilar, but I'm not sure I'm ready to hear Dr. Campbell's perception of my shortcomings. What if her opinions adversely influence the team's decision?"

Dr. Westerbrook stood and faced the man who'd posed the question. "Dr. Lock is absolutely right, Byron. At this stage in the process, interrogation must remain equally applicable to all candidates. Now, I think we've kept them on the hot seat long enough for one session. Shall we begin our campus tour?"

Everyone rose dutifully and shuffled toward the doors. Glancing at Byron Imes, Sherry could tell he hadn't liked being publicly chastised. From his scowl, she'd say his vote would, out of spite, go to Eli Aguilar. So far, it appeared she trailed miserably in the overall tally.

Still, it was decent of Lock to stick his neck out—unless he'd done it because he wanted to come off looking the hero. Sherry didn't want to be beholden to him for any reason. Needing to make that clear, she pulled him aside. "If that show was intended to prove your Southern chivalry, then you've made your point. Don't mistake me for Little Red Riding Hood. I can take care of myself with the worst of the big bad wolves. So back off."

Garrett's eyes narrowed as he watched her stalk away. That walk… He suddenly saw the swing of squared shoulders and a slim form disappearing through wisps of fog. He squinted, trying desperately to hang on to the vision as Professor Campbell melted into the crowd. It wasn't just her walk that reminded him of the spitfire who'd bopped him over the head this past summer. The memory floated in and out.

While panning for gold alone in a remote corner of Kansas, he'd stumbled across an apparition right out of a history book—a covered wagon. It was apparently being driven by two women. The night hadn't been fit for man nor beast, and he'd offered to help the women, who'd seemed lost and rather desperate. One, without provocation, attacked him with a stick of firewood. Then Nolan Campbell showed up—an affable guy, a historian writing a paper on how modern women handled trekking the Santa Fe Trail. The whole incident was so bizarre that after returning home, he almost believed he'd dreamed it. Except for the lump above his left ear that served to remind him.

The woman who'd hit him had had a mane of lush dark hair spilling over her shoulders. That was fact. Shaking his head to clear it, Garrett was jolted back to the present as two of the regents' wives flanked him, smothering him in a cloud of opposing perfumes.

"Mustn't dawdle, Doctor. If you're going to

win, you'll need to strip off those kid gloves and climb into the ring."

Garrett recognized Maxine March, wife of the board president. She clucked over him as if he were a prize at a silent auction. As if she saw in him an eligible bachelor to hook up with a friend's single daughter. He knew that look from Huntsville. Campus communities were alike in many respects. He needed to let the matchmakers know that he and Keith did okay as bachelors. His son went to school clean and well fed. As for a divorced dad's other needs, Garrett had learned to live with celibacy. Long periods of celibacy. He told himself it built character.

He wasn't looking for wife number two, and he had no intention of owing these women favors of any kind. Yet as he opened his mouth to set them straight, Garrett remembered why he'd tossed his hat into the ring.

Carla. Keith.

There wasn't another suitable opening on a campus within a hundred-mile radius. Tempted as he was to chuck it all, he knew he couldn't. He was stuck with this sideshow—because he intended to walk away with this job.

CHAPTER TWO

THE TOUR SEEMED to lift everyone's spirits. Brick buildings warmed by afternoon sun dotted a campus scattered with trees dressed in crimson fall foliage. Flowering shrubs lined interwoven walkways, scenting the air with a pleasant fragrance.

Sherry never tired of the ever-changing seasons here. She counted herself lucky to teach in such a stimulating atmosphere. In springtime the grass greened and the trees budded with new leaves. Rain washed everything clean. Summer heat brought a quiet period, lazy and relaxed, while autumn reinvigorated everyone with its briskness and beauty. Then winter winds blew in from the north, dropping a soft blanket of snow that students loved, and faculty and staff grumbled about good-naturedly.

Three generations of Campbells had received their higher education at Wellmont College, now in its seventieth year. All had proudly worn the burgundy caps and gowns on graduation day. At times Sherry stood at her office window and dreamed of seeing her own children among the students scurrying between classes. She'd never breathed that fantasy to a soul. Her yearning for babies contradicted how she felt about love, about marriage. Yvette, now, fell in and out of love on a regular basis. She attracted drop-dead gorgeous guys the way flowers attracted bees. And discarded them as ruthlessly as a bee sucked a flower dry. That never used to bother Sherry. Lately it did. She and Yvette were growing in different directions and that saddened Sherry. She supposed they should terminate their present arrangement as housemates before their friendship, which had spanned three decades, deteriorated beyond repair.

Ahead, administrators and board members trudged up the steps and into the counseling center where the departments of Women's Studies and Collaborative Programs shared space. Sherry had an office there, as did the dean of Human Services.

Sherry wondered what her opponents thought of the campus thus far. Maybe they wouldn't like it. It certainly didn't compare in size to the sprawling California institution where Aguilar worked. She hadn't caught the name of Lock's school, but she'd heard Texans were possessive about their particular portion of the vast state. So why was he hoping to move? Advancement, she thought glumly. He was already an assistant dean, and on paper at least, seemed the most experienced of the three.

She looked for the two men to see if their faces gave away their feelings. A casual glance over her shoulder had her sucking in her breath. Lock stood so close that when he exhaled, her skin absorbed his breath. His eyes, fathomless blue, reflected the ivy-covered brickwork. He'd stopped to read the words carved into the ledge circling the six-floor building. "'You must do the thing you think you cannot do,'" he read aloud. "Good advice," he said as if in response to Sherry's scrutiny. "A quote from Eleanor Roosevelt, isn't it?"

"Why, yes." The fact that he knew surprised Sherry. The quote was repeated on all four sides of the building, but Mrs. Roosevelt's name had only been carved on the south side when this building was added in the early 1940s. He couldn't have seen it from where they stood.

By now most of the entourage had disappeared, leaving them alone. Garrett laughed in the face of her amazement. "What can't you believe, Dr. Campbell? That I recognize the quote or that I deem it good advice?"

"Both, I guess," Sherry said honestly.

Bracketing his hips in a very male stance, Garrett shook his head. "Is that an opinion you formed because I'm a man or because I'm from Texas?"

Set to give a terse comeback, Sherry found

herself responding favorably to the deep grooves creasing his tanned cheeks. Annoyed by that, she linked her hands loosely over her stomach and pretended to study a crack in the cement. "My remark did sound sexist. I'm really not—no matter what you may hear." Her head came up and Sherry stared straight into his eyes. Why it was important to make herself clear, she couldn't say. Maybe because of what Yvette had said concerning remarks floating from campus into the community.

A small frown gathered between Garrett's straight brows.

Sherry was very glad when someone hollered for them to hurry. Lock was puzzling over her statement far too long. She didn't want to be forced to explain. He probably hadn't heard the rumors. Lies. Sherry didn't hate men. She got tired of playing second fiddle to them on this campus. Perhaps it wasn't true of all colleges, but here men got the best jobs. They were promoted faster and held most of the top positions.

Sherry was quick to respond to the summons, leaving Garrett behind. Or so she thought. She hadn't heard his tread and she gave a start when a masculine hand reached around her toward the door. For a second she gaped at the strong wrist and the long fingers gripping the knob. A thin gold watch lay in a dusting of light bronzed hair, gleaming below his starched French cuff. *Nice hands.* But then, she'd thought that earlier. With a jolt, Sherry discovered that he was staring at her quizzically. *Of course.* She needed to step aside and give him room to open the door.

"Excuse me," she mumbled, backing up and right into him. Her heel landed squarely on his foot and she felt him wince.

"Well, that's one way to eliminate the competition," he said pleasantly, a deep dimple winking briefly in his left cheek.

"Sorry. I didn't realize you were so close."

Dr. Westerbrook threw open the door, startling them both. "There you two are. We're waiting for Sherry. As department chair, she'd ordinarily give the grand tour. To avoid any perception of bias, I thought we'd ask the department secretary to fill in. What's her name?" he muttered behind his hand. "I should know."

"Angel," Sherry said. "Angel Baby Webster is her legal name. But I wouldn't advise using it," she said with a teasing grin.

Westerbrook grimaced. "Now I remember. She's rather, uh, flamboyant. Maybe you'd better do the honors, after all. You know how conservative the board is."

"Angel should talk to them. We hired her after she completed our program," she said for Garrett's benefit as they walked toward the waiting group. "Angel is the epitome of what we're about. The first time I saw her as a referral from the battered-women's shelter, she had a black eye, swollen lip and two broken ribs. The father of her six-month-old boy had thrown her down the stairs because the baby was sick and she couldn't keep him from crying. She has two older kids from a previous bad marriage. Our program offered her an alternative to living on the streets—or in prison. When the police arrived at her door, she was one step from carving up the boyfriend because he'd started to slap her kids around." There was more to tell, but Sherry felt a collective uncomfortable shifting of the VIPs.

Wishing she'd kept Angel's story to herself, Sherry elbowed her way to where the secretary sat. She quickly introduced the petite young woman, then said, "Angel, please explain how we operate. I've told them you're an expert on our work-study program." Sherry gave her arm a supportive squeeze, then stepped back.

Westerbrook sidled up to Sherry and whispered, "You've accomplished miracles. The dean brought me through the department right after you hired her. She looked like a...a vagrant."

"Many of our students arrive at the shelters with nothing. Did the dean tell you he opposed hiring her? Job placement is the final phase in whole-life training. Education isn't much good unless it puts food on the table and a roof over one's head. I hope no one considers it *fat* that needs trimming from our already meager budget," she said, looking pointedly at Garrett Lock.

The president coughed by way of response. Sherry was disappointed but not surprised. The old guard believed that degree in hand was the primary if not the only duty of this institution. They opposed funding anything that might be misconstrued as vocational training. Westerbrook and his henchmen would graduate ten thousand poly-sci majors, never mind that only one in a thousand would find work in that field.

Sherry decided to abandon the front row. Hassling the president wouldn't advance her cause. Again, unexpectedly, she turned and plowed into Garrett Lock.

This time, as his eyes cruised slowly over the stubborn set of her jaw, he wore a sympathetic expression.

Sherry pushed past him and ended up next to Eli Aguilar. The look on his face remained guarded. Great! She probably ran last in the field of candidates. And if either Lock or Aguilar won, she'd have the same walls to scale as she'd had with Kruger. Or worse, she groaned inwardly. Eli would study every issue to death, and Garrett would hack the life out of the program.

Sherry wasn't sorry when Westerbrook announced that interviews were over for the day. His secretary, Fern Mitchell, opened her briefcase and handed each candidate a revised schedule for the next day.

"As you'll note," Westerbrook said, "we meet at nine tomorrow in the lobby of the theater for coffee with the faculty. Immediately following, delegates from the Faculty Association will present a composite of their questions. So be prepared," he warned. "Lunch in the boardroom will give you a chance to relax and regroup. At two, you'll talk with students. Next day are the individual interviews, and after that friends of the college and other interested parties from the community will host a tea. At seven, there'll be a dinner, where we hope to finalize a decision. I think that's all until tomorrow."

"Wait." Garrett Lock stepped forward. "I don't know about Eli, but I'd like to see some of the city. Is that possible?"

"We'd be glad to chauffeur you around, Dr. Lock, wouldn't we, Sheldon?" Maxine March nudged her husband.

"I appreciate the offer, Mrs. March, but in the interests of fairness, I thought perhaps Dr. Campbell…" He let the suggestion hang a moment. "Then neither Eli nor I would have greater access to anyone on the selection committee."

"Good thinking, my boy." Westerbrook clapped Garrett on the back.

Sherry started to refuse until she realized Lock was absolutely right.

"I'd like to see the city," Dr. Aguilar agreed. "But my wife is at the hotel. I hate to leave her behind."

Sherry imagined squeezing them all into the Ford Escort she hadn't cleaned properly since school let out. The backseat was littered with folders and the floor with empty diet-soda cans. A brilliant idea struck. "I'm sure that, under the circumstances, Dr. Westerbrook will authorize us to use a vehicle from the motor pool. The white van," she hinted, referring to their newest acquisition, knowing full well he didn't like women to drive the state vehicles, period. She bit her lip to hide a smile as both Lock and Aguilar turned expectantly to the president.

"Ahem." He glanced at his secretary. "The white van? I...I suppose. But I want it returned before dark."

Sherry covered her surprise at his easy capitulation. "I'll go back to the office with Fern to collect the key," she said. "That'll give Dr. Aguilar time to call his wife. Gentlemen, the motor pool is building twelve on your map. We'll meet there in, say, fifteen minutes." She checked her watch. Expecting to see Mickey's gloved hands, she stared blankly at her arm for a moment.

"I'll take a cab to the hotel and wait with my wife. Do you mind? I have a phone call I need to make," Eli told Sherry.

"F-fine." She didn't like being left with Lock. "Maybe Dr. Lock would like to freshen up, too," she said with sudden inspiration.

"I'll just come with you," Garrett put in smoothly.

Sherry didn't want him tagging after her, although she couldn't put her finger on exactly why. Curving her lips into a false smile, she inclined her head graciously. It unnerved her further when he hurried to open the door, then placed a hand lightly on her back to guide her through. At the top of the steps his hand slid to cup her elbow. Did the man not think she was capable of navigating stairs, for pity's sake?

Once they'd reached the bottom, however, and he withdrew his support, for some strange reason Sherry felt like a barge cut loose from its tug. She quickened her steps to catch up with the president's secretary, who walked briskly along the path.

Garrett lengthened his stride, too. He shot her a sidelong glance, trying to recall the last time he'd encountered such a prickly female. Normally he was the one backing away from women who came on too strong. Garrett didn't know why he was annoyed, but he was.

"Nice campus," he said, taking his eyes off her to scan the brick courtyard where students gathered to study and talk.

"Yes, it's a wonderful place to work," she admitted grudgingly. Lock tucked his hands in his pants pockets, and Sherry heard the rattle of change.

"What can you tell me about the town's elementary schools?"

"In what regard?"

A light shrug rustled his crisp shirt collar. "Gangs. Drugs. Anything of that nature."

"Thinking of changing fields?" she asked, sounding hopeful.

"Nothing so drastic. I have a son going into third grade."

"A son. Oh. But I…I'd heard you were divorced," she stammered.

One sun-tipped brow feathered upward. "That's correct."

Flustered, Sherry scrambled to form an answer to his first question. All her dealings had been with single mothers. She didn't personally know any single dads. "I, ah, there're very few problems in our school system. My mom retired last year after teaching in the district for thirty-five years." Sherry waved her hands expansively. "I'm telling you this in case you think I'm whitewashing the situation."

"Frankly, I worried about the opposite." Garrett struggled to hide a sheepish grin. "We are after the same job, remember. You might have said the schools were infested to the max on the off chance I'd drop out of the race."

She stopped and blinked at him. "I do want this job, Dr. Lock. But I wouldn't lie to get it. I've worked hard to improve assistance offered by the crisis center and the rape-relief-counseling program at the Hub. I believe I'm the most qualified to direct Human Services."

"Fair enough." He hesitated. "Call me Garrett, please."

Sherry abruptly picked up her pace. "This afternoon I'm your tour guide. Tomorrow and the next day we go back to being rivals. If I'm chosen, we'll never see each other again. If you are, I'll call you Dean Lock."

"Ouch. You don't pull any punches. Most women—"

"I'm not most women, Doctor. We're here. Excuse me, please. I'll go sign for the car keys." This man *really* unnerved her.

Garrett rocked back on his heels as she strode through the door with the frosted glass. He watched her shadow, and for just a moment, a sense of familiarity knotted his stomach. Then it disappeared, leaving him with nothing but the sting of her rebuff. He studied the two women's silhouettes on the glass and noticed that his opponent talked with her hands. Both outlines were tall and slender, but Dr. Campbell was more... feminine.

Garrett seesawed from one foot to the other, briefly wondering about the woman behind that severe blue suit. He clamped down hard on the unexpected attraction he felt. He didn't have those kinds of feelings about women colleagues. And if he ever did, he'd pick one less abrasive than Sherilyn Campbell. She wasn't his type. In fact, she was the complete opposite of his type, in personality and appearance.

Her ultrashort hair was off-putting, Garrett argued silently. He frowned as her silvery laughter wafted through the narrow opening in the door, making mockery of the fact that he'd tried to convince himself he only found women with long hair attractive.

Discovering that he wasn't nearly as impervious to the professor as he wanted to be cooled Garrett's eagerness for the tour he'd instigated. Now he wished he'd let well enough alone.

They walked in complete silence to collect the van. Few words passed between them as Sherry drove to the hotel to pick up Eli Aguilar and his wife. She did slow once to point out the George

Caleb Bingham Gallery of Fine Art, adding, "Over there—the building with the black reflective windows—that's the insurance company where my dad's worked for nearly forty years." Thawing a bit, she smiled. "Mom bugs him to retire. They have a house on five acres east of town. Both are horticulture hobbyists. Ever since I was little, they've talked about building a greenhouse. But Dad's a conscientious agent. He can't say no to people who refer clients. I wish he'd slow down."

Garrett noted her wistful expression when she spoke of family. It softened her features. "Quite a feat to live in the same town for forty years. I had hoped— Well, never mind. Things happen," he said, turning to gaze out the side window.

It was on the tip of Sherry's tongue to ask what had made him apply for this job and leave a place he obviously disliked leaving—although she still didn't know what Texas college town that was. Nor was there time to probe. They'd reached the hotel. Sherry spotted Aguilar and a petite pretty woman standing at the entrance.

Garrett got out when Sherry stopped. He opened the van's side door, closing it again once Eli and his wife were buckled into the center seat.

"This is my wife, Marguerite," Eli announced proudly. "I apologize for asking you to go out of your way. I know it was an inconvenience, but we left our three children with their grandparents. I wanted to call and see how they're getting along."

"Three." Garrett whistled through his teeth. "I have one son. He keeps me hopping. 'Course, I'm a single dad," he said, in case Aguilar didn't know.

Sherry couldn't begin to explain the sudden yearning that struck her. Yet it'd struck with greater frequency this past year. When she found herself sitting with groups who discussed their children, she felt a gap in her life. To cover her discomfort, she smiled at Eli's wife in the rear-view mirror.

The woman smiled back. "It's kind of you to show us around."

"I thought I'd drive past libraries, museums and hospitals," Sherry said. "The insurance industry, medical services, colleges and a university make up the backbone of our city's economy. I'll circle our biggest shopping mall and go through a new housing development, as well as a more established neighborhood. Barring traffic problems, I'll have you back at your hotel in time for dinner."

The Aguilars nodded in agreement.

Garrett settled comfortably into the seat. "Fine as a frog hair split four ways," he said in a husky drawl.

His remark made no sense to Sherry. But the timbre of his voice had the same effect as someone using her spine as a piccolo. After that, she did most of the talking. Sherry's pride in Columbia was unmistakable. Her passengers were kept so busy craning their necks this way and that no one had time for questions.

Garrett asked the first after they'd completed the circuit and she'd again pulled under the awning at their hotel. "There were no For Sale signs in the residential areas. Not even in that new development. Do they not allow signs or what?"

"They do. Right now our growth exceeds available housing."

"But there are rentals?" Garrett had climbed out, shut his door and leaned in the side door where the Aguilars got out.

Sherry's hands tightened on the wheel. Did Lock sense he was the leading candidate? Was that why he pressed for details that wouldn't matter if he didn't get the nod? "I'm afraid you'll have to ask someone in real estate," she said stiffly. Purposely glancing at her no-nonsense watch, she added, "You might still catch an agent if you hurry."

"Here's your hat and don't trip on the way out?" Garrett deadpanned. "Seriously, Sherilyn," he said softly, ignoring her earlier insistence that they stick to titles. "Speaking for the Aguilars and myself, we appreciate your time and trouble."

Sherry bit her lip. "It wasn't any trouble…Professor."

"No? Then maybe you'll let me buy you dinner by way of saying thanks." *Where had that come from?* Garrett could count on one hand the number of women he'd asked out since Carla left. Most of those dinners had been job-related functions that required a partner.

For a few seconds Sherry actually considered accepting his offer. Why was a mystery. News of their hobnobbing would get out and reach the interview team. Shaking her head, she refused. "I can't. My roommate expects me home to cook dinner," she said. "I left meat marinating. But thanks for the offer. See you tomorrow." She pointedly shifted the van into drive so he'd take the hint and withdraw.

Garrett did, all the while picturing some dude in a suit and tie pacing from window to window waiting for her to get home to cook his meal. He had a hard time bringing that frame into focus. Once he did, he felt like a fool for assuming that just because Sherilyn Campbell wore no wedding ring she was free.

Sherry saw him glower at her taillights even after she'd waved to the Aguilars and headed off. Why that look? He had to know that college towns were notorious for gossip. Unless he *hoped* it would compromise her if she'd accepted his invitation. It was her town, after all.

She turned at the corner, effectively cutting off her view of the disturbing Dr. Lock. Sherry didn't want to think he'd play dirty politics, but the truth was she didn't know him at all.

And speaking of truth, she'd made a big deal earlier of her honesty, saying she wouldn't lie. But she'd known very well that Yvette wasn't waiting at home.

Sherry returned the van, then did what she did most nights. She went home to an empty town house and a solitary dinner in front of the TV.

Tonight was marginally different. Pictures of finalists for the dean's position had made the local news. Her phone rang off the hook. Friends called to congratulate or commiserate depending on their point of view. Not her parents or Nolan. They and Emily were probably grouped around the dinner table poring over wedding plans.

Getting up, Sherry put her plate in the dishwasher. Why couldn't she just be pleased for Nolan and Emily? No two people deserved happiness more. A man didn't buy a big house like Nolan had and toil to restore it unless he intended to fill it with a family. And Emily had been stuck too long in a loveless first marriage.

Depressed, yet not fathoming why, Sherry

switched the phone to her answering machine and went to bed.

In the morning she slept through her alarm. As a result, she was late for the second day in a row. Today there were more people to stare as she burst into the room. Half the faculty juggled plates and coffee cups while pitching pet projects to the regents. The other half didn't care. Sherry had done her share of politicking at these functions in the past. She'd forgotten how loud it could get until she walked in and a hush fell over the room.

"I overslept," she mumbled, making a beeline for the coffee urn. She felt a pair of eyes drilling her back as she fixed her coffee with two packets of sugar and a generous measure of cream. Normally she drank her coffee black. Somehow the thought of being grilled by peers this morning made her stomach churn. There was a lot of jealousy in academia. When she angled sideways to get a fix on where today's animosity came from, she encountered Garrett Lock's penetrating blue gaze.

Her hand shook and she dumped sugar all over the pristine tablecloth. What had happened between yesterday and today to make him look so fierce? Thank goodness she saw Nolan detach himself from a group and head toward her with arms outstretched. Sherry turned from Lock to meet her brother's bear hug.

Across the room, Garrett registered Sherry Campbell's lateness and her slightly rumpled appearance. He put them together with her remark about oversleeping and pictured her snuggled in bed with the man she had offhandly referred to as her roommate. Was that him now—the long-legged galoot making a spectacle of them center stage?

But no, when Garrett got a good look at the two side by side, it was easy to see their resemblance. That made the man Nolan Campbell. Garrett's jaw sagged. He wouldn't have recognized the historian if they'd bumped into each other on the street. That night on the prairie, the man who'd ridden into his camp—after the crazy woman and her companion had taken off—had badly needed a shave. Rough outdoor clothing had made him appear huskier, too.

What came as an even bigger shock to Garrett—viewing brother and sister together like this—was knowing exactly why Sherilyn Campbell had niggled at his memory. She was the wild woman who'd done her best to brain him. A fire caught slowly in Garrett's belly.

Nolan Campbell had known it all along. He'd accepted Garrett's hospitality, drunk his coffee and shot the breeze amiably, the way men out camping did. All the while lying through his teeth. How could Campbell not have known that his sister had applied for this job? The job he'd been well aware Garrett was applying for! And he must have known she was the one who'd bloodied Garrett's head, too. Well! The distinguished history prof had some explaining to do.

Garrett excused himself from the pocket of faculty members. "I see an old friend." Grinding his teeth, he set a straight course for the Campbells, and as he drew near, heard their raised voices. He wasn't close enough to sort out what the argument was about.

Listening to Nolan, Sherry felt guilty and annoyed in equal parts.

"I can't believe you kept news like this from the family, Sherilyn." He sounded more than a little hurt.

"You were all submerged in wedding plans. And I know you spent every spare minute on the house so that Emily and the kids'll be able to leave Mom and Dad's by the wedding and move out to your place. How's the remodeling going?"

"Fine. Emily's nose is out of joint because you've dropped out of sight. At least now she'll understand. She's counting on you to be her maid of honor, sis."

"I don't know, Nolan. If I get the dean's job, I'll have to really burn the midnight oil." She hoped he didn't pick up on her ambivalence.

But Nolan wasn't listening. His attention had

flown to the man approaching from behind her. Sherry knew it was a man from the heavy tread. Nolan's wide smile branded the person a friend. She hoped it wasn't that obnoxious Lyle Roberts.

Her brother stretched out his hand and stepped around Sherry. "Well, well, after hearing your name on the news, I wondered when we'd meet. You clean up pretty good, Lock."

Garrett didn't take the offered hand. "I'm wracking my brain to remember what we discussed this summer. I trust you got a kick out of sharing bits of my personal history with another candidate. When can I expect it to rise up and haunt me?"

Nolan curled his fingers back into his chest. "There's no call to be rude, Lock. When we met, I didn't have a clue that Sherry had aspirations of becoming a dean."

"That's not surprising," Sherry blurted. "Since you fell head over bootstraps for Emily, you haven't been able to see the nose on your face, Nolan Campbell."

Ignoring his sister, Nolan turned back to Garrett. "No offense, pal, but I judged you a hundred-to-one long shot to even get an interview. What with having hair down to your shoulders and being none too clean in spite of an unplanned dip in the river."

Campbell might have missed the subtle message in his sister's words that she was jealous of his impending marriage; Garrett did not. "I suppose it's possible you didn't know about Sherry's plans, Campbell. Difficult to argue with a guy too blinded by love to see that his own sister's pea-green jealous over his getting hitched."

"I'm no such thing," Sherry snapped. "Who asked you to butt in, anyway?"

"Whoa!" Laughing, Nolan held up a hand to stave off the angry pair. "I am deliriously happy, Lock." Nolan provided Garrett with a sketch of what had happened in his life since their chance meeting on the prairie. "I'm afraid I'll have to renege on the good luck I wished you. But if you should get the job, you're invited to Emily's and my wedding. Thanksgiving weekend. Hey, come even if you don't get it." Nolan's grin spread from ear to ear.

Sherry looked in amazement from one man to the other, finally adding things up as she flipped back to that foggy night in August. She didn't much like how the score tallied. With an artist's eye she layered Garrett Lock in the ragged trappings worn by the lunatic who'd materialized out of the fog. Run-down scruffy boots. Longer scraggly hair, as Nolan had said. A beard and…and a *gun!* They were one and the same man. Sherry took a step closer to Nolan, exhaling on a partially restrained gasp. For all she knew, the man was unbalanced.

Her own brother had unwittingly led Lock straight to her.

And who would believe her tale? Not the administrators who looked at him as if he'd hung the moon. Blindly she groped behind her for the cup of coffee she'd filled.

Garrett saw her grab something from the table. He automatically feinted left. She'd cut her hair and dressed like a corporate executive—but this was the same madwoman who a short month ago had tried to brain him with a stick of firewood. What should he do now? He wanted this job. Needed it for Keith's sake. But if he got it, he'd have to work with *her*.

"Nolan Campbell, you're a rat!" Sherry rounded on him. "Not one word did you breathe about meeting my victim. The guy I…fended off. Not one! You knew I was sick with worry."

"Well, why didn't *you* mention Kruger's retirement? I would have supported you for the deanship. Do support you. I think we should discuss this later. After we all calm down."

"Calm down?" She stared at one man, then the other, furious with both.

To Garrett's relief, Dr. Westerbrook stepped up to the podium. "Break is over," he announced. "This is faculty members' chance to measure each candidate against the others. You know the time allotted for questions. Candidates, on stage, please."

Working hard to compose his features, Garrett carefully placed Eli Aguilar between himself and the woman he'd once jokingly told Nolan Campbell he hoped never to meet in a dark alley. They'd both laughed as they parted that night. Neither so much as cracked a smile now.

CHAPTER THREE

IT INFURIATED GARRETT that Sherry Campbell acted as if *she* was the injured party and *he* was Jack the Ripper. He leaned around Eli to scowl at her. "I think the least you could do is apologize for hitting me."

"Stay away from me," she warned, putting up a hand to ward him off.

"Same goes," he snapped.

Dr. Aguilar's head whipped first one way, then the other. "Uh…shall I move?"

"Stay," they both hissed.

"All right, all right," Eli said. "Calm down."

The bombardment of questions began the minute they each received a microphone. The delegate from Business stepped to the podium first.

"Relative to your position on the joint deans' committee, if faced with cutbacks, would you—*a* support buying more computers for classroom use, or *b* argue to spend the limited funds for women's special interests? Sherry, you go first."

A setup. The School of Business Management recruited widely, attracting a large number of students, which qualified them for bushels of grants. No program on campus received more support from local business. They needed more computers like a shark needed a snowmobile, but Sherry was determined to be tactful. "Our current computer-student ratio is reportedly the highest in the state. My vote for distribution of funds would depend entirely on what other issues were on the table."

The delegate smirked. "I see. Dr. Aguilar, same question."

"I assume each request would be accompanied by adequate documentation. I'd have to carefully study all petitions before voting." When it was apparent that Eli had said all he was going to, the delegate turned to candidate three. "What would you do, Dr. Lock?"

"I'm pro-student, male *and* female. And pro-technology. I fail to see a conflict of interest."

Sherry glared around Eli at Lock's Cheshire-cat grin. That answer landed the sneaky son of a gun right in the pocket of a big contingent. Throughout the audience, men visibly relaxed. Women leaned forward to give Lock a closer look.

It might seem a small matter, but Sherry, with her background in psychology, read the body language as favorable toward the Texan. If they were playing tennis, it would be fifteen-love for Garrett.

Business had set the tone. Sherry likened the

barrage that followed to enemy fire. Lock, however, breezed through unscathed.

Eli came out ahead during questions from Integrated Programs, and again through a grilling by Minority Affairs. It was, after all, his bailiwick.

Overall, hands down, Lock walked away with the match. Feeling sort of shell-shocked, Sherry was glad to have the session behind her. As President Westerbrook called a halt, her main objective was to escape the crush of faculty descending on the other two candidates. Faculty knew her. Knew where she stood.

But that was supposing the crowd aiming for Lock had any interest in discussing campus issues, she thought, running a jaundiced eye over the mob of females rushing him like a pack of hounds. Disgusted at her peers' shameless flirting, Sherry slipped behind the blue velvet stage curtains to regroup. Even then, the curtain gaped, providing a panoramic view of those jockeying for Lock's attention.

Sherry sucked in her breath. *The man did ooze charisma.* Lock threw back his head and laughed at something a female faculty member said. Lights from the stage emphasized his lean jaw and glistened along the strong tanned column of his throat. Nolan's earlier words skated around inside Sherry's head. *You clean up pretty good,* he'd told Lock. An understatement if ever there was one.

Chills marched up Sherry's spine. So why had Professor Lock appeared that night looking like a derelict? She didn't know, but in all probability she did owe him an apology. She might have killed him. Would he believe she'd paced the campsite, fearful she'd done just that? Not even Nolan knew how utterly relieved she'd been when he came back with the news that his search hadn't turned up a dead body. But that was *all* he'd said. If only he'd told her of his meeting with Lock, she'd have been better prepared.

An irritating pain began to pulse behind her eyes.

She absolutely wouldn't permit any man to cause her a headache. Sherry charged out from behind the curtain and into the fray.

The more Garrett charmed the faculty, the greater the pounding in Sherry's head. She could have kissed Westerbrook's secretary when Fern announced that it was time for the candidates to convene for lunch.

Only fate would be so cruel as to seat Sherry directly across from Lock. Worse, he noticed her distress. Seconds after they sat, he caught her eye and murmured, "Headache? I'm not surprised. Faculty really raked us over the coals." Unfurling his napkin, Garrett shifted his attention from

Sherry to the somber interviewers filing into the room. "Here comes the SWAT team." Lock pretended to shiver. "Or more like a convention of undertakers. Almost enough to cause second thoughts, right?"

Sherry dropped her hands from massaging her temples. The twinkle in his blue eyes sent blood galloping through her veins. She concentrated on his shirt collar. "If you're having second thoughts, Lock, why don't you drop out of the race now and go back to…Huntsville?"

A muscle at the base of his jaw tightened. She couldn't know how close he came to saying he'd gladly leave the field to her if he could. Already he felt homesick for Texas.

If it were up to him, Garrett would tell her what she could do with her belated motherly instincts. But his lawyer had blown that notion out of his head. He said judges believed shared custody was best for a child. Something else he said was even scarier—now that Carla was married, she might actually appear to be the better parent should Garrett press for full custody.

His stony silence started wheels grinding inside Sherry's head. "Maybe the team should delve into your reasons for leaving Huntsville."

"They're personal," he said, then wished he hadn't played into her hands.

"Ah, the term 'personal' covers a multitude of

possibilities. We farmed a professor out on leave last year when he couldn't keep his hands off female students. Officially he's on sabbatical for *personal* reasons."

Garrett heard both accusation and challenge in her statement. He wadded his napkin and half rose from his chair. Never mind the place cards, he'd find a new seat. But he sank back down as interviewers pulled out chairs on either side of him. They filled the empty space between Sherry Campbell and Eli, too. He appeared oblivious to their squabbles.

The college vice president claimed the seat to Garrett's right. The instant the waiter left after delivering salads, Phipps turned to Garrett. "What was the dispute you had this morning with Nolan Campbell all about?"

Fork poised over his shrimp salad, Garrett's gaze flicked over Sherry's tense face. He tried ducking the query with a minimal shrug. If she wanted to explain the bizarre facts, let her try. Frankly, he wouldn't know where to start.

The ploy didn't work. Barnard—or "Barney"—Phipps repeated his question. People on both sides of the table put their conversations on hold to listen.

Garrett broke a roll and calmly buttered half. "It was nothing really. We had a chance meeting this summer during the study Campbell conducted—

the wagon train reenactment. We talked about this and that. I don't know how it came up, but I mentioned that I'd applied for the dean's position here. Campbell claimed he didn't know Dean Kruger was leaving. Today that struck me as odd, given his sister's candidacy."

"Can you answer that, Sherilyn?" The vice president switched to grilling her. "By the way, how did you manage to meet the application deadline? According to a news report, Nolan's group returned from Santa Fe a week after the final date."

Sherry stiffened. "Dean Kruger dropped hints around the department about retiring. I filled out an application in advance. Is there a rule against doing that?"

"None," boomed Dr. Westerbrook from the head of the table. "I'd say it shows initiative. Where is this line of questioning leading, Barney? It's clear Sherilyn was home to receive the supplement we mailed out to semifinalists."

Phipps twisted the stem of his water glass. "I made no secret of the fact that I thought her answers read like those of a man. And we know her original application was mailed locally."

What was he implying here? That she'd had some *man* complete her application? "That's right," Sherry said, trying not to sound defensive. "I asked my roommate to mail it when the position was announced. Out of curiosity—" Sherry's grip tightened on her fork "—how do women's answers differ from men's? Do we get a different form?"

"Certainly not." Barney touched his napkin to his lips. "Everyone knows men approach problems more analytically than women."

"Indeed?" Sherry's voice quivered with indignation, although she shouldn't have been shocked by his answer. She knew Barney Phipps didn't believe that women belonged in administration. And maybe not on the planet.

"Books have been written on the subject, for goodness' sake." The floundering VP looked to the row of administrators for help. None came to his aid.

When the silence had stretched long enough for Sherry to hear the ice in her tea melt, she decided she didn't want a job she had to cry foul to get. "I kept all my rough drafts," she said lightly. "Anyone know a reputable handwriting analyst?"

"More like a good lawyer." Lock glared first at Phipps, then at Westerbrook, who appeared unhappy with his second-in-command.

Phipps stood. "Excuse me, I just remembered a prior engagement." A collective sigh rose from administrators as the door closed.

"May I remind you," cautioned Westerbrook,

"that this institution prides itself on its commitment to equal opportunity."

It seemed a pointless statement in light of the previous exchange. Garrett reached across the table and shackled Sherry's wrist with a warm hand. "You know, you may have grounds to force them to give you the job."

She shook him off and picked up her fork. "How would *you* handle it?"

His lips twitched. "Call for sabers under the dueling oaks."

"I thought Texans used six-guns at high noon."

"Sorry, I was born and raised in Louisiana." He pronounced it *Loosyanna* in the slowest way.

Sherry stabbed more salad with her fork than she could eat in one bite. Then she set the fork down, feeling a need to explain. "My method may appear passive to you. But when I started teaching here, there were no female department chairs. Now we have two. If I play by the old guard's rules, maybe I'll be the first woman dean."

Garrett leaned back. She had guts. Not a response he'd have expected from the hysterical woman he'd met on the prairie. Which one was the real Sherry Campbell?

"Look," Sherry said in an undertone when she caught him staring at her across the table. "I'm no wimp. I can fight in the trenches when I have to."

He gingerly touched two fingers to a spot above his left ear. "I can certainly attest to that."

"Yes, well, I do apologize," she said stiffly. "You burst out of the fog, and…and…looked so scruffy. Then when you mentioned Huntsville, I panicked. I thought…prison." She cleared her throat. "Perhaps if I'd seen you at your campsite the way Nolan did, things might have been different."

He laughed, a deep rumble from his belly. "Yeah. You'd have finished the job you started. When Nolan stumbled in, I'd shucked my wet clothes. He caught me buck naked, my skin blue as Babe, Paul Bunyan's ox."

Sherry felt heat stealing up her neck into her cheeks. Still, it was hard not to laugh with a man capable of joking about himself. Sherry had met so few men who could do that. Except for Nolan, most of the men on campus took themselves far too seriously.

Garrett frowned; he hadn't meant to make her blush. That was not his style. He wasn't looking to start anything, especially not with a woman who might end up his subordinate. More like *in*subordinate based on his experience so far with Professor Sherilyn Campbell. He slid her a glance and was surprised to discover her fighting a smile. So she did have a sense of humor. Garrett wouldn't have thought it. Up till now, he'd labeled her tempestuous, if not shrewish.

As if reading his mind, Sherry shrugged. "I'm afraid we started off on the wrong foot. Blame it on knee-jerk reactions linked to our first disastrous meeting. Truth is, you're no chain-gang escapee and I'm not a menace to society." Genuine contrition tinged her words. "The thought of physical abuse sickens me. I can't explain what made me hit you after all I've seen and heard...." Her voice faded to a halt.

"I believe you," Garrett said. And he did. He'd heard the passion in her voice when she discussed the services she struggled to provide for abused women. A far greater range than those available on his campus in Huntsville. Yet if he believed the rumblings he'd heard from some faculty, several claimed that Sherilyn Campbell had a tendency to be too passionate on behalf of the Hub. That maybe she bought too readily into the women's stories. Or had quit looking to see if there were two sides. Even her advocates feared loss of objectivity with regard to men if she became dean. Her enemies, and Garrett knew it was impossible not to make them in the academic community, said she already wore blinders. Case in point, they said: check out how negative she was on the subject of her brother's marriage.

As lunch wound down, Garrett decided to test

the waters. "I hope Nolan rented the convention center for his wedding."

"Why?" Sherry pushed her dessert cup away. "Are you in favor of elaborate weddings?"

"No, but from the sound of it, everyone on campus plans to attend."

"Probably."

That didn't leave much of an opening for further discussion. Garrett backed off. What was he after, anyway? He'd never met the prospective bride. And he certainly wasn't a walking advertisement for a long and happy marriage.

Sherry stood up. "I'd advise a run to the men's room. If you think faculty hit hard, wait till the students strike. They have so little control over what happens on campus, these forums afford them the illusion of power."

"Are you always such a cynic?"

"A cynic?" Sherry raised a brow. "More like a realist. Student concerns rank low on the academic totem pole. That's fact."

Garrett eyed Sherry as she set her course for the door. Her suit today was gunmetal gray. Silk, he thought, and soft enough to allow fluid movement. She had nice legs. Mouth suddenly dry, Garrett darted a guilty glance around the table and discovered his weren't the only appreciative eyes glued to Professor Campbell. Why not? Looking didn't hurt, did it? Crumpling his napkin, he adjusted his new Brooks Brothers tie. Garrett sure hoped it impressed the team members, because it had cost what he considered an outrageous amount of money. Not only that, it was choking him.

Man, he hated ties. He could almost believe what a friend said, that they'd been designed by a woman bent on torturing men. He had to smile. That was the reverse of Carla's complaint about panty hose—muttered as she hung them wet on every surface in their minuscule bathroom. He recalled weaving his way through a sea of nylon to reach his shaving gear. Thinking back, Garrett guessed he hadn't minded so much.

Guiltily he caught himself up short. It'd been ages since he reminisced fondly about any aspect of his life with Carla. That cracker-box-size apartment was all they could afford on a first-year instructor's salary. More materialistic than he, Carla had wanted to drop out of school and work so they could get a bigger place. He'd insisted she finish her degree and encouraged her to go for an MBA. Then their method of birth control failed, and Keith was born before Carla graduated from the master's program.

Catering staff cleaned the table around him. Lost in memories, Garrett recalled begging Carla to take a year off. She'd refused. As a result, he'd spent more and more time juggling his job with domestic chores. Which delayed his receiving tenure. Then Carla became obsessed with banking, and that was the beginning of the end of their marriage.

"Dr. Lock."

Garrett roused himself as President Westerbrook called his name. He glanced around, surprised to find he was the only one still seated.

"Did Dr. Campbell leave that sour look on your face?"

Garrett smiled. "She said I'd be smart to hit the men's room before our meeting with the students. I'm weighing the pros and cons."

"Hmpf. Nothing students love more than extracting their pound of flesh from faculty and administrators."

"Will you be there?"

"Are you kidding? Avoiding confrontations with students is ritual with me. Each crop is more inventive than the last. Brr!" He clapped Garrett on the back, pointed him toward the men's room, then took off in the opposite direction.

Garrett arrived last of the three candidates. He noticed students who wore buttons that read Minority Affairs had Eli boxed into a corner. Professor Campbell gestured with a diet soda while chatting with some tough-looking women. Two were tattooed. At least two more were pregnant and in dire need of maternity clothes. Garrett felt a stab of sympathy. They looked so young. One of his first published papers had been titled *Babies Having Babies*. Something he liked about Wellmont's disadvantaged women's work-study program was that it provided parenting classes and a semester on nutrition. Also one on money management. Whole-life training was a concept few campuses embraced. Garrett wondered if Sherilyn had done any follow-up studies. If they made him dean, he'd suggest it.

A beanpole of a girl with wire-rimmed glasses blew a whistle to gain everyone's attention. Laughter and talk subsided. After introducing herself as student-body president, she read off several names. Those students went to stand beside her.

"We have some concerns that aren't being addressed now," the student president said. "Naturally we're interested in learning how each of you feel before we give our input to the interview team. Dr. Aguilar, if you'll respond first, followed by Dr. Lock and Dr. Campbell."

An angelic young woman with blond hair that brushed the waistband of her jeans took the mike. "Two years ago condom dispensers were installed in the men's rest rooms on campus. Administration won't even discuss placing them in ours. We want them. Where do you stand on this issue?"

Eli's skin turned splotchy red all the way to his bald spot. "I, ah, I'd have to see the statements already submitted. And there's cost to be considered."

All eyes shifted to Garrett. "It should be a line item in the dean of students' budget package. For men and women," he said without hesitation.

The dean of students vaulted from his chair, clearly agitated. "Last year, to kick off National Condom Week, our health department provided packets of condoms to put in campus newspapers. The students *stapled* the packets inside. Not only did I have to deal with their blunder, but parents who saw the paper were outraged to think we'd condone promiscuity on this campus."

Sherry faced him. "Harold, our mission is to teach. Shouldn't we teach responsibility?"

"A student's sexual activity is not our business, Professor Campbell. If anything, we should promote abstinence."

"So," Sherry said softly, "are we removing the dispensers from the men's lavatories? Or is it just women you're saying should abstain?"

Garrett hid a smile behind his hand as Harold's eyes bugged out. Then the dean abruptly got up and stalked from the room.

After that, the questions switched to academics. Students complained that faculty refused to give make-up exams. They claimed to need more night classes. Lively discussion ensued over the cancellation of a popular yearly conference called Women's Vision, Power and Potential.

All three candidates agreed those were requests worthy of a second look. By four o'clock they were ready to call it a day.

The minute they cleared the building, Garrett stripped off his suit jacket and loosened his tie. "Want a lift to the hotel, Eli? I drove my own vehicle today."

"Sure. I hope my wife's amenable to room service, this evening. I only want to hibernate."

"How about you, Doc?" Garrett turned to Sherry and said unexpectedly, "I'll spring for dinner at your favorite bar and grill, and even throw in dessert."

"Sorry, I already have plans." Sherry didn't, but the thought of accompanying him to some dim smoky pub caused her to break out in a cold sweat.

Garrett slung his coat carelessly over one shoulder. The offer had again sneaked out. For a minute there, he'd forgotten she lived with some fancy dude.

Sherry watched his shoulders slump in spite of the casual wave he tossed when they reached the fork in the path separating staff and visitor parking. She almost said she'd reconsidered his offer. Then because Garrett and Eli struck up a conversation, she kept going, pretending to search her purse for her car keys.

IF THE CANDIDATES believed they'd been raked over coals by the students, the individual interviews with the team were even tougher.

"Whew!" Garrett exclaimed as the three met again after their sessions. "Anybody who thinks deans are just figureheads ought to go through the interview process. From the questions, you'd think these guys were building a dynasty."

"Keep the sense of humor, Lock," Sherry said around a chuckle. "Wait'll the barracudas from the business community chew you up and spit you out."

And she was right. Townspeople vetting the candidates appeared innocent enough with their flashy rings and flashier smiles. Turned out each had a private agenda. All operated on the premise of "Scratch my back if you want endowments." At the end of the coffee hour, the candidates felt worked over by a battering ram.

Later, on their way out the door, Eli shook his head. "Am I such a babe in the woods? Deans here spend half their time politicking and the other half fund-raising."

Garrett, looking the least frazzled, shrugged. "Where I work now, fund-raising falls to the assistant dean. Yours truly." He gave a mock bow. "I try to take it in stride. Hey, it keeps the job from getting boring."

Sherry shouldered her purse. "Thankfully the wait's almost over. May the best man win. Or woman," she added cheekily, swinging down the path toward her car.

"My kids will be happy if I lose," Aguilar announced unexpectedly to Garrett as they watched her angle between the rows. "The oldest one says he won't leave California. What about your son?"

"He's bummed about leaving his friends. But this job puts us closer to his mother."

"I see. Well, if you get the nod, watch your back. I hear the current Women's Studies chairperson tends to blame men for *all* domestic discord."

"How so?" A little surprised by Eli's uncharacteristic remark, Garrett watched Sherry disappear from sight.

"Haven't you heard that Campbell's a man-eater? I'm not sure I could work with her," Eli said.

"Mm," was Garrett's only response. "Shall we go? I need to call my son before I dress for tonight's slaughter. He's staying with one of his friends in Huntsville. He doesn't like my being gone this long. I'd hate to miss touching base."

Eli thrust his hands in his pockets and fell in beside Garrett.

SHERRY MADE SURE she arrived early for the banquet. She'd dressed carefully for this event in basic black linen. Her only adornments were her grandmother's pearls and the discreet pearl studs at her ears. Strappy heels and a patent-leather evening bag completed her ensemble. As she entered the banquet room and stepped into a sea of chiffon and glittering sequins worn by the regents' wives, she felt drab. She should have known they'd put on the dog. Oh, well. She didn't have sequins and chiffon in her wardrobe.

Taking care to skirt the knots of people already deep in conversation, she turned down an offer of champagne and requested ginger ale. Tonight's interrogation would be subtle. If she hoped to win, her answers needed to sparkle. Wandering around the table, Sherry noticed that her place card sat between the other two candidates'. She didn't want to sit next to Garrett Lock. He muddied her thinking.

The minute no one was looking, she switched her card with that of Eli's wife. Twice. Each time someone put it back. Afraid of discovery, she gave up and decided to bite the bullet.

The three candidates didn't meet until they were seated for dinner. Eli wore tweed over a sweater vest. His wife was elegant in green satin. Lock had on a notch-collared tuxedo with a houndstooth checked tie and matching cummerbund.

His stomach was so flat not even one pleat on his cummerbund bunched when he sat. As soon as he took his seat beside her, a light clean tantalizing scent that Sherry couldn't quite place tickled her nose.

Garrett and Eli both asked the waiter for a drink.

"I'll stick with water," Sherry told the waiter as she let the talk flow around her. To her surprise the topic under discussion was gold-panning.

"You don't do it to get rich," Garrett said, bumping Sherry's arm as he swirled the ice in his glass. "'Scuse me," he murmured before returning to the conversation. "I look at gold-panning as a chance to spend time with my son while teaching him to appreciate the environment."

"Three cheers for that old male fire-in-the-belly, let's-commune-with-nature routine," Sherry quipped. "Definitely not the polished academician you see here. Give Lock a tent in the wilds and he becomes the outlaw Josie Wales. I know."

"So you met Garrett this summer, too?" President Westerbrook smiled at Sherry, then turned to Garrett. "Did Sherilyn look like herself, I wonder?"

Garrett's gaze shifted, inching slowly over her slender frame. He said nothing.

Sherry feigned interest in the soup the waiter had just brought. She'd said enough already.

Maybe too much. Clearly the men at the table envied Garrett's footloose lifestyle. And the women—the women, hooked on his slow Southern drawl—imagined what it'd be like to spend time alone with him in the wilds. Sherry dipped her spoon in her soup, only to have her arm jostled again by Garrett.

"Sorry," he said. "Banquet seating is a curse when you're left-handed."

Sitting next to him was a curse. Throughout the main course their arms constantly brushed, making Sherry all too aware of his broad shoulders. Worse, a member of the interview team asked Sherry's opinion on the proposed raise in tuition. Right in the middle of her answer, Garrett's leg accidentally bumped hers, and her mind blanked. She completely lost her train of thought, and as a result, she broke off lamely, prompting a row of elevated eyebrows.

With delivery of the main course, questions to the candidates turned personal. From living all her life in a city with more than one institution of higher learning, Sherry knew that during these interviews no area of a candidate's life was sacred.

Garrett appeared dumbfounded when a team member inquired about the details of his divorce. "We split over six years ago," he muttered. "I see no relevance. My ex-wife is remarried."

"You told Sheldon's wife that your boy lives

with you, Lock. Our deans often meet early in the morning or late into the evening. Will child care be a problem?"

Garrett stared at the speaker, his right hand squashing his napkin.

Sherry didn't know why she should resent the invasion of his privacy, but she did. "Our women's crises center, the Hub, is something of an authority on local child care," she put in smoothly. "We have a whole rack of brochures." Her response seemed to satisfy team members. They tossed the next barbed question at Eli.

"Thanks," whispered Garrett, scooting his chair closer to Sherry. "I guess I haven't thought ahead to child care. I had no idea they'd ask anything like that."

"Why would you? It's a question working mothers get asked. A woman thinks of her family first. A man thinks of his job."

"Now wait just a minute. You don't know me well enough to make snap judgments."

Sherry snatched her dessert spoon and made craters in the chocolate mousse a waiter set in front of her. She glanced around to see who'd heard, already regretting the childish display of temper.

Several sets of eyes were trained on her and Lock. Sherry squirmed in her chair. Her elbow and Garrett's made contact. She jerked aside, knocking over a newly topped-up water glass. The contents, ice included, were dumped in Garrett's lap.

"Oh, no!" She lunged for the glass and in so doing, upset his water goblet, too. She fluttered about, sopping up water with her napkin until Garrett grabbed her hand and said tersely, "That's enough!"

Sherry dragged the dripping square of linen to her breast. Gulping, she realized everyone but the three candidates—and President Westerbrook—had fled the table.

Eyes flinty, Garrett rose and shook ice onto the floor. "It seems Dr. Campbell has found a way to clear the field. Excuse me," he said. "Dinner was delightful. I trust someone will call my hotel with the results."

Before Sherry could deny knocking over the glasses on purpose, he vanished.

Folding her napkin with shaking fingers, she reached under her chair for her purse. "It was an accident," she stated firmly. "And it isn't fair to go on without him."

College administrators and team members huddled for a moment. "We probably have sufficient information to make a decision," Sheldon March announced. "Sherilyn, you and Eli may leave. We'll poll the team and I'll call everyone later."

Summarily dismissed, Sherry wrestled with a

sick feeling as she slunk out a back door. It was probably petty, but she hated the thought of receiving that call tonight. By tomorrow the results would be on local TV. She could wait for the bad news.

Yvette was still out of town, so once Sherry reached the safety of her home, she turned off the phone and her cell and went straight to bed.

CHAPTER FOUR

REPEATED POUNDING on Sherry's front door dragged her from a sound sleep. "All right, all right. I'm coming," she shouted, stumbling around the dark room searching for her robe and slippers. Her heart skittered wildly. People just didn't knock on her door in the middle of the night. Giving up on the slippers, still struggling to get one arm in the robe's sleeve, she hopped barefoot across the cold slab of entryway granite and tried to see through the peephole who was making such a racket.

Her parents. Panic made Sherry forget the sleeve as she worked to release the chain with fingers that shook. "What's wrong?" she cried, at last throwing open the door. "Did something happen to Nolan? Oh, no. Not Emily or the kids?"

"Nothing like that, dear." Her mother stepped inside and gently thrust Sherry's arm through the empty sleeve. "We were worried about you. Sheldon March phoned. He said he'd been trying to reach you since ten. He thought you might be at our house. We tried you, too. When it was after midnight and still no answer, well, your father and I thought we'd better check."

"We know you're an adult," said her father gruffly. "But it's not like you to stay out all night. So we got worried. Not even our community is exempt from nut cases."

Sherry smiled to assure them she wasn't angry. However, she only listened with half an ear. Would March bother her folks to deliver bad news? She shivered against a cool night breeze.

Mr. Campbell noticed. He herded them all inside and shut the door. "You're not sick, are you, Sherilyn?"

She shook her head. "I unplugged my answering machine and turned the ringer down on the phone. Did Sheldon give you a message?"

Her mother's eyes clouded in sympathy, and Sherry's hopes plummeted.

"He did, dear. What with Emily and the children staying with us, and Nolan dashing in and out to complete the remodeling of his home, I feel terrible that your father and I didn't even know you were being considered for a promotion. Why didn't you tell us?"

Sherry thought she'd steeled herself to lose, but from the way her stomach constricted, evidently she wasn't ready to face it. "All of our lives have been so hectic. I would have told you if I'd been selected."

Her parents exchanged guilty glances. "We've been running hither and yon helping Emily square away the wedding. You still should have called. But it does explain why you haven't dropped by. Emily's relieved it was business that kept you away. She's afraid that you're…unhappy about her marrying Nolan. Emily so wants you as her maid of honor, Sherilyn."

Sherry recoiled from the slight censure in her mother's tone. She'd hoped Emily would ask someone else to stand up with her. But she supposed her future sister-in-law felt it was appropriate, not only because they were friends, but because Sherry had been the one who'd invited Emily to take part in Nolan's study. But only to prove that today's women could function fine without men. Not Emily, apparently. It hadn't taken her three months to fall head-over-heels in love.

So okay, Sherry admitted it. Her nose was out of joint.

"Sherry? You look upset. I'm so sorry you lost out on the job, honey." Sherry's mother gave her a bracing hug.

"Who did get it?" Sherry asked dully. "Did Sheldon say?"

"Oh, yes." Mrs. Campbell turned to her husband. "I told you the man's name, Ben. Do you remember?"

Sherry's dad rustled his keys. "Not anyone we knew. Jared, or maybe Garth. Sounded like a cowboy singer."

"Garrett Lock," Sherry supplied. It was no big revelation, but having it spelled out cracked the dam on feelings she'd held at bay thus far. Now she faced real concern for the future of a program to which she'd dedicated so much energy. Coupled with that, a sense of failure seeped in. Personal, yes, but more than that. Her loss set back the upward mobility of women on campus.

"I'm sure it's a crushing disappointment at the moment, Sherry," her mother said gently. "But I've found things usually work out for the best. I'm sure something good will come of this. Give it time, dear."

"Yes," agreed her father. "Maybe it's a blessing in disguise. Your mom and I have been trying to find a way to broach one of our worries—we think you've given up all semblance of a private life for your job. We see more of Yvette than of you. She's always going to parties or out on a date. All you do is work, work, work."

A tic fluttered in Sherry's left eyelid. "Dad. It's after one, and I have to be at the office by eight."

"She's right, Ben." Sherry's mom slipped her arm through that of her spouse and hauled him toward the door. "It's enough that we had to be the bearers of bad tidings. We should have the decency to let her lick her wounds in private."

"Won't work, Mom," Sherry said, all the while wondering if she'd have half of Nan Campbell's verve when she reached sixty. "Your 'good cop, bad cop' routine doesn't work anymore. I've wised up."

"Pity," Nan murmured. "But then, I guess it's time you started working our old flimflam on your own offspring."

"Guilt isn't effective, either." Sherry crossed her arms and leaned a shoulder against the door frame. "I have a Ph.D. in psychology, remember?"

"Then I know you'll march right in there tomorrow and congratulate the winner," her mother whispered, tiptoeing into the dark courtyard that fronted the U-shaped complex of townhomes.

Sherry shut the door with enough force to rattle the stained-glass panels on either side. *Congratulate Garrett Lock?* "It'll be a cold day in… in Texas," she mumbled. Rats. Her mother could still lay on a guilt trip to beat all guilt trips.

As sleep was now out of the question, Sherry went into the kitchen and brewed a pot of Red Zinger tea. Forty minutes later, she dug out the telephone book and looked up the number of the hotel where her rivals were staying. Lifting the receiver, she quickly punched out the main number. A cheery voice answered.

"I'd like to leave messages for two of your guests," she said. "One will be checking out in the morning, so please tuck it under his door. Tell Dr. Eli Aguilar that I enjoyed meeting him and Marguerite. Say it's too bad there was only one job. Sign it Dr. Sherilyn Campbell." She spelled her first name. Even after the staff person read it back, Sherry wasn't sure what she wanted to say to Lock.

"You said two messages?" the clerk prompted.

"Yes. The second goes to Dr. Garrett Lock. Just say, congratulations on your appointment. And sign it the same way as the first."

After she hung up, Sherry worried that her message sounded too terse. She did have to work with the man. Somehow she couldn't bring herself to say work *for* him. Technically they were a team. That had been a big problem with Kruger. He hid in his office, preferring to issue edicts in rambling memos. She hated those memos—and the fact that she could never get an appointment with him to discuss any of his preposterous decrees. He required memos in return, too. Some of hers were so hot Angel joked that she needed to fan the keys on her computer as she typed them.

If Lock wanted to get off on the right foot, he'd make himself more accessible to staff. Come to think of it, Sherry didn't envy him having to listen to all the initial gripes that got tossed at a new dean. Faculty members all had their petty complaints and pet projects. The classified staff lobbied for less pressure and more help. As a department chair, she bullied for growth and expansion. And if the board's questions these past three days were any indication, they planned to tighten the old purse strings even more.

Sherry sighed. Maybe she was a teensy bit relieved to know that Garrett Lock would be the one tearing his hair out attending all those ulcer-inducing meetings and not her.

The clock in the living room struck three. Why go back to bed for a few short hours? Stifling a yawn, she got out her cookbook and decided to make something gooey and chocolate to take into the department tomorrow. One thing staff agreed on was that chocolate solved a lot of woes. If she appeared bearing chocolate fudge squares, no one would comment on her loss or the road maps in her eyes.

Would Lock be surprised? She'd bet he had her pegged as a sore loser. A sore loser without domestic talents, if he was anything like Nolan's pals in the history department.

By seven, Sherry had showered and dressed in her favorite baggy, hot pink pants, bright orange poet's blouse and comfy Birkenstocks. Mickey was once again ensconced on her wrist. Back to her old self. Almost, she lamented, running gel through her shorn locks. But her heavy hair had always been so difficult to tame. She might just stay with this cut for a while.

Feeling refreshed, she hummed along with a Sugarland CD she'd popped in the player before smoothing chocolate glaze on the cooled cake. In the middle of slicing finished squares, her doorbell pealed. "What now?" She licked chocolate off her fingers. She might be resigned, but that didn't mean she wanted well-meaning friends stopping by to commiserate. As her mom said, she preferred to lick her wounds in private.

"Yes?" She yanked open the door. The knife she'd been using to cut the cake slipped from her fingers, bounced off the floor and splattered chocolate across the light khaki pants of the man standing there.

Garrett Lock danced back too late to save himself. In doing so, he spilled water down the front of his shirt from the bud vase he held.

"I'm sorry." Sherry leaned down and brushed at the spots on his pant leg only to watch in horror as the chocolate smeared and spread. "Oh, no!" she gasped. "I've made it worse."

In trying to see what she'd done, Garrett tilted the vase the other way and poured a stream of water over Sherry's head.

"Stop! I just washed my hair." She leaped up, accidentally knocking the vase out of Garrett's hand. It flew through the air, crashed on the entry floor and exploded. For a heartbeat they both stared at the pale pink rosebud swimming in chocolate-muddied water. Sunlight streaming over Garrett's shoulders glittered off particles of glass embedded in the bruised petals of the delicate flower.

"Oh. Oh," Sherry said softly as she sank onto one knee to rescue the poor bedraggled rose.

"Wait." Garrett quickly jerked her to her feet. Too late. He saw a dark splotch of blood seeping through Sherry's pink pant leg. Hauling her into his arms, he strode into her living room where he dropped her unceremoniously into a rocking chair, still clutching the soggy flower.

Sherry's squeak of protest was cut off by the sound of rending fabric. In one fluid motion he'd ripped her pant leg from the bottom hem to three inches above her knee.

"What…what are you *doing?*" A tic hopscotched beneath her eyelid. "Look what you did to my best linen pants!" she gasped.

"Best…?" He blinked. "I thought they were pajamas. I also thought you'd bloodied your knee. I see now that you hit a blob of chocolate." Closing his eyes, he massaged the lean contours of his cheeks. "I have a cab waiting. I intended to cart you off to the emergency room."

"I can't believe you mutilated my pants." Sherry

smacked him with the rose she'd rescued from the muck, much as she would have done to Nolan. Hopping up, she literally shoved him out the door.

"Ouch! Are you nuts? That thing has thorns." Garrett put his arms up to ward off her swats. "I swear, for someone who claims to abhor violence, you get plenty physical," he grumbled.

Sherry slid on the wet flagstone and almost fell. He caught her and held her upright until she shucked off his hands and toppled into the decorative railing that edged her small porch. "You bring out the worst in me, Lock. Shouldn't you be meeting with Westerbrook and the rest of the deans?"

The blue eyes assessing her narrowed marginally. "I got your note of congratulations and decided I'd been rude last night. The hotel gift shop was open and...well, I bought the flower. I was out the door before I happened to think what people would say if I gave it to you on campus. I found you in the phone book. I don't know the area, so I called a cab. You look different, by the way. What have you done to yourself?"

"I've gone back to my old job, as if you didn't know. And let me say again—dumping that water on you last night *was* an accident." Her gaze strayed to the pathetic flower now bent and mangled. Softness crept into her voice. "The rose was a nice gesture, Lock."

"Then do you mind telling me what happened

here? Do you throw knives at every man who knocks at your door?"

"I didn't throw it. You were the last person I expected to see. The knife sort of…fell out of my hand. Um, I really feel bad about the chocolate on your pants. I'll give you the name of my dry cleaner. Tell him to put it on my bill. If you hurry, you should be able to change and still make it to campus to meet the brass." He'd be on time, but she'd have to rewash her hair. Rumors would fly, after all, about her being a sore loser.

"Are you sure you didn't cut your knee?" He leaned down to check again.

His breath tickled her skin. It was all Sherry could do to stand still for his examination until he muttered, "Yup. You're fit as a fiddle." He stood abruptly and she flinched and flattened against the railing.

"You're sure one jumpy female. Hey, I feel awful, tearing your pants like that."

"We could call it even. I take care of my ruined pants. You take care of yours. And don't feel obliged to replace the rose. Is that your cabbie honking?" She leaned over, trying to see out to the parking strip.

Like a shot, Garrett pulled her back. His fingers flexed around her upper arms. "Stop. You make me nervous. That top rail wobbles." He set her nearer the door.

She looked amused. "The railing has always wobbled, and I've lived here five years. That *is* your cab's horn," she said pointedly.

He still seemed unsure whether to go or not. "I hate leaving you with this mess. If you have a broom, I'll sweep up the glass. I'm paying the driver. He can wait."

Somehow picturing this man, who as of today was her boss, inside her home with a broom in his hands, drove Sherry's nerves to red alert. "I'm not the one with an early meeting," she said firmly. "Go."

He did, but only because the cabdriver lay on the horn and Garrett didn't want any of Sherry's neighbors calling the cops. "I feel like we're still off on the wrong foot," he called as he walked backward along the center walkway.

Sherry's stomach stayed in knots until he totally disappeared. She'd never met a man who made a habit of throwing her into a tailspin.

Once she'd cleaned up the glass and the watery mess and washed her hair, Sherry peeled off her pants and tossed them in the trash.

"For pity's sake!" Lock attracted accidents. Or else she did.

His concern for her welfare had been commendable, however. That warm pleasant thought kept him on her mind as Sherry yanked a wild print skirt from the closet. Its riot of colors further lightened her mood.

LATE AGAIN, Sherry detoured past her office to the staff break room. Angel intercepted her, the secretary's cool gray eyes assessing. "Those goodies don't fool me, boss lady. You stayed up half the night crying, didn't you?"

"Nary a tear. I wouldn't give them the satisfaction." Sherry lifted her chin.

"The prez sashayed his drugstore cowboy by here to see his new digs half an hour ago. Think you oughta know I'm probably the only woman on campus who isn't tripping over her feet to kiss up to macho man."

Sherry placed her chocolate squares on the break-room table, along with paper plates and plastic forks, as she listened to Angel. "I expected as much."

"What are we going to do?" Angel asked when Sherry headed into her office.

"Do?"

"Yeah. Are we gonna roll over and play dead or give him the business like we did old man Kruger?"

Sherry stuffed her purse into the locking file where she kept it during working hours. For some reason she recalled how he'd looked, standing in her doorway, holding a rose. "The man deserves a chance, Angel."

"Don't tell me you've fallen for his pretty face, too?"

"Certainly not. It's just…well, I believe a person is innocent until proven guilty. If Lock rides the fence like Kruger, then we'll take him to task." Sherry's lips twitched in the barest hint of a grin.

"He's a man, isn't he? Already has three strikes against him."

Sherry watched Angel turn and dash out to answer the department phone. She remembered the accusation Yvette threw at her the other day—how friends thought she'd become a man hater. It wasn't true, even if her attitude toward men had become a little…jaundiced. Angel, now, had good reason to be bitter, hooking up with two losers before the age of twenty-five. Still, there *were* good men out there.

Sherry made a mental note to watch what she said from now on. She was the teacher—the one charged with straightening out her students sometimes warped views. Taking a moment to give the situation serious thought, Sherry realized her disenchantment with the opposite sex had come about gradually.

The people she dealt with day in and day out were mostly women whose spouses had left them for someone younger. Wives whose husbands abused them physically and mentally. Mothers fighting for custody of their kids. Women unable to get minimal maintenance from the men who'd fathered their children. Who *wouldn't* be jaundiced?

Rearranging a stack of files, Sherry's thoughts turned to her new boss. What was the reason for *his* divorce? He'd certainly evaded the team's questions on that subject. Was it because the truth would hurt him?

Sherry slammed the files into a box. There she was, doing it again. Condemning a man on the basis of his sex. She'd told Angel she was going to give Garrett Lock a fair shake, and she would.

It didn't bode well for him, however, that he didn't bother showing up in the department again all day.

At five minutes to five, Dr. Westerbrook paid Sherry a visit.

"I want you to know, Sherilyn, the decision to hire Garrett was unanimous. Dr. Lock had more administrative experience. Our decision would have been harder if you'd been an assistant dean. There are larger institutions elsewhere in the state that may have openings for assistant deans."

Sherry rocked back in her chair. "Am I to gather that Lock objects to working with me?" Anger clenched her stomach. It took every ounce of professional acumen to keep her tone level.

"Not at all." Westerbrook appeared ruffled. "Sheldon wants assurance that you'll play ball with the new dean. Will you cooperate, Sherilyn?"

"It's not hard to be cooperative with an invisible man. Where is the boy wonder?"

"That's the attitude that worries us," Westerbrook exclaimed. "According to the contract, Garrett has two weeks to relocate his household before he starts the job. It's not his fault that Kruger waited until so late to declare his intent to retire. We'll have to begin classes next week without Lock."

"A lot goes on in the first two weeks that needs the dean's attention. Who'll sign overloads and make decisions about adding and dropping classes based on enrollment?"

Westerbrook puffed out his cheeks. "Routine matters. Kruger said he relied heavily on your recommendations." He grasped the doorknob as if wanting to escape. "What if I authorize giving you the title of interim dean? It'll look impressive on your résumé."

Sherry trailed him to the door. "Do I need a résumé?"

"No, of course not," he blustered. "But I assumed that since you'd put in for one administrative post, you'd naturally try for another."

Sherry crossed her arms. "Tell Sheldon March

not to get his hopes up. Every college needs a watchdog. I think I'm rather good at it."

"Um…yes. So you'll oversee the department's opening weeks?"

"Lock will owe me big time, but yes, I'll do it." She sounded reluctant but inside she jumped for joy. She and Kruger had always fought bitterly over his dropping classes from the schedule too early. This was one semester they'd be safe.

Still humming happily on the drive home, Sherry had barely cleared the door to her town house and kicked off her shoes when her phone rang. It was Garrett Lock.

"I'm looking at a registration printout," he said without identifying himself. Not that he had to. Sherry would have known that drawl anywhere. "I see two classes with low enrollment. If there's no change by tomorrow, cancel them."

"Where are you? How did you get a printout?"

He chuckled. "I'm in Huntsville. I had the college computer guru link my laptop to the administrative computer program before I left today. You didn't think I'd shirk my duties, did you?"

That was exactly what she'd thought. So the title of interim dean didn't mean diddly. A figurehead. That was all they wanted. A warm body to take the flak from disgruntled students. She felt her temper sizzle on a short fuse.

"Hello! Are you there?" he asked loudly.

"Cancel them yourself. You don't need me if you have access to enrollment."

There were shouts in the background, then muffled mumbling. "Sorry." He came back on the line. "What was that you said? Things are squirrelly here. Movers are trying to give me an estimate and my son locked them out of his room."

Sherry thought he did sound harried. *The busier, the better.* "You must have a million and one things to do," she soothed. "Leave this kind of stuff in my hands, okay."

There was silence except for the hum of the wire, as if he was weighing her suggestion.

"You can trust me." Sherry injected enough indignation in her tone to push his guilt buttons.

"All right, but keep me posted." He reeled off his email address.

She scribbled it down, never intending to use it. They rang off. She'd no more than hung up when the phone jingled again. This time it was her mother, inviting her to a family barbecue. "Saturday night. To celebrate your birthday, dear."

"Don't, Mom. I'm acting dean until Dr. Lock completes his move. I'll probably have to work Saturday." Her family meant well, but on each successive birthday, more was made of her single status. She didn't need that this year, what with losing out on the promotion and with Nolan so sappy in love. Talk was bound to turn toward weddings. In fact, she'd be willing to guarantee it.

"Nonsense," Nan Campbell chided. "You shouldn't work as late as seven, and you have to eat. Dad's lighting the barbecue at six-forty-five. Be here." Sherry found herself staring at a buzzing receiver.

The jarring reminder that she faced turning thirty-two in a few days left her feeling melancholy. It didn't help that in the day's mail were two invitations to wedding showers for Emily and Nolan. Sherry went into the kitchen and threw herself into a cooking frenzy. After dirtying half the pans in the cupboard making chicken cordon bleu for one, she set the table with her grandmother's fine china, lit a taper and poured a glass of wine.

She was perfectly happy being single. A woman didn't need a man to enjoy a romantic dinner. It was just random bad luck that the songs she'd slipped into the CD player were all about everlasting love.

Sherry picked at her food. In a fit of feeling sorry for herself, she wished she'd gone out more with friends. If she had, on evenings such as this she'd feel free to drop by the pub where the old crowd tended to hang out.

What was wrong with her? For crying out loud, she was a psychologist. She was a woman in her prime. There wasn't a reason in the world for her to feel as if life had passed her by. No reason at all.

AT WORK THE NEXT DAY, Garrett Lock phoned her four times.

Five times the day after. More on Friday.

By Saturday Sherry viewed the prospective party at her parents' home as an escape from his infuriating meddling in every decision she made.

Emily met Sherry at the door and engulfed her in a hug. Megan and Mark, age fourteen and twelve respectively, Emily's two kids from her previous marriage, blindfolded Sherry the minute their mom returned to the kitchen.

Calling her Auntie Sherry, the kids led her to a stack of presents. Amid boisterous shouts, they instructed her to guess what was in each package. Sherry had developed a soft spot for these two. Although Megan had started the wagon-train journey as a trial, she'd turned out to be quite a plucky young woman by the end of summer.

"Hey, you guys, I've never been an aunt. I think I'm going to like it." Sherry poked and prodded the many gifts. "It means more packages to open," she teased.

"You rascals," Emily scolded her two. "Untie that scarf and let Sherry see. I think Megan hid a box under the couch that she hoped you'd miss."

As the blindfold came off, Sherry noticed Megan's blush. "Isn't that always the way?" Sherry said gently. "We buy other people what we're dying to have ourselves."

"It's not so much that I want what we bought you as I want *something* new. Everyone here is so busy with wedding stuff Mark and I haven't shopped for school clothes. We start our new schools next week."

Nolan, who'd come in from the patio, shot a worried glance at his bride-to-be. "Emily, maybe you and Mom should take a day off. Clothes are important to kids starting a new school. If it's a matter of money—"

"It's not," Emily rushed in. She gazed helplessly at her future mother-in-law.

Nan turned to her son. "Nolan, you're the one insisting on a big church wedding. These things take time. I'm afraid we don't have a free minute next week."

Sherry was moved by the kids' long faces. And if she spent another interminable week at the beck and call of Garrett Lock, she'd probably go berserk. "Tell you what, guys, any aunt worth her salt would rescue you. How about if I take you both to the mall next Saturday? All day. We'll grab hamburgers or a pizza and do the concert in the park that evening." She named a well-known rock group scheduled to perform.

Megan and Mark shouted with glee.

Emily bit her lip. "Sherry, are you sure? Nan said your job—"

"Positive," Sherry broke in. "Mom and Dad think I'm working too hard. Besides, the new dean needs to get rid of the notion that I'm his flunky."

"How are you and Garrett getting on?" Nolan asked casually.

"Swell." She made a face and picked up one of the gifts. "He hasn't even been in the office and already I feel like his personal gofer. Do this, do that. He's good at barking orders."

"Give the guy a break. Among other things, he's having trouble finding a place to live."

"Really? On his salary I shouldn't think it'd be a problem." Sherry did the fake violin thing, and the kids laughed.

Nolan silenced their antics. "Garrett called in a panic yesterday and asked me to keep an eye out for houses for sale or rent. He'd like three bedrooms and a yard."

"Tell him to call a Realtor." Sherry's conscience niggled as she recalled the corner town house in her complex; just today the owner had posted a sign for sale or lease. It had three bedrooms and a nice backyard. Also a loft bedroom with a city view. But it was much too close to where she lived. From porch to porch, less than a hundred yards.

Sherry pretended interest in folding the paper she'd removed from the gift, which turned out to be a CD carrying case from Mark. Thankfully her terse response motivated a change of subject. Garrett Lock's name didn't come up again all evening. Sherry actually relaxed and enjoyed herself. She even let them ensnare her in the wedding plans. Before she left, she caved in and agreed to be Emily's maid of honor. Something about weddings was infectious.

By the end of the week following her birthday bash, Sherry was ready to wring Lock's neck. If she talked to him once a day, she talked to him fifty times.

Five o'clock, Friday night, she fumed into the telephone, "You're being unreasonable. I have ten students on a degree track who need that class. If they don't get it this semester, they'll have to delay graduation until summer. Six of them won't qualify for grant money if they extend."

"The rules are clear," Garrett said, equally exasperated. "It takes twelve students for the class to run. Find two more students."

"I can't," she wailed. "Cut me some slack here, Lock. The money isn't coming out of your pocket."

"Technically it is. Or it soon will be when I become a home owner/taxpayer. The best I can do is hold off another day. Phone me names and social security numbers of two students by six tomorrow night, and I'll punch them into the system myself."

She thought of her proposed shopping trip with Emily's kids. "I can't tomorrow. My…my mom is sick and I'm needed at home," she said on impulse. "I'll do it Sunday. Will you give me two days?" Sherry felt guilty for lying. But he'd already run her ragged today. Her back ached. Her eyes burned. She was dead on her feet. She couldn't stay late. To find students to fill a class meant tedious hours at the computer going through individual class schedules of everyone in her program.

"I'm sorry to hear about your mom. Nothing serious, I hope."

"Flu," she mumbled, feeling the flush of guilt warm her neck and cheeks.

He waited a heartbeat. "All right. Two days. Give me your folks' phone number. Since I'm not sure if I'll be at the hotel or if the Realtor's going to find me something, I'll call you."

"Use my number. I'll access my machine. Their phone's unlisted," she said lamely, wishing she could take everything back. One fabrication only seemed to beget another.

"All right. Good luck, Sherilyn. For the record, I dislike putting a hardship on students as much as you do." He clicked off, leaving her with mushy insides because of the soft way he drawled her name. And leaving her feeling embarrassed and ashamed because of the ease with which he'd accepted her lie.

"'Oh, what a tangled web we weave, / when first we practice to deceive,'" she muttered, vowing this was the last time she'd go out on a limb like this.

CHAPTER FIVE

SHERRY RECALLED THAT very quote when at ten sharp on Saturday, she and the kids elbowed their way up to a jeans sale table at the mall and she found herself facing none other than Garrett Lock.

Nobody deserves such rotten luck. Nobody.

Garrett recovered first from the shock of seeing her. "Either this sale is a sleeper and worth more than it looks or your mom underwent a miraculous recovery."

"I, ah, she…is better, thank you. Come on, kids, let's check other stores to compare prices." If ever Sherry wanted to sink through the floor and disappear, it was now.

Megan glanced with interest at the man talking with her soon-to-be aunt. Then in the blunt way of teens, she said, "I didn't know Gram was sick. She looked okay to me when she and Mom left to see the florist this morning."

Sherry dropped the jeans she'd been inspecting. She stared in horror at Megan. Now she was truly nailed.

The girl flung the pair of jeans she held onto

the table. Eyes defiant, she pushed her brother toward the door. "Your mom said for us to call her Gram, didn't she, Mark?" The statement was carelessly thrown at Sherry.

"Oh, Megan, I'm upset with myself, not you. Never tell even a tiny white lie," she groaned. "They have a way of backfiring. Kids, I'd like you to meet Dr. Lock, my boss at the college. I told him Mom had the flu so I could skip work today and bring you shopping." Her story emerged in nervous spurts.

Garrett smiled at the kids. "I'd have known you anywhere from Nolan's description. He brags on you shamelessly. So? Are you all shopping for school? My son and I are, too. Keith? Where'd he go?" Garrett searched the aisles, then stepped back, practically trampling a small blond boy.

Sherry's heart went out to the child, whose huge blue eyes were framed by thick dark lashes most girls would kill to have. He seemed awkward, as if he hadn't grown into his feet. Or frightened, the way he stared at his sneakers, barely mumbling hello in response to Mark and Megan's greeting. Garrett Lock was so outgoing his son's shyness struck a sympathetic chord in Sherry.

Her imagination kicked into overdrive as Garrett tried unsuccessfully to draw the boy out. Sherry judged that Keith felt intimidated by his dad. Who knew what Garrett was like as a parent? As a husband? She'd heard somewhere that Texas law had a tendency to favor men in cases of divorce. Did the poor tyke miss his mom? Was that it? Had Garrett taken this job to spite his ex-wife? To keep the boy from her?

"What?" With a start Sherry realized Lock had spoken to her.

"I said, I don't expect you to work weekends. I realize now that we set a Sunday deadline. It didn't register at the time. My mind's been jumpy as a frog in a hot skillet. Keith's school starts Monday. If we don't find a house, I may be forced to transfer him a second time when we do."

"Your Realtor…?"

"Isn't worth ten cents in Confederate money. He claims the market's bad because of heavier than normal enrollment in all the area colleges." His eyes clouded. "Everything we own is stored, which is why we're shopping. Most of Keith's clothes ended up in boxes at the back of the storage unit."

Megan shifted from one foot to another, a frown of concentration wrinkling her forehead. "I saw a For Sale sign this morning."

Sherry sucked in a breath. Megan must mean the sign outside the corner town house. Sherry purposely closed her ears. Who in their right mind would want their boss next door? She picked up the jeans Mark had said he liked. "I'll go pay for these. Megan, if you want those—" she pointed to the pair Megan had tossed aside "—bring them." Sherry headed for the cash register.

Garrett detained Megan. "Where did you see a For Sale sign?"

Her frown deepened. "On our way here, I think...but I can't exactly remember."

"Oh. Too bad."

"Look," Sherry called back, "I hate to be unsociable, but the kids have long shopping lists. This is the last weekend before school opens, so the stores will get crazy by afternoon." She aimed a smile at Garrett's son, who peeked at her from behind a rack of shirts. "Opening day of school is pretty exciting, Keith."

He continued to watch her with solemn eyes.

Garrett joined his son. "Guess we'll go." He tossed Sherry a wave, and she fluttered her fingers, wishing he'd hurry up and leave.

Megan bounced over to where Sherry had moved up in the line. "He seems nice. A fox. Don't you just love how he talks? Southern drawls are sooo dreamy."

Sherry mumbled something unintelligible. The very last thing she needed was to agree and have it somehow get back to Lock. Chatterbox that Megan was, she might blab anything at the dinner table. Not that Nolan gossiped. But if he somehow let news of that nature slip in his department, those guys would have a field day spreading rumors.

Sherry craned her neck to watch Lock's broad back disappear out the door. Only then did her breakfast settle. In a mall this big she naturally assumed they'd seen the last of the Locks. After paying, she guided the kids to the next store. And the next.

"So we meet again." Garrett's lazy greeting an hour later grated on Sherry's frazzled nerves. She spun toward his voice and landed squarely on the toe of his shiny black boot. "What are you doin—" Thrown off balance, Sherry fell against him.

Garrett caught her. Hopping on one foot, he polished the toe of his damaged boot against the opposite denim-clad leg. "I do believe you're trying to maim me for life, Doc."

All ten of Sherry's fingers dug into the soft fabric of his shirt for a moment—until she felt singed by the heat of the hard flesh underneath. It was she who scrambled out of his grasp. "Why are you shopping at Victoria's Secret?" she whispered loudly.

"I...uh..." He glanced around, noting for the first time racks of satin-and-lace undergarments. Taking her arm, he dragged her and her many packages toward the door. "We ran into Mark. He said as soon as you're finished here, y'all plan to eat lunch. I thought we might go together."

She dug in her heels and ground to a stop. "Why?"

"Why what?" He flashed another nervous glance around. No one appeared to be paying attention, but Garrett felt more at ease after stepping out of the store and into the mall.

Sherry signaled to Megan that she'd be right back. Garrett's obvious discomfort stirred amusement and a modicum of sympathy in her. She realized, too, that inviting himself to lunch hadn't been a come-on. So what *was* his purpose? "I repeat, why should we eat together?"

His gaze swerved to his son, who was seated on a bench beside Mark. Garrett's expression changed. Softened. "Keith's having a hard time adjusting to the move. Huntsville is the only home he's known. Mark's older, but the two seem to be getting along. I thought—"

"If Keith's feelings were such a big priority, why did you go after this job in the first place?"

"My reasons are personal." Shutters clicked firmly into place.

What reasons? Too bad she was an advocate of a person's right to privacy. Anyway, secrets didn't stay secret for long on campus. She felt herself giving in. Lunch for the sake of a little boy wasn't a major sacrifice. "Mark knows the way to the pizza parlor. You guys go stake out a table. Megan and I'll join you when we finish here."

"Thanks. I owe you, Doc." He said it as if he meant it.

"No biggie," she mumbled. "And stop calling me Doc. You're one, too."

"I know, but referring to women by their last name goes against my Southern upbringing. I was taught to call ladies ma'am. A courtesy I had to unlearn as times have changed. Genderless titles are safest. Especially with you. You did object to our being on a first-name basis, remember."

She had. She'd been pretty annoyed, and it'd be a cold day in Panama before she'd apologize for being a feminist. "At work I insist on formality. Off campus, I guess there's no harm in our using first names," she grudgingly agreed.

The good Professor Campbell was as bristly as a hedgehog. *Oh.* Did she think he wanted them to be more than colleagues? Garrett tensed briefly until he recalled the ear-dusting campus gossip and relaxed. She wasn't a big fan of men. "Okay, since it's settled, the boys and I will take off. Shall we order or wait?"

"Order yours. Megan and I'll decide after we get there. I'd better go keep her from buying out the store." She waved toward the window.

"Good luck with that. I believe I hear my pizza

calling." He walked off, leaving her looking bemused.

Garrett had sprung from Confederate stock, so he knew better than to provoke a battle he had no hope of winning. Considering who he'd taken on, it was better to sound a retreat.

Sherry watched him collect the boys. In those square-toed boots, Garrett Lock had an intriguing walk. A walk that defied definition. But walk or no walk, he was her boss. She fanned suddenly hot cheeks and ducked back into the store.

Bitten by the shopping bug, Megan didn't want to stop for lunch.

"Mark's already gone to save us a place," Sherry said.

Megan flounced along beside her. "Pizza is so fattening."

"Serious shopping burns a lot of calories," Sherry returned dryly. "Not that you have to worry. What are you? A size three?"

"Five." Megan said it as though five was one step from requiring the services of a tentmaker.

Sherry rolled her eyes. "This place has a salad bar." They were still heatedly discussing what constituted fat when they arrived at the table occupied by Garrett and the boys.

"Fat? Who's fat?" Garrett demanded. "Present company excepted, of course." His assessing blue gaze skipped over Megan's skinny frame to loiter on Sherry's more womanly curves.

She felt like a rabbit caught in the crosshairs of his sight. That look was precisely why she'd had second thoughts about this impromptu lunch date. *No, not a date. Not by any means.* She dropped her purse on the empty seat between them, then relieved Megan of her shopping bags to build the buffer higher.

"Girls always think they're fat," Mark informed Keith Lock with the superiority of his advanced age. "If you hadda sister, you'd hafta listen to girls gripe about stuff like that all the time. Girls always think they're fat."

"'Least you've got company," Keith said wistfully.

Megan leaned across the table and slugged her brother in the shoulders.

Rubbing the spot, Mark said to Keith, "You're the lucky one being an only kid. Look at the abuse I gotta take. 'Cause guys can't hit a girl back and they know it."

"Girls shouldn't hit boys, either," Sherry put in after noting a faint frown between Garrett's brows. Although he appeared to be staring at Keith, Sherry thought his disapproval must be aimed at her for not having better control of her charges. "Mark, if you've ordered, would you go tell them Megan and I want the salad bar?"

She dug in her purse and handed him some bills. "Take out enough for your pizza, too."

The boy pocketed the money. "Can I keep the change? When Keith and me finish eating, we wanna drop some coin in the techno peeps."

Sherry gaped. "Say what?"

Megan interpreted. "He means they want to play the video games. They have cool ones here. Can I play, too?"

"You may," Sherry said. "All of you may, if we have time."

Keith slouched. "My dad probably won't let me."

"It's just in the back room," Sherry informed Garrett, again wondering if he was a real tyrant. Or did he resent not having a macho son? How many times had she heard that complaint from the moms she counseled? Her heart pinched. Where was Keith's mother that she'd allow him to suffer through this machismo routine?

Garrett was genuinely puzzled by Sherry's harsh expression. *Now what?* What had she read into his thoughts this time? Well, he'd put up with her attitude for Keith's sake. His son had been so down since their move it worried Garrett.

"If you clean your plate," he murmured, "you may do the videos." Garrett hated resorting to bribes, but lately Keith only picked at his food. He'd always been wiry, and it wasn't so much the boy's ribs sticking out that Garrett found troubling as his inertia. Keith didn't seem to care about anything. Not where they were going to live or the prospect of starting school, though he'd always loved his classes. More baffling, he seemed angry at Carla. And wouldn't you know she'd told her lawyer Garrett was turning their son against her. He'd been so careful to hide his feelings from Keith.

Mark's getting up to go and place Sherry and Megan's order jostled Garrett from his private thoughts. "I'll buy drinks," he said, rising, too. "What would you like?"

"Water for me," Megan said.

"Me, too, but I'll fetch mine after we get our salads," Sherry said.

"You'll *fetch* it?" Garrett laughed, his good humor restored for the moment. "Don't razz me anymore about coming from Cowpatty college."

"I never did. I love listening to you talk." The instant the admission left her lips, her face flamed, and so did his.

He muttered something about buying sodas while the line was short.

Megan pushed her chair back. "Hey, there's a girl I met at registration. I'll be right back. I want to ask her what kids are gonna wear the first day of school. Go on through the salad line,

Aunt Sherry." She left Sherry alone at the table with Garrett's son.

"Um, Keith, around here kids your age wear a lot of denim shorts and T-shirts at the start of school. It's still hot and humid in the classrooms."

He sat straighter. "Really? That's what we wore in Texas. Will you tell my dad? He's been lookin' at dweeby plaid shirts."

Sherry tried not to smile. "Our schools do have strict rules about the kinds of logos on the T-shirts," she cautioned.

"What's a logo?"

"Pictures and advertisements." Then she reduced it to his level. "No shirts with bad words and stuff."

"Oh." He wriggled forward in the seat, swinging his knobby knees. "My dad'd never buy me those."

"What won't Dad buy you, buddy?" Neither Keith nor Sherry had heard Garrett return. Smiling, he pulled out a chair, sat and placed a pitcher of soft drinks and several empty glasses on the table. "My line went faster than Mark's," he said, tilting back in his chair. "Now, what is it you want that I won't buy you, Keith?"

"Nothin'." Keith shut down.

Sherry recognized the sullenness. Exactly how Megan had acted toward Emily at the start of the wagon-train expedition. Taking pity on Garrett,

Sherry apprised him of what he'd missed. Except for the remark about dweeby plaid shirts. That was for Keith to relay.

"See, son? Your new school won't be much different from your old one. That should make you happy."

"I still won't know nobody," he said defiantly.

Garrett sighed. Unconsciously he turned to Sherry for support.

She didn't know what he wanted from her. Clearly his son was no happier than she that Garrett had come to Columbia. What could she say? That it wasn't too late for him to bow out? It was. Who'd step in knowing he—or she—was second-best? The person would never get respect.

The silence dragged out between them.

Mark clomped up in his size-eleven unlaced sneakers and threw himself into the chair next to Keith. "Sheesh! What a dork taking orders. Like, how hard is it to punch in two salads? Here's your plate, Aunt Sherry. Where's Megan?" He waved a second platter in the air.

"Talking to someone she met about school."

Nudging Keith, Mark said, "I really like livin' here. Things are…comfortable, you know?"

Keith's shrug said he didn't agree.

Sherry felt Garrett had been left in the dark. "Emily's in-laws were pretty controlling. They ran the town and everyone in it. Columbia's a much bigger city, so life here is a very different experience for these guys."

"A better one!" Mark threw in.

"Uh, thanks," Garrett mumbled. "As new kid on the block I still have a lot to learn about this place."

She rested an elbow on the table. "I've never lived anywhere else. I can't imagine moving, although I like to travel."

Keith Lock's lower lip trembled. "I don't see why we hafta move closer to Mom." Leaping up, he knocked his chair over as he ran toward the rest room.

Sherry gasped. "I'm sorry if I caused that."

Garrett fumbled to right the chair. "This isn't like him. Excuse me—I need to go straighten things out."

Megan, who'd wandered back to the table in time to hear Keith's outburst, winced, remembering, no doubt, her recent shouting matches with her mother.

Still shaken by Keith's blowup, Sherry wished she'd declined Garrett's invitation.

"You'd better hurry and get him," Mark hollered after Garrett. "Here comes our pizza."

Needing space, Sherry announced that she was going to the salad bar.

"Me, too." Megan trotted after her. "Keith Lock

is one unhappy puppy," she said, heaping lettuce on her plate. "I feel bad for him, don't you?"

"You and Mark are starting new schools," Sherry said, bypassing the croutons and other toppings. "Is transferring really so hard?"

"No. But we're getting a new dad, a big house and a dog. What do you suppose happened that Keith's so bummed at his mother?"

"I don't know, Megan. Those aren't questions one asks a new boss." Although Sherry was more curious than ever. She'd assumed Garrett's move had to do with trying to avoid his ex. Now it sounded as if the opposite was true. Maybe he still loved her.

Sherry's hands tightened involuntarily on her plate. Maybe he was one of those men who obsessed over a wife who'd rejected him. Last year they'd accepted a young woman into the program whose ex-husband wouldn't let go. First he stalked her. In the end he killed her, then turned the gun on himself.

Heart pounding, Sherry watched Garrett and Keith navigate the rows of tables as they returned. The man's face was positively grim. He kept a firm grip on his son's shoulder. Sherry felt so sorry for Keith that she lost her appetite.

"Is that all you're eating?" Megan asked, eyeing the small lump of salad on Sherry's plate.

She thrust her Mickey Mouse watch under Megan's nose. "Look at the time. We still have a lot of shopping to do."

"Gotcha. So let's eat fast and split. Amy—she's the girl I went to see—she bought this really great dress at a boutique on the lower mall. She said they had one left in my size. It's lime green and *so* cool."

"By all means." Sherry sighed with relief. "Eat and we'll split."

Keith ate in silence. Garrett tossed out various topics that nobody took up. Sherry responded with a sentence or less, spread her salad around and kept staring at Garrett in a strange way.

"Have I done something to offend you?" he finally asked, a little exasperated.

"No." She pushed her plate away. "Are you kids finished?" She gathered her purse and packages and stood.

"What's the rush?" Mark asked around a mouthful of pizza. "Me'n Keith were gonna do videos, 'member?"

Sherry started to say no but caught sight of Keith Lock's blue eyes resigned to yet another disappointment. "One game," she said, slipping back to balance on the edge of her chair. "Two, max. And make them short ones, Mark."

"You got it!" He stuffed the last bite into his mouth, latched on to Keith's hand and dragged him toward the dark cavern that housed the noisy games.

Megan rose with more grace, then—forgetting her age—chased after the boys.

Garrett set his slice of pizza aside to pour another soda. "I appreciate what you just did," he said. "I know it's biting into your day." With a quick glance toward the room that'd swallowed the kids, he said, almost too softly for Sherry to hear, "Carla is forever making him promises she doesn't keep."

A million questions whirled through Sherry's mind. She didn't ask a single one. Always conscious that counseling was her job, she tried hard not to grill her friends. She stayed out of people's problems unless they specifically asked for her advice.

The longer she sipped at her water, the more apparent it was that Garrett Lock hadn't been seeking advice. In fact, if anything, he regretted letting slip what he had. On the heels of his unexpected statement, he'd plunged right into shop talk. He quizzed Sherry about the department she chaired—asking how she managed enrollment, determined outcome assessments and handled student quotas. He kept the questions rolling, never giving her an opening to mention Keith's mother.

"Whoa!" She finally held up a hand. "These are

things you should bring up at a staff meeting. You *do* plan to meet with us on a regular basis, I hope."

Eyes hooded, he tipped back in his chair and laced his hands over his flat belly.

"You're not," she accused, setting her glass down with a crack. "Dean Kruger kept his department staff in limbo. It was a big mistake."

Garrett walked his fingers together one at a time, starting with his thumbs. "Do you intend to undermine my efforts to administrate unless I agree to play the game your way?"

"You call dissemination of information a game?" Sherry hadn't intended to let her voice rise, but it did. The boys came barreling back, interrupting her glaring match with Garrett. "Don't sit down," Sherry ordered Mark, scrambling up herself. "I'll phone you tomorrow regarding enrollment in that class," she snapped at Lock. "At least information will flow *one* way."

Garrett balled his napkin. "If our work relationship starts off rocky, I don't have a hope of striking a positive chord with the faculty who report to you. How long are you going to hold it against me that I got the job?"

"What?" she bristled. "To couch this in Texas terms, Lock, except for that teensy lie I told yesterday, I'm about the squarest shooter of all the Human Services chairs you'll deal with. Yes, I'll fight for program expansion, but you'll see me coming. I don't strike from ambush. If there's an uprising in the ranks, I won't be involved." Chin held high, she wove through the tables like a blue-ribbon slalom skier. Megan and Mark caught up with her halfway down the mall.

"He called you a hard-boiled egg," Mark said, puffing in his effort to match his steps to Sherry's. "I said you fly off the handle quick, but cool off fast, too. I didn't want you to get in trouble, Aunt Sherry. I mean, you said he's your boss."

Her steps lagged. Already she felt bad for having lost her temper in front of the kids. She reached over and ruffled Mark's hair. "So, which of us is the psychologist, huh, kid? Okay, I'm calm now. I doubt we'll see the Locks again today, but how about if I promise to apologize tomorrow when I phone him about enrollment?"

Grinning, Mark strode ahead, whistling.

"He'll have a big head for a week," Megan complained. "How can you be so nice to my dorky brother and rag on a hunk like Dr. Lock?"

Sherry stepped on the escalator, pretending she hadn't heard Megan. Why worry about it right now? As she'd told Mark, she didn't expect to see Garrett again today.

Wrong. The father-son duo lurked outside the boutique where Megan's friend said they'd find the lime green dress.

Deciding there was no time like the present to

clear the air, Sherry immediately said, "I apologize for mouthing off."

Garrett pushed away from the wall, caught her wrist and at the same moment she spoke said, "I was out of line at lunch."

Pinpricks of heat spread from his fingers to the underside of Sherry's arm. When it seemed as if the silence was stretched so tight it was about to crack, they both laughed and Sherry pulled free.

Garrett sobered first. "I had no call to go on the attack. If I have an excuse, I guess it's because the dean at my old college called meetings for the purpose of putting faculty on the hot seat. He pitted faculty against department chairs and vice versa."

"Kruger did everything by memo. After ten or so memos filled with backpedaling and double talk, ideas always ended up being shelved. The previous dean was never in his office. Under his leadership all the departments stagnated. The chairman before me got so frustrated he quit. Faculty elected me, and I've spent two years smoothing ruffled feathers. The apathy is terrible. No one likes to lose out on a promotion, but when it comes right down to it, I'm relieved you inherited the whole mess."

He crossed his arms and chewed on his bottom lip as he listened. "I don't claim to be a miracle worker," he said after she'd finished. "We've both taught and you still do, so we know what happens in a house divided. If the dean and department chairs disagree, faculty is always split. I need your support in front of staff, Sherilyn."

The soft pleading way he said her name tracked tiny shivers up Sherry's spine. Coupled with those blue eyes and crooked smile, his voice launched an assault on her senses impossible to thwart. "Ho…kay." She sucked in a deep breath, trying to get out from under his spell. "We'll keep our battles private."

Garrett dropped his chin to his chest and massaged the bridge of his nose. "I prefer not to battle at all, but I'll do my best to see our skirmishes don't turn into war. Now that's settled, I'd better take off. Once I outfit Keith, I have to go sign a contract for his after-school day care. Then…another visit to the Realtor."

As Megan beckoned Sherry to come and look at the dress, she said she had to go, too. Later, when she and Megan emerged from the shop with the dress, Mark was waiting there alone. Sherry actually found herself looking around for Lock—and couldn't believe she was doing it.

The three shopped so long they were almost late to the concert. Garrett didn't enter her mind again until nearly midnight when Sherry pulled into her complex and her headlights illuminated the For Sale or Lease sign on the corner unit.

She leased her place. Some people in the complex owned their houses. Either way, she didn't want Garrett Lock that close to her.

Would Megan notice the sign and remark on it? she wondered. But no. Both kids bubbled over with news of their purchases and tales of the cool rock band.

Nolan, who awaited their arrival, stuffed the kids and their bags into the car. "Whew," he said to Sherry once the noise subsided. "Have they been like that all day?"

"Not really. We had a good time. They're great kids, Nolan."

"Emily and Mom sent their profound thanks. They accomplished a lot today. I finished sanding floors. Things went so well I finally believe there'll actually be a wedding at Thanksgiving and that my house will be ready to move into."

His joy was contagious. Watching him and the kids all brim with happiness made Sherry's earlier notion that somehow they'd all end up hurt seem silly. She rose on tiptoe to kiss his bristly cheek. "Tell Emily I'll drop by Monday after work, and we'll go pick out material for my maid-of-honor dress."

"Hey, sis, that's great. I know you're as skittish as I was when it comes to weddings. But I guarantee, when love strikes, you'll fall like a ton of bricks."

"Me? No way. Get these sleepy kids home before Emily thinks you've all been kidnapped."

She waved as Nolan backed out, realizing that Lock had probably been right—she'd been jealous of Nolan and Emily's close bond. Sighing, she let herself into her dark empty house. What was this? An admission that she might need someone else? No way. Once all the lights were on, she felt fine again.

THE EARLY PART of the week flew by. Garrett reclaimed his job on Monday. From then on, Sherry didn't have a moment's peace. A flood of paperwork flowed from his desk to hers as it did to all department chairs who reported to him. For three days a steady stream of people marched in and out of his office. Whenever the traffic stopped, it meant he was in meetings and would come back with double the workload.

Sherry grew adept at sidestepping personal questions concerning her new boss—mostly from unattached female faculty wearing a certain gleam in their eyes. They refused to believe Sherry didn't know anything personal about the handsome Texan.

They'd better believe it. She and Lock had barely exchanged two words since their encounter at the mall. Which was why Sherry was stunned when he stuck his head in her office Wednesday afternoon and announced he was leaving early to meet his movers.

She peered up from one of many student folders piled on her desk, her eyes requiring a moment to focus on the rangy figure lounging against her door frame. He wore close-fitting blue jeans, black boots and a blue shirt that matched his eyes. He carried a soft gray Western-cut jacket slung over one shoulder. "Movers?" she managed to blurt, after running her tongue over dry lips. "I thought your stuff was here in storage."

"I bought a place. Well, actually I've filled out the paperwork. Luckily it's vacant. The owner agreed to rent it to me until the deal closes."

"Where—" The phone rang, cutting her off. "A student," she mouthed, covering the receiver. "Troubled." Listening a moment, she glanced at Garrett again and sliced a finger across her neck.

He studied the credentials on her wall and the plaques he thought said a lot about her. One read: We will find a way—or make one. Another said: Success is an inevitable destination. When it became apparent that she'd be on the phone indefinitely, he tapped his watch, gave her a two-fingered salute and pulled the door closed on his way out.

Sherry raced to her four-o'clock intermediate psych class with only seconds to spare. It was six-thirty by the time she trudged to her car. Tired and hungry—she'd skipped lunch—she was ready to spit nails when she pulled into her complex and found the entry blocked by an enormous moving van.

Her stomach growled as she parked on the street, gathered her briefcase and hiked back to the inner courtyard. A cluster of neighbors lined the walkway, shouting suggestions to movers struggling to push a leather couch through the front door of the town house that'd been vacant when Sherry left for work.

Even in the dusk, she recognized the waitress who lived next door, Alicia Jones—the beautician from three places down—and Yvette. Sherry wondered vaguely when she'd gotten home from her road trip.

Her roommate's back was to Sherry, but she recognized Yvette's seductive pose and her habit of twisting her long blond hair around one finger while she flirted shamelessly.

This time, however, she happened to be flirting with Garrett Lock.

Sherry's stomach pitched and rolled. Feebly she pushed forward.

Garrett glanced up and saw Sherry at the same time she saw him. He knew because of the way her amber eyes opened wide. His own eyes narrowed warily as they exclaimed in unison, "What are *you* doing here?"

In the next breath both chorused, "I live here."

"I signed papers last night." Garrett waved a hand at the corner unit, while Sherry pointed to the lighted house catercorner across the courtyard. "Mine," she whispered.

Yvette, always a toucher and always possessive when it came to men, slid her arm through Garrett's. Sherry understood the warning in her friend's cool green eyes, a warning that said, *back off.*

A noise, not quite recognizable, strangled its way past Sherry's lips. "How…how did you find this particular town house?" she demanded of Garrett.

"Nolan told me about it Sunday. He said it was a nice place—but neglected to say you lived next door." Garrett appeared every bit as disconcerted as she. "Honestly, the morning the cabbie brought me here, I was too turned around to notice."

About to mutter that she'd kill Nolan, Sherry happened to glance up over Lock's head and into the lighted loft bedroom. Keith Lock was outlined there, hugging some sort of stuffed toy. A bear, she thought. His nose was pressed to the glass, his small face pale in the lamplight.

If ever anyone needed a home, that child did. And the truth was, Sherry didn't see much sense in wasting energy railing at situations over which she had no control.

"Tell Keith I said welcome to the neighborhood," she said to Garrett, shoving her way past the milling throng. Without a backward glance, she stalked into her one-time haven of rest.

CHAPTER SIX

SHERRY STRIPPED off her work clothes and stared at the shower, but then decided she needed something physical to work off the head of steam that'd built. Not even the hottest shower would dissolve the irritation knotting her muscles. She pulled on her bike shorts and a crop top, shouldered her in-line skates and collected her helmet, then left the house again.

A big golden harvest moon hung low in the sky, and though night shadows were falling, the evening remained pleasantly warm. The park directly across the street from the town-house complex boasted a wonderful set of lighted trails. From the start of fall classes until Halloween, one of the fraternities patrolled the pathways. At a point where the trails crossed to form a figure eight, their sister sorority operated a hot-dog stand to help pay for a yearly Christmas dance. Sherry was such a steady customer the girls who worked the booth knew her by name.

She was far from ready for a heart-to-heart chat with Yvette, so this spur-of-the-moment outing provided an opportunity to slay three dragons at one time. Sherry's dragons tonight were irritation, hunger and the need to keep peace in the household. She'd seen the same scenario time and again. Yvette threw herself into relationships with abandon. She blundered through the steps like a ritual and to the exclusion of everything else in her life. In Sherry's opinion Yvette always smothered the object of her affections. Love burned bright only so long, then it flamed out.

Sherry's steps slowed as she passed Garrett's house. The crowd had scattered. Through the curtainless window she saw Yvette pointing and waving her hands, obviously helping arrange his furniture. Maybe by this time next week she'd be moving in with him.

As she rounded the moving van, Sherry asked herself why that mattered to her. It couldn't be because she cared for Lock—or cared if he suffered when Yvette found someone new. And she would. Yvette had left a string of casualties. But for all Sherry knew, so had Lock. That might be why Keith looked so sad. Had Garrett moved closer to his ex because mother-son visits would give him greater freedom to sow wild oats?

Now who had an overactive imagination? She'd gone from suspecting Lock was obsessed by his ex-wife to branding him a world-class Casanova. Sherry peered inside the van as she passed and noticed it was nearly empty. That made Garrett's moving into her neighborhood suddenly very real. She actually hoped she'd somehow dreamed the whole incident. But of course she hadn't.

She dropped onto the first bench at the park entrance to change from her sneakers into her skates. Tying her shoelaces together, she draped the shoes around her neck and immediately glided off.

"Dr. Campbell. Hey, I thought maybe you'd given up skating. I've been here every night since we opened and I haven't seen you around."

Sherry circled and stopped beside a sun-freckled student who flashed her a huge grin. Robert Dickson was the catalyst behind this park project. "Robby, after three years, you must know that opening week is a killer for faculty. And since I'm also a department chair, I work double the time."

"Boy, you must really be under siege. This is the *second* week, not the first."

Sherry wrinkled her nose. "See how time flies when you're having fun?"

"I hear you got a new boss. The sorority women think you should've gotten the job."

"Really? I'll thank them when I stop at the hot-dog stand." Sherry enjoyed a close rapport with the sororities. Most of the girls she'd advised when she'd served as a full-time counselor had graduated. But word filtered down and the current sorority members dropped by if they needed to talk. The older she got the more she felt like an advice columnist.

"So, is the new dean a pretty good guy? Letty has an appointment to see him next week. She got two *D*s last semester, and she received a letter saying she can't work in the cafeteria and carry a full class load. But without a job she can't pay tuition."

Sherry gazed at him sympathetically. "That is the rule. I don't know what Dr. Lock will do, but Letty needs to tell him she had a bad time when your dad died. I wondered if either of you'd even be back this year. Who's running the farm?"

"I am. Well, sort of. Dr. Temple adopted the farm as our Ag project this year. His summer class helped with tilling and planting. My class will harvest and ship."

"That's wonderful, Robby. When exactly is Letty's appointment? I'll put in a good word for her with Dr. Lock. I can't promise anything, but I believe he'll be fair."

"Thanks. She won't fall behind. Guys in my fraternity offered to tutor her in chemistry and physics. You know Letty and I have two brothers and a sister still to put through college. We have to stay on schedule. If Letty misses the nursing boards this spring, she won't get the job she's been promised at the valley hospital."

Sherry nodded and waved goodbye as someone

else claimed Robert's attention. She skated off, worrying that she'd stuck her neck out. Frankly, she wasn't at all sure Garrett would make allowances for Letty. He hadn't been willing to bend the rules on the class some of her students needed. Because she'd found only one extra student, instead of the minimum two, he'd canceled the class. Sherry hoped he wasn't by-the-book about everything. Sometimes you had to take a chance on a kid.

She concentrated on the uphill leg of the cinder path, working out in her head what she'd say to Garrett on Monday—provided, of course, that he could give her five minutes.

Her opportunity to speak on Letty's behalf came a lot sooner than that. On her way home after completing the circuit, she took the opportunity to move her car from the street to her covered space, since the van was now gone. Just as she climbed out with her skates and turned to lock the car, Garrett showed up to unload something from the back of his pickup, which was parked beside hers.

"You skate in the dark?" He rested a heavy crate on the tailgate, and in the soft pool of light cast by the carriage lamps hung at intervals along the car park, he took in her windblown hair, sweat-damp neck and arms and the bulky knee pads.

"Isn't it dangerous this late?" Frown lines formed between his brows.

She downed the last swig of her bottled water and blotted her face before she told him about the park. It had crossed her mind to ignore him. She certainly didn't want him horning in if he also skated. Although on second thought she figured it was a foolish worry with Yvette occupying his spare time.

"Are the park trails only for adults or can kids use them, too?"

"Whole families," she said. "Why? Do you and Keith skate?" Her heart sank.

"Keith has in-line skates packed somewhere. And a skateboard. He and his friends taught themselves in our previous neighborhood. I hate to think I may have to learn at this age." His smile faded as he cast a worried glance toward the brightly lit town house.

"Keith will soon make friends." Sherry felt compelled to ease the man's obvious anxiety if she could. "The only children in our complex are babies. But on the days I go to work at nine, I see a group of boys walking to the elementary school."

"That's another problem. With my hours, I'll have to drive him. He'll take a bus to the day-care facility when school's out."

"That's too bad. Well," she said brightly, "after you meet some of the other kids and their folks, maybe you'll turn up a mom who baby-sits in her home before and after school."

"You think?" He scanned her with apprehension. "Where kids get their notions I'll never know, but Keith has it in his head that only babies go to day care."

"Yeah, kids talk. The most ideal setup is when one parent is able to stay home, but very few people can manage that these days."

"Boy howdy, don't you know it. And since we're discussing parental responsibility, I'd better be getting back so I can deal with Keith's bed."

"Do you mean you still have to assemble the beds?"

He shook his head as he hoisted the box to his shoulder. "Not assemble. The movers set them up. I just need to find the sheets and put them on."

"Well, I'm sure Yvette will lend a hand."

He caught the sharpness of her tone and delivered a frown that Sherry missed because she stepped aside and let him pass. "I sent Yvette home. I appreciate her offer to help, but if I don't put things away myself, I'll never find them later."

"Really?" Sherry examined him with new eyes, although her mind darted to other things. Absently she asked, "Will you be in the office tomorrow?"

"I hadn't planned to be. I didn't use all the time allotted for my move. I told Westerbrook I'd be out both tomorrow and the next day. Any special reason you ask?"

"You have an appointment on Monday with a student by the name of Letty Dickson. Or she may be listed as Letitia. I'd like a few minutes to talk about her."

"What am I seeing her for?"

"Low grade point average. She got two *D*s last semester. She's scheduled to work twenty hours a week in the cafeteria, so the computer kicked out a letter saying she couldn't. It's mandated that she meet with you to discuss her poor grades."

"That sounds logical." They'd arrived at his gate. He shifted the box to see Sherry more clearly. "Someone who got two *D*s should concentrate on her studies. I agree, she shouldn't work."

"She had a family crisis last semester."

"Okay. Let her drop out of work this year, retake those two classes and better her grades. If she brings her GPA up, she can work again next year. Say ten hours."

"Right, Mr. Hardnose," Sherry flared. "Only next year she won't be back because the family lost its breadwinner, and Letty needs to be working full-time to help send three younger sibs to college." Reaching around him, she opened the gate for Garrett. Then without another word, she walked away.

"Sherilyn, wait," he called, softly drawling her

name. He sighed angrily when she didn't turn back. "Can't we ever have a discussion without you getting hostile? Run her scores for me and drop them by on your way home tomorrow. Please," he added.

A backward wave was all she gave to let him know she'd heard.

Garrett stood at the gate, slow to shake off the frost of yet another encounter with Dr. Campbell. As he wandered toward his front door, he mulled over the difference in the two roommates. Yvette, attractive as she was, showed the potential of draining a guy with her clingy ways. Sherilyn was the type to leave skid marks on a man's soul. How did those two ever end up living under the same roof? They were as different as sugar and vinegar.

Sherry had no sooner stepped through the front door than Yvette pounced.

"What were you and Garrett talking so chummily about?"

"A student," Sherry said, dumping her helmet and skates in the hall closet.

Yvette flipped her long hair out of her face. "I suppose you think having a job in common with him gives you the inside track."

Bending, Sherry unbuckled her bulky knee pads, tossed them into her helmet and closed the closet door with a loud bang. "Inside track to what?"

"To dating Garrett of course. Don't play coy with me, Sherry."

Sherry rolled her shoulders tiredly. "When, in all the years you've known me, have you seen me act coy? You'll have plenty of competition without me if the parade of women staffers beating a path to his office door is any indication of his popularity."

"He's not the type to get involved in an office romance. Living in his hip pocket is much better. When he comes home, he'll want to relax. And I'll make sure relaxation is synonymous with little ol' me."

"You do that, Yvette. Excuse me, I'm going to take a shower."

"Okay. What and when is dinner?"

Sherry stopped and turned. "It's your night to cook, according to the calendar."

"You must have planned something. You didn't know I'd be home."

"No, I didn't. Whatever happened to us letting each other know about our schedules?" When Yvette didn't answer, Sherry said, "I bought a hot dog at Gamma Sigma's stand."

"Oh. Then I'll go to the pub and grab a burger. Your turn tomorrow. Make something yummy, all right?"

Sherry sighed. She had papers to grade tonight, but Yvette had been on the road two weeks. She was probably sick of eating out. Maybe a little compassion was in order. "How about lasagna? I bought all the stuff the other day. Lasagna and Caesar salad?"

"Great. And peanut-butter-brownie cups for dessert?"

"Yvette, are you all right? I can count on one hand the number of times you've eaten dessert with a meal."

"So? You baked chocolate squares and took them to work last week. You always do that. I might eat sweets if you'd ever leave any here."

"How do you know what I took to work last week?" Sherry asked suspiciously.

"Garrett mentioned it."

Sherry was even more astounded. She hadn't thought he'd come back to the office that day. Obviously he had. "I'm not making brownies. As it is, I'll be up late making the lasagna for tomorrow. If you get home at a decent hour from the pub, you can fix dessert. The recipe's in my box, and it's simple."

"Like anyone would eat anything I cooked. Cooking isn't my thing, as you well know. Even your mom gave up trying to teach me. Anyway, don't count on me being home early tonight. All I've seen for two weeks are snippy clothing-department managers. After I eat I'll probably play some pool." She paused. "Garrett plays. But he doesn't have a babysitter for his kid. Hey, does Emily's daughter babysit?"

"Megan? She'd be more apt to play pool," Sherry said dryly. "Just don't put any money on the game. Nolan says she's a real shark."

"Well, I'll call Emily and ask. Garrett needs to be able to come and go as he pleases. He'll need a regular sitter."

Sherry thought about the unhappy little boy she'd met. Keith Lock needed more of his dad's attention, not less. She'd thought Garrett seemed worried about his son. But if he'd indicated otherwise to Yvette, then she must have been mistaken. "I'll likely be in bed when you get home, Yvette. Shall we have dinner at seven tomorrow?"

"Seven-thirty? I have a trunk show for a boutique in Kansas City at noon. They're hosting a champagne brunch to promote one of our new lingerie lines. So please walk softly in the morning. I'm sleeping until ten."

Nodding, Sherry stripped off her sweaty top as she walked down the hall. For a minute there she'd given a fleeting thought to going to the pub with Yvette, just to see what she was missing. But apparently pub crawlers didn't have eight-to-five jobs. No way could she socialize and play pool until closing time and still hit the ground running first thing the next morning. It was just as well she preferred puttering around the house and left being a party animal to Yvette.

The shower refreshed her. She hummed along with Carrie Underwood's latest while assembling ingredients for two pans of lasagna. One to cook and one to freeze for later. Taking pity on Yvette, as she'd eaten in restaurants all week, Sherry relented and fixed a double batch of peanut-butter brownies. While they baked, she corrected papers from her first-year psych class. If the placement test was any indication, things did not bode well for this particular class. On the whole, their handwriting was bad and their spelling atrocious. Comprehension wasn't great, either. One said Jung was a game where you stacked blocks. No one believed B. F. Skinner had raised his daughter in a box. If they hadn't copied each other, they'd probably all flunk. Monday she'd crack down on their copying.

Snapping off the kitchen light, Sherry checked to be sure the outside light was on for Yvette. She expected Lock's place still to be aglow as he unpacked, but the windows were dark. Another huge difference between men and women, she mused. Most women wouldn't go to bed until every last thing in the kitchen was in order.

SHERRY REFUSED to tiptoe around in the morning for Yvette's sake. Thursdays were long full days for her, since they included counseling in the Hub. For comfort she teamed baggy linen trousers with an oversize poet's blouse and clogs. Never one to wear much makeup, Sherry decided on none. She quickly brushed her short hair, thinking it made her look younger—or was it the mismatched earrings? Tweety on one ear, Sylvester on the other. She deliberately mismatched earrings to make students laugh. Most of the women who timidly drifted into the Hub didn't have a whole lot of laughs in their lives. Administration preferred staff to dress more conservatively, but too bad.

It was such a nice sunny morning that Sherry thought it'd be quieter if she took her coffee and newspaper out on the front porch. Halfway through both, a noise made her glance up. Garrett Lock stood before her looking vaguely rumpled. Hair that was usually tamed flopped over his brow. A slight stubble fuzzed his chin. Barefoot, he had on gray sweats that looked as if they'd once been washed with something red.

"Uh…I don't suppose you'd lend me some coffee and a filter? I found the pot, but I've unpacked three boxes and still no coffee. There's no room on my counter to put anything else."

Sherry grinned. It did her heart good to discover his small imperfections. At the office he was a man of precision. "It's pathetic, Lock, to hear a grown man whine. I thought you'd have every box numbered and labeled as to content." She stood and wafted her cup in the vicinity of his nose. "Who had a fit on Monday when I couldn't lay my hands on J. J. Perry's incoming student record?"

"Have a heart, Campbell. We're talking major caffeine attack here."

"In that case I'd like to see some major groveling."

He dropped to his knees, clasped his hands and beseeched her plaintively—an action that took the wind right out of her sails. Going a step further, he leaned down and kissed her feet. Sherry jumped back and slopped coffee everywhere.

"Stop it, you nut!" she gasped. "What if one of the neighbors sees you?"

Grinning, he sat back on his heels. "If anyone else was up this early, hard-hearted Hannah, I'd already have a cup of java."

"I'll get it. Now. Just please sit in a chair like a normal human being. I'll be right back. Do you have a grinder or do *I* need to grind a batch?"

"Juan Valdez and I have this deal. He grows coffee and then he grinds it. I buy what he exports in industrial-size cans."

"A real connoisseur, huh?"

A crease dented one cheek. "Hot as Texas. Muddy as the Mississippi. A bottomless cup. My only criteria. What can I say? I have no taste."

"I'll grind three batches. Should tide you over till afternoon. Just beware, after three pots of high octane, you might be hooked on the gourmet stuff."

"I'll chance it."

Sherry was still chuckling softly as she burst into the kitchen. Seeing Yvette, hair combed, makeup on, grinding coffee beans, wiped the smile right off her face. Wasn't she going to sleep late?

"Run along to work, Sher. I'll take care of Garrett's...needs."

Taking in the loaded implication, Sherry let her mind hopscotch over a gamut of possibilities. Especially as Yvette wore a minuscule pair of hot-orange shorts and a top that left a great deal of midriff bare.

Crossing her arms, Sherry propped a shoulder against the refrigerator. "That outfit's a little obvious, don't you think? But be my guest. He wants his coffee black."

"*I'm* obvious?" Yvette arched a carefully penciled brow. "You were giggling like a teenager and falling all over him out there."

Sherry straightened, extending her palms. "I offered the man three batches of ground coffee. That's *all*." She spun on her heel and marched out of the kitchen, down the hall and into her bedroom, where she just managed not to slam the door. Closing it quietly, she began shoving books and case studies into her briefcase. Then, ear to the door, she listened for Yvette to leave. After a decent interval, one long enough to ensure they'd gone to Lock's to make coffee—and Sherry tried not to imagine what else—she hefted her briefcase and strode to her car.

THE DAY FLEW BY. Sherry loved counseling, even though in some cases what she provided was a Band-Aid at best. It saddened her that so many women lacked the funds to get the psychological support they needed. All who came through the Hub had one thing in common, regardless of age. They were women who'd fallen through the funding cracks. Middle-aged, divorced and suddenly dropped from hubby's insurance. Young yet no longer eligible for care under dad's policy. During her first years on the job, Sherry took all their problems home. But the burden was too great. After much soul-searching, she'd come to the realization that she couldn't provide miracles. So she'd put together a strong referral system for women teetering on the edge and gave the others her undivided attention in the fifteen-minute slots allotted her. Today that meant she had to flush her mind of her roommate and her boss.

Well after five, Sherry walked to the door with her last appointment. She'd talked so much that her throat felt raspy. Now she was glad she'd stayed up last night to prepare lasagna. As she locked up, she looked forward to unwinding; she also needed time to set up the best way to proceed with her new cases. If fate was really kind, she'd have an hour to herself before Yvette rolled in.

Concentrating on her plans for the evening, Sherry almost didn't see Keith Lock sitting dejectedly on his porch as she entered the courtyard. The flash of his red T-shirt caught her eye. "Keith," she called, a smile automatic. "Are you taking a breather from unpacking boxes?"

He raised his head from his hands and clambered slowly to his feet. "Hi," he said, moving to the gate. "Where's Mark and Megan? Dad said maybe they'd visit you sometime."

"And so they may. Probably not tonight," she told him honestly.

"Oh." His shoulders bowed as he buried his hands deep in his front pockets. "Are you going skating now?" His eyes brightened momentarily.

Sherry's muscles still protested after last night's rigorous workout. "Sounds like you found the box with your skates. Maybe your dad will take you to the park later."

"He's too busy. He said for me not to bug you, either. But I thought if you were going, I could maybe tag along. I skate pretty good," he added.

Sherry gazed into the hopeful blue eyes and

saw her plans for a relaxing evening disappear. "As a matter of fact, I did plan a short turn around the trails. Give me fifteen minutes to change, throw together a salad and stick a casserole in the oven. Meanwhile, you make sure it's okay with your dad."

"It is," Keith said confidently, bestowing her with a gap-toothed grin that altered his appearance to that of a normal happy-go-lucky kid.

Striding off after an involuntary smile in return and a quick glance at her watch, Sherry rushed by Alicia Jones, her beautician neighbor, with barely a nod.

"Did you just come from Garrett's?" The statuesque woman caught Sherry's sleeve with her long curving purple fingernails.

Puzzled, Sherry shook loose. "No. His son, Keith, was outside. Why?"

The woman waved a bakery bag. "I bought extra corn muffins and thought I'd be a good-doobie neighbor. Lorraine," she said, referring to the flight attendant from another unit, "already dropped off a gelatin salad. I mean, really— gelatin'll hardly appeal to a Texan. Everyone knows they have big appetites." She patted her hair.

"Mm." Sherry narrowly managed to suppress a chuckle. "Gotta run. I have my own dinner to pop in the oven."

"What are you taking Garrett? Sweet potato pie, I'll bet. You're such a good cook it's not fair to the rest of us." The woman pouted.

Sherry lost the battle and did laugh. "I'm not taking him anything. I figure he can do like everyone else who moves—order in Chinese." Leaving her neighbor looking perplexed, Sherry went inside.

Keith was sitting on her porch when she came out fifteen minutes later.

"Hey, those are classy red skates," she said. "You have a helmet and pads for knees and elbows?"

He held them up one at a time for her inspection.

"Okay, sport. And you told your dad we'll be back after one turn around the park?"

"Yep. He's busy tryin' to get rid of another dippy woman. They've been comin' round all afternoon with food."

"They're called housewarming gifts, Keith. A welcome from the neighbors."

He slanted her a sidelong glance through indecently thick sooty lashes. "When my gramma phoned, she said they're women who think Dad'll marry them."

"How old are you, Keith?" Sherry asked, placing a hand on his shoulder to guide him across the street.

"Almost nine. Well, I'll be nine in January."

They stopped at the park bench to change into their skates. Sherry showed Keith how to knot his sneaker shoelaces to carry them around his neck. Then she asked a question that was really none of her concern—and blamed the fact that it'd slipped out on her having been in counselor mode all day. "Are you hoping your mom and dad will get back together, Keith?"

He stumbled a little and she put out a hand to steady him. "Nah. Mom just married Crawford. He don't know nothin' 'bout kids. And he smells prissy. Dad says it's 'cause he's president of a bank. I don't like going there, but Dad says I gotta."

"Oh." Sherry's heart beat faster. She had judged Garrett wrong; apparently he was neither obsessed with his former wife nor trying to get her back.

The path that wound through the trees grew steeper, and they were both panting. Talk died down until they reached the hot-dog stand. Sherry dug out money for bottled water for herself and fruit juice for Keith. He wanted a hot dog. "Too close to dinner," she said.

"Sheesh. You sound just like dad."

Sherry laughed. The girls running the stand asked veiled questions about Sherry's new buddy. She introduced him as the new dean's son, then wished she hadn't because she saw speculation in the students' eyes.

"I wish you had kids," Keith mumbled after they'd deposited their containers in the trash and started along the trail again. "There aren't any kids here to play with."

"I know. It's too bad," she said sympathetically. "The people who moved out of the house you're in had two girls about your age."

"Dad won't even let me get a puppy. He said the Homeowners' Association rules say no pets."

"That's right. But my brother has a dog and so do my folks. If your dad doesn't object, one of these days I'll take you to play with them."

"That'd be cool…but you'll prob'ly forget."

"I won't," Sherry said fiercely, her heart squeezing with pity for the child who'd so obviously been disappointed a lot in his young life.

"Mom was s'pose to take me to see a paddle-wheel boat on the Mississippi this weekend," he said listlessly. "She phoned this morning and said she can't 'cause of a party she and Crawford got invited to. Dad was ticked off. I told him it didn't matter, but he yelled at her, anyway."

Sherry skated on in silence. She recalled the remark Garrett made at the mall when they met for lunch, about how Carla made promises she didn't keep. Still she felt honorbound to stand up for the woman she'd never met. "I'm sure your mother feels bad, too," Sherry ventured, not sure at all but guessing, based on the women she counseled. Jobs too often dictated a single mom's schedule. Keith's mother had remarried, but that was recent. And maybe her new husband was to blame for this current situation.

"Yeah." Keith shrugged as he plopped down on the bench where they'd sat to don their skates. "I had fun tonight," he said shyly. "Can we do this again?"

"You bet. I don't go every night, but between now and Halloween the trails are pretty safe. Once you're unpacked, though, your dad will probably take you."

"He's got a lot of meetings. I hafta stay at that dorky play school. I don't see why I can't come home by myself. I'm not a baby."

"Your dad would worry, Keith. Anyway, you'll make friends at school. Maybe you can join one of the soccer or Little League teams. I'm sure there are parents who transport kids whose folks both work. Give it time."

He kicked a rock as they crossed the street. "You're nice, Sherry. Can you come in and play with me while Dad's busy? I have Mr. Potato Head."

"I can't tonight, sprout. I have dinner in the oven and notes to look over before tomorrow."

The boy appeared so crestfallen Sherry wished

she was free—though she wouldn't want to join the parade of women throwing themselves at Lock. Speaking of parade, there was Yvette sashaying through Garrett's gate. As Sherry and Keith drew even with her roommate, Sherry saw that Yvette juggled a square casserole dish and the covered container in which Sherry had stored the peanut-butter brownies.

"Hey!" Sherry quickened her steps. "Where are you going with our dinner?"

Surprised, Yvette turned and tossed her silky blond hair over one bare shoulder. "Sher. You're back so soon. I thought you and the kid would skate a lot longer."

Sherry glanced at her watch. "No, I set the oven timer. You should've known I'd be back in time to get the lasagna out."

"It's out. I'm afraid I must confess—I've stolen it to feed Garrett. The poor man is famished after unpacking boxes all day. If you were a real pal, you'd take you know who out for burgers." Yvette gave an exaggerated wink. "I guess not," she murmured, eyes locked on Sherry's stony face. Then she turned to Keith. "Well, c'mon kidlet. Late as it is, you can eat, then hop off to bed."

Keith tossed Sherry a long-suffering I-told-you-so look before he put his head down and trudged up the sidewalk after Yvette's swishing short skirt.

The nitro in Sherry's stomach had burned

high enough to explode as Garrett's front door slammed on Keith's heels. If she wasn't so dog-tired and if she didn't have case reports to dictate, she'd march right up there and barge in on them. Of all the gall. After she'd slaved over that lasagna.

She'd make sure Yvette got an earful tonight, even if it meant staying up till midnight. Unless…Yvette spent the night at Garrett's. The very thought made Sherry's stomach queasy. But that was probably just hunger, she told herself.

In the end, she ate the Caesar salad Yvette had left behind—left because Sherry hadn't yet mixed the dressing. In the end, she laid a blistering note on Yvette's pillow and went to bed without dictating her reports. Frankly, if Yvette didn't come home, Sherry would rather not know.

But by the time she fell asleep she'd managed to convince herself the only reason she cared was because it might color her work association with the dean.

That was the *only* reason, too.

CHAPTER SEVEN

AT THE END of another hectic day on campus, Sherry marched up to Garrett's front door with Letty Dickson's folder and punched the bell twice. She shouldn't have been surprised when Yvette opened the door, but she was—or disappointed.

"Garrett's busy breaking down moving boxes." Yvette stepped outside and pulled the door almost closed behind her. "Sher, I need a favor. Will you take the kid skating or rent a movie tonight? So I can show Garrett off at the pub. It's Friday night," she wheedled. "I called Emily to see if Megan could babysit, but her school has a ball game tonight."

"Why should I do you favors after the stunt you pulled last night?"

"Oh, don't be a spoilsport. The lasagna was a big hit. C'mon, Sher. It's not as if you have a date or anything. You never do."

For some reason that statement rubbed Sherry the wrong way. Was her life so predictable? She chewed the inside of her mouth, thinking back to when she'd had her last date. Valentine's Day a year ago—the new psychologist in town who'd spoken to her class that week. Or was that two years ago? The door, suddenly jerked out of Yvette's hand, ended Sherry's trip down memory lane.

Garrett, who stood a head or more taller than Yvette, stared over her shoulder. "Hi! Keith said he'd heard the doorbell."

Sherry struggled with hello. Garrett wore snug-fitting blue jeans, a navy short-sleeved pullover and sneakers that had seen better days. His sun-streaked hair, boyishly tousled, reminded her of Keith.

"Is that the student's records I asked for? Come on in and we'll go over the case. Yvette was just leaving, isn't that right?"

From Sherry's perspective, he'd issued her roommate a plain "here's your hat" type of good-bye. Yvette was either obtuse or chose not to understand.

"I have plenty of time. The pub doesn't liven up until nine. Sherry was just saying she plans to rent *Snow White and the Huntsman* and fix pop-corn. That'd give Keith something fun to do while we run down to the pub for a couple of hours." Yvette straightened the points of Garrett's collar and trailed her palms down his chest.

His gaze moved to Sherry. She read a combi-nation of reserve and frustration. "I, ah... That's nice of you, Sherilyn, but Nolan called. He's taking Megan and Mark to her high-school football game and invited Keith and me to tag along."

Sherry didn't know how to respond. Yvette took answering out of her hands. "Fine." She curled against Garrett's shoulder. "Tonight we'll do your macho football thing. I'm sure Sherry won't mind saving the movie for another time. The pub's more fun on Saturday night, anyway."

Garrett gently disconnected their limbs. "Sorry, this is dads' night with the kids. And tomorrow I'm helping Nolan put up paneling in his family room. Keith and I are eating with them." He reached out and pulled Sherry across the threshold. "Excuse us, Yvette. Our discussion concerning this student is confidential."

Yvette hovered a moment, as if she considered staying despite his dismissal. Then, with a shrug and a coy smile, she rose on tiptoe and pressed a kiss on Garrett's mouth. By the time he stumbled backward out of her reach, she aimed a not-so-coy smile at Sherry and left.

The reserved Dean Lock looked so alarmed that Sherry almost laughed. However, Keith, who'd been skipping down the stairs and was treated to a bird's eye view of the kiss, didn't find it funny. "Yuck, Dad." He navigated the remaining stairs in two jumps. "Why were you kissin' her? I thought you said—"

"I didn't kiss her, son," Garrett broke in. "She kissed me. There's a difference."

Keith's lashes drifted down over skeptical blue eyes. At some point he realized he and his dad weren't alone. "Sherry, hi!" The boy loped to where she still hovered in the entryway. "Are you here to take me skating? I can't tonight. Me'n Dad are goin' to a football game. Wanna come with us?"

Sherry savored the shock that crossed Garrett's face before she let him off the hook. "A little bird told me the game is a father-kid night out. I wasn't going skating, anyhow, Keith. I'm here to talk to your dad about a student."

"Oh. Okay." He turned to Garrett. "Can I have a bowl of cereal? I'm starved."

Garrett ruffled the boy's unruly curls. "Are you getting ready to shoot up another foot? Isn't this the third bowl of cereal you've eaten since you got home from school?"

"Yeah...but if I had a dog, I wouldn't sit around eatin' and watchin' TV."

"Don't start on the dog bit again," Garrett warned. "Keeping you in cereal is infinitely easier. Besides, I told you, the Association rules don't allow pets."

"I know." Keith hunched his shoulders and shuffled toward the kitchen.

"Now, where were we?" Garrett swiped a hand

over his mouth and chin. Then he gestured Sherry toward the living room. "Can I offer you water or a soda?"

"Neither, thanks. I'm really anxious to get home. Hey, before I forget, thanks for calling a staff meeting for next week. We got your memo today."

Garrett seated her on the couch and took the opposite chair. "I've heard the gripes. I don't want any confusion over the changes coming down the pike."

"Changes? What changes?"

"Ones I want the entire staff to hear at the same time," he said dryly. "Since you're in a hurry to get home, shall we skip to the Dickson girl's problem?"

"As you wish," Sherry said stiffly. She relayed Robby's concerns for his sister and added her own recommendations. "They're a hardworking family. Letty has had her sights set on being a nurse for as long as I can remember. She's a credit to our nursing program."

He flipped through the folder. "An honor student except for last semester." Closing the folder, Garrett tapped it against his lips. "The rules—"

"Forget the rules. Letty isn't just some statistic. She's a person."

His eyes widened marginally at Sherry's outburst. Was Ms. Success-is-a-destination suggesting he flout the rules? "I've never even spoken to this girl. Yet you expect me to step out on a limb. How do I know you aren't waiting to saw it off behind me?"

Sherry looked offended. "I guess I can see where you might worry. After all, we were on opposite sides of the fence during the interviews. Ask someone else. Ask Temple in the Ag department." Sighing, she got to her feet. "Ultimately it's your call. Will you return the folder or shall I? It came from a stack on your desk."

He jumped up, too, and tossed the file on a glass-topped coffee table. "I'll authorize her to work this semester. Second semester I'll reevaluate. If her grades don't dip, I'll lift the restriction altogether."

She mockingly bowed. "Letty won't let you down."

"Hey, we're on the same team. Shall we start the clock over?"

She turned from the door. "Being on the same team doesn't make me a yes man."

His gaze, which rested on her wine red toenails, traveled up her legs to her paisley print sarong skirt. Somber blue eyes paused momentarily on her sleeveless teal blouse. Garrett's eyes ignited briefly before moving on to stop at lips that might have started out the same color as her toenails but had long since been licked bare.

Sucking in a nervous breath, Sherry yanked open the door just as Garrett exhaled.

"You're absolutely right," he said. "You'll never be a yes man. Or any other kind of man," he muttered.

"That's right," she shot back, his next statement cut off in the squeak of the hinges. She caught sight of Keith, idly bouncing a ball down the steps. Either he hadn't eaten the cereal or he had and slipped out the back door. "Yo, Keith. Enjoy the ball game. And tomorrow, maybe you and Mark could go fishing in the creek that runs through Nolan's property. If you do, guard your pole against Pilgrim."

"Who's Pilgrim?" He caught the ball one-handed and cocked his head in a gesture reminiscent of Garrett.

"Pilgrim is my brother's golden retriever," she said. "A lovable mutt. But if you don't keep an eye on him, he'll steal your fishing pole just to get attention."

The boy giggled. Sherry thought it was perhaps the first time she'd heard him laugh out loud. Glancing over Keith's head to his dad, who'd followed her to the door, Sherry saw from the soft quirk of his lips that Garrett had also been affected by the joyous sound. Her heart tripped awkwardly. She quickened her pace and hurried past the gate.

It bothered Sherry that she didn't know quite how to pigeonhole Lock. She had a place for men like her dad and granddad. Devoted husbands and fathers who stayed married to the same woman for fifty years. Next came the consummate bachelors. Until recently, Nolan had fit that mold. A separate category held men embittered toward women in general. Last came the dregs. Ex-husbands of the women she worked with every day. Rotten men.

Garrett Lock didn't seem to fit anywhere.

As Sherry inserted her key in the door, it opened and Yvette pounced. "I saw you flirting. What are you trying to do? He's *the* man for me, Sher. Mr. Right. I feel it in my bones."

Sherry's eyebrow vaulted skyward. "Is your new motto get 'em young and raise 'em yourself? I was joking with Keith."

"Don't try to buffalo me, pal. I saw the look on Garrett's face."

Sherry could have said that look was for his son. But Yvette's jealousy got pretty tiresome. "If I had a dollar for every time you claimed a new man was *the one,* I'd be a millionaire. I know you and Vonda had it rough after your mom died and your dad went through all those twenty-year-old babes. But you should take a page from Vonda's book. Ask for the name of her therapist. She's been happily married for eight years now."

"I don't need a shrink. If you were such an almighty expert, you wouldn't sit at home seven nights a week. So stay out of my head. And hands off Garrett." Yvette slung her purse over her shoulder and stormed out.

Sherry flinched as the door slammed. She was buffeted by puffs of the sultry fragrance that permeated the hallway. The scent made it difficult for Sherry to breathe. Or was that because of the situation? Maybe she should move, get out of here. Except the lease was in her name and had eight months to run. Given the trouble Garrett had experienced finding a place, she knew it'd be next to impossible to get anything as nice as this. And why *should* she leave?

Taking refuge in her bedroom, Sherry kicked off her shoes. When they were kids, Sherry and her family had acted as Yvette's anchor. Yvette's dad, a wealthy cardiologist, had overindulged his motherless children with material things. During fling number five or six, he'd forced Yvette off to college. Being neighbors, she and Sherry had drifted into rooming together. Yvette's ability to have fun was a trait Sherry had liked back then. Because she herself was too serious. The bald truth was that neither woman had changed, and what worked at eighteen didn't work now.

Sherry hated these lengthy self-assessments that she'd been subjecting herself to lately. Counselors rarely healed themselves. Those who tried had fools for clients, as the saying went. At least that made her laugh. Frankly, she still found her best therapy in cooking. So that was what she did. Cueing up a dozen old Elton John tunes on her iPod, she gyrated into the kitchen and rattled pots and pans to her heart's content.

The house was silent the next morning when she slipped out. She didn't know or care if Yvette had come home. She ate breakfast at a nearby café, and when she was sure Nolan, Emily and the kids must have left Sherry's parents to go work on Nolan's house, she drove out to visit the elder Campbells.

"Behold a stranger," Nan quipped when Sherry appeared at the back door.

"Oh, Mom. Hardly a stranger. Just last week Emily and I went out to buy the material and pattern for my dress."

"Almost two weeks ago, Sherry. And you popped in and popped out. I hope you stand still long enough today for me to measure you."

"Emily said you wouldn't start sewing it until mid-October. She also told me Nolan inundated her with handwritten pages of notes from our trip. They're serious about writing a book about the wagon train reenactment, aren't they?"

"Absolutely. I have to admit they have a knack for humor. I know all those things really happened, but it reads like a farce. I laughed so hard I cried at the account of your meeting with that nice dean Nolan invited for breakfast today."

Sherry whirled from the coffeepot, where she was helping herself to a cup. "Does Lock know they're putting that horrible tale in their book? Mom, everyone'll know it's us! I'll sue Nolan, I swear."

"You signed a release, dear. That was your idea, I believe."

"Ha!" she fumed. "*Lock* didn't sign anything." She gestured with her cup, paying no attention to the liquid sloshing over the sides.

Her mother patiently wiped up the spill. "He did this morning."

"Why? Doesn't he realize we'll be the butt of jokes around campus?"

"Who on campus will admit they read light-hearted travel-adventure stories?"

Sherry met her mother's laughing eyes. "You're right," she said, at last allowing a smile. "They'll dissect Nolan's academic paper and blow off the book. So, what are you doing today? I really came to see if you wanted to run to St. Louis to shop. Emily said you hadn't found a mother-of-the-groom dress yet."

"I'd love to go with you. Is something wrong? I can't remember ever seeing you not work week-ends at the start of a new semester."

Sherry hesitated. "Mom, I need your advice."

"Ah." Nan gave her daughter a big hug. "Advice I'm delighted to give. I didn't think you'd ever meet your match. I say grab the brass ring with both hands."

"Mother, what are you talking about?"

Cloaking a conspiratorial grin, Nan patted her arm. "I mean, go for it, girl. If I was twenty years younger, I'd be in a hurry to snap up that handsome Dr. Lock myself."

"What?" Sherry yelped, and drenched the floor in coffee again. "Oh…but I suppose he is the problem in a roundabout way," she muttered, doing the mop-up this time. "Get your purse and tell Dad we'll be back before dark. I'll explain on the drive to St. Louis."

She did. And for probably the first time in Sherry's life, her mother didn't have answers. Or, rather, she gave bad advice. Nan said Sherry should either make a play for Garrett and tell Yvette to buzz off, or Sherry ought to find another man she could be serious about and show Yvette she wasn't a threat. Both were stupid ideas. Furthermore, they couldn't even find an appropriate dress for Nan in all those hours.

Sunday, it was mighty chilly around the town house. Yvette flounced around and for once, Sherry didn't try to make peace. By Monday, she was actually reconsidering her mother's suggestions. On a scale of one to ten, dating Garrett earned a four. She assigned a lowly one to going out with other men she'd met through intercampus committee work. And the farmers in the community tended to want wives willing to stay on the farm, which she wasn't.

That afternoon at the staff meeting Garrett blew the first proposition right out of the water—not that it had ever really been viable.

The sneaky man met each staff member at the door with a handshake and his killer smile. He'd even bought doughnuts to go with a fresh pot of coffee he'd heisted from Sherry's department, which earned him extra points with the staff.

Sherry took a seat in the back of the room. Thinking of Lock in other than a strictly professional way caused her to feel giddy. Sort of unbalanced.

Everyone else acted relaxed. They munched doughnuts and listened to Garrett toss out solutions to their concerns. Sherry's mouth was full when he moved to item two on his agenda—and drove a knife through her heart.

"I have here a request from the board of regents. Mandate, I guess you might say," he offered with a shrug. "They want us to spend more time on academic counseling and phase out time spent on students' personal and social deficiencies."

Sherry jumped up, gagging on the doughnut she

couldn't swallow. She whirled on colleagues who suddenly acted as if she didn't exist. "Where's your backbone?" she demanded. "We spent two years getting Kruger to at least ride the fence with regards to whole-life counseling for students who have precious little impetus to attend class. Maybe you're all willing to let this metropolitan cowboy waltz in and set our program back fifty years. I'm not." She thumbed herself in the chest so hard, tears sprang to her eyes. "I'm not," she repeated, a quaver creeping into her voice. Before she lost her composure altogether and embarrassed herself with tears, Sherry scooped up her things and fled the room.

In the hall, with the door safely closed between her and the dean, she gulped in air, hating to admit that she more than half expected Garrett to stop her mad flight.

He didn't. Sherry squared her shoulders and strode purposefully past the cubicles where secretaries typed furiously with their heads bent. It occurred to her then that she might have committed a grave error in judgment. Back a new broom into a corner and he had no choice but to sweep his way out. So what if one insignificant department chairperson got caught in the debris?

She sighed as she let herself into her office. From the interviews she should've seen that Lock, unlike Kruger, wasn't a fence rider. He acted.

He'd also called the entire division together. Something his predecessor had avoided like the plague. Good grief. She'd let her temper override good sense again.

She glanced up eagerly as a tap sounded on her door. Through the frosted glass she saw Angel's outline, not Garrett's.

"Come in."

Angel crossed the room and shoved a cup of steaming coffee into Sherry's hands. "Not like you to hide under a rock, boss. Scuttlebutt says the new dean clipped your wings."

Sherry accepted the cup, mouth turned down. "Who said? How?" She waved a hand as if to say, *Don't bother explaining.*

"You asking how I know what happened behind closed doors?" Angel winked. "I have my sources, boss."

"I should have guessed." Sherry lifted her cup in salute. "It pains me to ask, but what went on after I left? Did the dean blast me with both barrels?"

"That's the part I don't get." Angel rolled innocent-looking eyes. "He just went on to the next agenda item. They're up to number six."

Sherry took a seat behind her desk, a faint frown forming between her brows. "Can you lay your hands on a copy of his agenda?"

"Ta-da!" Angel pulled a scrunched paper from

her jacket pocket. After smoothing the page, she offered it to Sherry.

Sherry's lips twitched. "You are amazing. Devious but amazing."

"I give you permission to put the amazing part on my next evaluation. Leave off the devious bit, if you don't mind."

"Evals? Didn't we just do them?" Sherry's muscles tensed at the dark thought of who'd be doing *her* performance evaluation. Garrett Lock.

Angel hesitated. "Lock's secretary is typing names on the forms even as we speak. They'll be on his desk by noon waiting for his memo."

Sherry groaned.

"Aren't you glad you have tenure?" Angel said cheekily, speeding out and closing the door on her ear-to-ear grin.

It forced a smile from Sherry in spite of herself. Angel was right, though, when she'd said Sherry usually didn't run from a battle. Before she'd finished her coffee, Sherry opened her door wide and dug into the million and one tasks that befell her as teacher, counselor and department chair. She dictated the case notes she hadn't gotten to the previous night and handed Angel the tape on her way to her ten-o'clock intermediate psychology class. Her route took her down the corridor, past the room where the meeting had been held. It had just broken up. No one spoke, and the brief glimpse Sherry had of Garrett showed him surrounded by staff. *Female* staff. Be that as it may, she owed him another apology. She could do that—even if there were several issues on his agenda she took exception to. During the break between classes, she practiced sounding properly repentant.

Her fifty-minute class stretched to an hour. Then she got tied up helping a new student straighten out a computer glitch in her schedule. Sherry didn't get back to her office until two. Garrett's office was dark, so she approached his secretary.

"He left campus after receiving a call from his son's school."

"Is Keith sick?"

"I really can't say." The woman's icy tone said she wouldn't pass on the information even if she did know.

"If he gets back before three, will you tell him I'd like a word with him?"

The woman nodded, although she plugged her earphones in without writing anything down.

Sherry tried to connect with him again at three-thirty. This time his secretary was away from her desk. When Sherry let herself into her own office, she discovered why. A memo requesting that she make an appointment for her evaluation had been shoved under her door. Kruger had always put off doing evals until the president's secretary rapped his knuckles. Lock obviously had no compunction about rating a staff he barely knew.

She never caught up with Garrett. The next day, she counseled in the Hub. Efforts to reach him by phone during her few breaks didn't pan out. She didn't leave messages because she was hardly in her office and wasn't in the mood for hours of telephone tag. She would never have approached Kruger at home, but she would've talked to Lock if either he or Keith had been around the two evenings she went off to skate.

Yvette, too, was conspicuously absent. A logical assumption might be that the three were together. A possibility that depressed Sherry. These days, even colleagues avoided her on campus. If staff sided with Lock, she'd never win the battle to expand whole-life training services.

By Friday Sherry had given up hope of seeing Garrett. Midafternoon, with Angel gone to a secretaries' meeting, Sherry answered the department phone on the third ring and was shocked to hear Garrett asking to speak with her.

"This is me," she squeaked. "Angel is out and I don't know what happened to our student helpers," she said in a long breathless blur.

"You and I have passed like the hare and the turtle in a footrace all week," he drawled in the slow molasses way that always melted every last shred of Sherry's composure. "I think we need to set up an appointment to talk."

"Sure." Sherry tripped over her tongue agreeing. "Anytime. You name it."

She heard him flipping his calendar. "How about now?"

"On my way."

Garrett stepped to the door of his office to greet her.

As Sherry didn't hear the click of any computer keys, she assumed his support staff had gone to the same meeting as Angel. Digging a notebook out of her briefcase, she perched on the edge of the leather chair Garrett indicated—one of three grouped at the other end of his office. She'd a whole lot rather have had his desk between them. But she could hardly refute his choice of the more informal conversation area.

After taking a deep breath, she plunged right into the apology she'd spent the week polishing. "I'm sorry I walked out of the staff meeting, Dean Lock. A department chair should set a better example."

He waited and she fidgeted—she wouldn't apologize for defending her position in favor of whole-life training. He studied her so long and with such intensity that she eventually scraped a nervous hand through her short hair, making it stand in spikes.

"Why do I get the feeling you're not really sorry about anything?" he asked.

She hadn't expected such a frank statement and so had nothing to say.

"Truth is, you make a pressure cooker look calm, Sherilyn. Don't ever run out on me again after slinging manure. I need ammo to take back to the board. Testimony from law enforcement, women's shelters or from your students' employers. The regents don't want to reduce services at the Hub. They want to scrap the program altogether."

She looked stricken. "Since we're being honest, I'll tell you why I left. Sometimes when I get mad I cry. Men expect that of a woman. I was afraid it would hang me and negate anything I said."

"Fair enough." He pondered, then discarded the notion of telling her he considered tears a human trait. He'd shed some at Keith's birth and after Carla's exit from their lives. But Sherry rushed on before he could. Anyway, it wouldn't have been wise.

"I have another bone to pick," she said. "Agenda item four regarding standardized competency-based assessment. The women who enter our work-study program through the Hub aren't standard. It's unfair to expect them to make any kind of showing compared to the skill levels of normal college students."

"Eloquently put, Dr. Campbell. Did your spies tell you Jess Fowler made essentially the same point at the meeting?"

"Spies?" Sherry tongued a dry bottom lip.

Garrett glanced away, squeezing the bridge of his nose with his thumb and forefinger. "Yes, spies," he growled. "That's a copy of my agenda you're holding. I typed it on my computer and I thought there was only one copy."

"You typed it? Then how did Angel— I mean, I assumed the secretary who typed it...well, I, ah, I do have my sources." She resorted to Angel's pat response.

"Never mind. It's my fault for keeping Kruger's computer password. I can see I need to change it before I start typing evaluations."

"You type evals, too? Isn't that a waste of *expensive* time?"

"You think I can't type as fast as I can dictate?" He laughed. "Thank goodness your sources aren't omnipotent. Guess they didn't inform you I have two undergraduate degrees. One in sociology, the other in computer science."

"I'm impressed. I keep meaning to take computer classes."

"Well, I believe in staff development. I realize computer classes fill up fast, but if you find one you'd like to take and can get in, I'll authorize the department to pay for it."

"That's very generous, considering the board ordered you to trim the budget."

"Ouch. I said I'd cut fat. I didn't promise to cut from the areas *they* pick." He leaned back and tented his fingers. "Enough said. I have a fair idea of the general workings of the program for disadvantaged women. Fill me in on the exact steps. I'll save questions for when you finish." He rummaged for a yellow legal pad.

Sherry explained the lack of services for displaced homemakers in the original design. She listed classes she'd badgered them to add. Extra counseling. Child care on campus and whole-life training. "That's what sets our program apart. Our success rate is more than double other similar programs."

"Successful, but terribly expensive."

"Compared to what? For the women referred to us from the penal system the alternative would be jail—and you know how much that costs the taxpayers. These women come with a load of baggage. Nine out of ten resent any form of authority. Three counselors brainstormed and designed a series of preliminary requirements that include courses on nutrition, self-esteem, grooming and interactive people skills. These are taken before we discuss academics. The board of regents thinks the extra classes are frivolous."

"Have you had students from the program attend board meetings and explain how much the introductory classes mean?"

"Several times. And not just students from the penal system. We have physically challenged students whose self-esteem needs shoring up. We serve single mothers and divorcees of all ages. Most of them married before they graduated from high school and suddenly found themselves out on their ears with virtually no marketable skills."

Garrett opened his mouth to interrupt when the phone shrilled.

Sherry let it go to the third ring, then just about knocked a funny clay pig paperweight off his desk in her attempt to snag it. The pig's owner motioned her sharply back to her seat.

"There's a student clerk filling in," he said. "She'll answer it. Now where were we?" The phone rang again, more insistently, as he shuffled notes.

Unable to let the call go unanswered, Sherry dove over Garrett's desk. "Dean Lock's office," she said crisply and efficiently. She listened, then asked the party to hold. Covering the mouthpiece, she whispered, "It's Keith's day care. Do you want to take it or phone them back?"

Garrett looked startled, then grim. "I'll take it." He all but ripped the receiver from her hand. "This is Garrett Lock. My son did what? No, we do not have a dog!" Resting the phone on his shoulder, Garrett shut his eyes. "Why would the driver let him take some scruffy pup on the bus?"

Sherry wondered if she should slip out and give him privacy. She did her best to tune out his end of the conversation. Not easy, as his face grew red and the veins bulged above the collar of his white shirt. Before Sherry could decide whether to leave, he said goodbye and slammed the phone back in its cradle.

It appeared he'd forgotten her presence. Then his eyes lit on her, and he cleared his throat. "I have to go and take care of a matter that's come up. I'd like to talk more about this. If it's not an imposition, could you drop by the house tonight? Ordinarily I wouldn't ask," he said, noting her wary expression. "But we are neighbors. It seems absurd for both of us to drive back here."

Still she hesitated. What if news of their cozy meeting got out? He was an eligible bachelor and she a single teacher. Exactly the juicy stuff rumormongers loved.

"Just say if you have plans. Really, I have to run. Keith found a stray dog. He told the bus driver it was his—that it followed him to school."

"I don't have plans," Sherry said. Her need to convince him to save the Hub won out over what campus gossips might say. "What time is convenient?"

"Is eight or eight-thirty too late? This isn't the

first time Keith's been in trouble at school and day care this week." He sighed. "I think he needs more of my time right now. Even so, he'll be in bed by eight-thirty."

"Eight-thirty it is," she said. "Go easy on him, huh? He talks a lot about wanting a dog. Spending last Saturday with Mark and Pilgrim probably made matters worse."

"If I've explained the rules of the Home Association once, I've explained them twenty times. I hate to run out on you like this. Would you ask the student to log messages?"

"Take off," she said, shooing him with her hands. "I'll turn out your lights, set the alarm and tell the staff."

Grateful for her understanding, he thanked her again and dashed out.

She watched the swing of his broad shoulders and felt an uncommon tug on her heart. For Keith, she insisted, unconsciously running her fingers over Lock's silly pig.

CHAPTER EIGHT

AN UNSCHEDULED COUNSELING appointment detained Sherry at work. Unusually heavy traffic further delayed her. It was nearly eight when she walked into the house and met her housemate who was already showered and dressed to go out.

"Where have you been?" Yvette railed without warning.

"At work. Why? Is there some emergency?"

Yvette snatched a DVD lying on the couch. "I rented this so you could entertain Garrett's kid while we go out."

"Tonight?" Sherry didn't take the plastic case. "Yvette, if you and Garrett had a date, he didn't remember." She glanced at her watch. "I'm due at his place in half an hour to go over the details of one of our programs."

"You sneak! I told you Garrett Lock is the man I want. How can you stab me in the back like this?"

"I didn't. He set the meeting. And four months ago Tony Meyer was the man of your dreams. Darrell Bauer last fall. Kurt somebody before that.

Anyway, if you're serious this time, you should be including Keith in your outings."

"A lot you know. The boy's mother is making a big stink over custody. I didn't get the whole story, but I heard Garrett talking to his lawyer. He moved here to appear more accommodating. You know she'll win in the end. Judges always favor mothers. Garrett's going to need consoling when he loses the fight." She twisted a piece of hair. "I intend to be the one he turns to. So be a pal. Call him and cancel the meeting."

Sherry wondered if the custody battle was why Keith had been acting out at school and day care. "Canceling isn't up to me. He's the boss. Besides, he said Keith would be in bed by eight-thirty. That wouldn't allow time for a movie."

"Oh, you can be very persuasive when you set your mind to it, Sher. The incentive is having a house to yourself. If we get married, it'll be all yours."

"Married? That's a big step when you haven't even gone out with the man yet. Has hunting for Emily's wedding dress scrambled your brain?"

"Unlike you, I want to be a wife."

Sherry had a hard time visualizing Yvette as a dean's wife. But, hey, that wasn't her problem. Maybe Yvette *was* serious this time. "Okay," Sherry sighed, and pulled a file of papers out of her briefcase. "But the decision will have to be Lock's."

Yvette opened the door with a jangle of gold bracelets. "Here's the movie. Tell Garrett to drop by here for a drink. If I get lucky, you may have to spend the night with the kid."

"No." Sherry shook her head. "I'm sleeping in my own bed tonight and that's final. You want somebody to stay all night, you'd better call a babysitting service."

"Okay, okay. No overnighter. Just go."

As Sherry rang Garrett's bell, she wondered how she'd let herself get talked into this. But if they'd truly had a date and he'd forgotten— She almost jumped out of her skin when he bellowed, "Come in!" She eased open the door.

He had a cell phone tucked against one ear and two mitted hands wrapped around a smoking pot. Behind him, the room was blue with smoke. Even as he waved her inside, the smoke alarm bleated. "Oh, no," he said, gesturing helplessly with the blackened pan. "No, not you," he said into the phone. "I've got a crisis here," he snapped. "All right, I'll continue to hold."

By now Sherry saw that Keith wasn't in bed, but huddled in the leather recliner. He had his arms around the most disreputable excuse for a dog Sherry had ever seen. The boy's nose was red as that of Santa's lead reindeer. Huge tears made muddy furrows down ashen cheeks, and giant sobs shook his skinny chest.

Sherry closed the door quietly. Or maybe it only seemed quiet because the alarm made such a racket. Dropping the printouts and the movie on the glass-topped coffee table, she went straight to the alarm box, set a straight-backed chair beneath it, climbed up and pried the top off, dropping the batteries.

"Thank you," Garrett mouthed, and went back to talking on the phone.

Sherry hurried to open the front windows, then the back door to let the smoke out. The kitchen was in chaos, she noted as she waved her way through the smoke and navigated around nearly empty packing crates. Dirty cereal bowls still sat on the table. She even tripped over one on the floor. Gazing at it blankly, she finally decided either Keith or Garrett had fed the dog Lucky Charms. She gingerly picked up the bowl, put it in the sink and ran it full of water as Garrett came in and dumped the charred kettle into the other half of the divided sink.

With a dazed expression, he punched the phone's disconnect button. "That was the Humane Society," he announced. "They claim they can't tell me if anyone called about a missing dog, because I don't know what breed this one is." He closed the phone and tossed it on the counter. "I'm not even sure it *is* a dog, except the thing barks. I know it has fleas because the manager of the day care is going to make me pay to have the facility sprayed. She spent ten minutes lecturing me on health regulations. Then she suggested I find a new day care for Keith."

"Oh, no. By now most of the good ones are full and have waiting lists."

"Right now that's the least of my worries. First I have to get rid of the dog. Will you go tell Keith I'm not lying about the rules? We can't keep the dog and that's that."

"Slow down." Sherry placed a hand on his arm to calm him. "You have two bathrooms. I'll bathe the dog in the tub. You stick Keith in the shower. Once the pup's clean, we should be able to tell the breed."

"You think so?" Garrett scowled. "If it didn't growl every time I got close, I'd say it was a mop someone threw out with the dirty water."

"So you don't like dogs?"

"Me? I love them. I didn't make the rules here. I do obey them. I can't afford to be thrown out before my deal on this places closes."

"Did you feed the dog sweet cereal?"

"Keith did even after I said not to. I put bean soup on to heat for us and went to phone the animal shelter. Keith insisted the dog was hungry."

"He probably is. I have a solution," she said,

all memory of Yvette's mission flying out of her head as she walked over to Keith and knelt to look at the dog. "No collar. Very likely he is a stray."

"Your solution?" Garrett prompted.

"Oh…I was going to say my folks have an old dog who's pretty easygoing. They're well stocked with dog food, flea soap and combs. Let's take the pup there. My mom's home all day. I'm sure she'd keep him while you run an ad."

Keith brightened considerably at that. He scooted forward, his tears abating.

Garrett gazed at Sherry as if she'd lost her mind.

She stood and faced him. "Do you have a better idea?"

"No. But what if no one claims him? Then what?"

She waved a hand airily. "Cross that bridge when you come to it." She offered the boy an encouraging smile.

"All right," Garrett agreed slowly. "We'll take my pickup. It already has muddy paw prints on the seats. Don't say I didn't warn you about fleas."

The dog whined, burying his nose in Keith's neck the minute the truck door closed. Sherry absently scratched behind the pup's matted ears. She was rewarded with a hearty lap and Keith's grateful smile.

"It's hard to tell, but I think the dog is part poodle and maybe terrier."

"Ninety percent ragamuffin," Garrett muttered.

Keith glanced up in surprise. "I'm calling him Rags. I think it's his name. He came the first time I used it."

Sherry sympathized with a lonely boy's desire to own a pet. During her own childhood, with her parents and Nolan spending long hours at work and school, she didn't know what she'd have done without Murphy, their lop-eared beagle. "Exactly where did you find Rags?" she asked, inspecting a tender pad on the dog's right foot.

"When Dad dropped me off, Rags was lying outside the fence. He was still there at recess. At lunch I gave him half my sandwich. He crawled under the fence and followed me. A big kid kicked him." Keith's lower lip trembled. "It hurt him, Dad."

Garrett glanced over at his son, eyes dark and enigmatic. "Nevertheless, Keith, what you did was dangerous. You should have told the playground teacher or gone to the office. He might have bitten you. Strays can have rabies."

"Turn here," Sherry said when it seemed Garrett was so intent on lecturing Keith he was about to drive past the Campbells' street.

"He didn't bite me," Keith said stubbornly. "He's scared and hungry is all. He needs a home.

If you won't let me keep him, me'n Rags will run away."

"Nonsense, Keith. You don't know what you're saying."

"The driveway's coming up on your left." Sherry raised her hand to point and managed a warning squeeze to Garrett's shoulder before she dropped it again. She might not have kids, but she'd worked with enough parents and children to know that too often such threats weren't idle.

"Let's not make plans until we have him bathed and fed," she said. "Rags will be safe, Keith. I know you'd rather not think about the fact that he might already have a home. But what if he belonged to you and accidentally got out and became lost? Wouldn't you want the person who found him to try and locate you?"

The boy's skinny arms tightened around the dog. "I guess."

Garrett felt himself relax at Sherry's touch. Did she think he didn't realize the seriousness of this mess? He did. Before the move he'd thought himself capable of handling anything that came up with Keith. Carla's demands to be let back in her son's life changed all that. And where *was* she? If she'd taken Keith to see the stern-wheelers as she'd promised, this entire episode with the dog would probably have been avoided.

Secretly though, Garrett didn't mind that Sherry

Campbell had come by a bit early. Or rather, he wouldn't mind *if* she figured out a way to extract him from this debacle. *No,* a little voice argued, *that's not entirely true.* It helped having someone around when push came to shove. Someone as calm and unruffled as Sherry. This was a new side of her. A nice side.

Garrett slowed, peering into the darkness. "Did I miss their driveway? Last time we were here it was daylight."

"After the next block."

Keith slid forward and tried to see around Sherry. "I wish we had a house out here or closer to Nolan. They don't have stupid rules that say you can't have dogs."

"Your dad didn't have much choice, Keith. How about your mother? Will her home accommodate Rags? Provided no one claims him when you run the ad?"

Keith hunched. "Her house is big 'nuff. Everything in it's white. Crawford's afraid I'll get stuff dirty. Don't think he'd like a dog. But I'll ask. Can I call her, Dad?"

Garrett glared at Sherry over Keith's head. He took the corner into the driveway pretty fast and was forced to brake harder than he'd intended. "Let's get this smelly mutt washed first, shall we?" He killed the engine and was none too gentle setting the emergency brake.

Sherry got the message that she'd overstepped her bounds. Boy, was Lock a hard man to please. He didn't want the dog. She'd thought the idea of pawning Rags off on his ex might please him. Obviously not. Well, at least Mark and Megan's presence ought to ease the tension some. It might turn out to be a lucky thing that Nolan had insisted Emily and the kids stay here until after the wedding.

Leading the way through the side gate and into the mudroom off her parents' kitchen, Sherry called out a greeting. Nan Campbell appeared at once.

"What have we here?" Nan aimed the question at Sherry, but smiled at Keith.

"Keith found a dog today, Mom. No tags. He's in bad need of TLC."

"Well, we have plenty of that. If I had a nickel for every stray you dragged home, Sherilyn, I could retire in style."

Keith cocked an ear. "What happened to the dogs you brought home?"

Nan tweaked his button nose. "Practically everyone we know is blessed with man's best friend. Sherry found them all good homes."

Sherry backed out of the pantry, dragging a bag of kibble. "Got a bowl, Mom? After a good meal we'll bathe this little guy—and see what we have under the grime."

"Where's Mark?" Keith glanced around. "I wanna show him my dog."

"Not yours, son," Garrett was quick to correct him.

"He's gonna be. Look at him eat, Dad. I bet he hasn't had food in a long time. We can't let him go back to bad people, can we?"

Sherry waited to see how the man with all the answers worked his way around that logic. Turned out he didn't have to. Nan offered him an out.

"Ben's in the family room watching a football game, Garrett. He'd love company. Nolan, Emily and the kids went out to dinner and a movie. I've been making favors for the wedding. Ben came in here during the quarter and said it's too quiet."

Garrett's eyes lit. "I forgot about the game. I've waited all week to see the Chiefs play the Cowboys. Nothing like starting the season out with divided loyalties."

Nan made a face. "Better not venture into the family room if you aren't rooting for the Chiefs. Few things turn my mild-mannered husband into a snarling beast. One of them is anyone making even a slightly disparaging remark about his team. I swear you'd think he owned them."

"Thanks for the warning, Mrs. C. Man, switching allegiance is tough. Keith, do you think we can go in there and not root for Troy?"

"You go, Dad. I'll stay with Rags."

Garrett frowned. "What? But you love watching the Cowboys play."

"It's okay," Sherry urged the boy. "I'll take good care of Rags. However, I make no promises that you'll recognize him after a bath."

"I want to help." Keith thrust out his jaw. "Dad doesn't think I can take care of a pet. Mrs. Curtis in the school office said keeping dogs clean is important. Even Dad said Rags smelled. Can I stay and watch how you give him a bath?"

Sherry shrugged. "You may. And it's time. Look, Rags licked his bowl clean. Cleaner than clean. Nab him before he licks a hole in Mom's dish."

They all laughed watching the pup lick the bowl across the floor. All except Garrett. Sherry eyed his frown with some misgiving. For his sake, she hoped Rags did have an owner. But not for Keith's.

"Wow, HE'S ALMOST white," Sherry said half an hour later after she'd changed the water in the tub twice. They'd bathed him first with a flea soap, then with a better-smelling herbal doggie shampoo.

Keith sat back on his heels and shook water from his shirt and hair. "Boy, is your mom gonna be mad. We got water everywhere."

"I'll clean it up—" Sherry laughed "—while

you dry him with the blow-dryer set on low. I hope the noise doesn't scare him, but I don't like seeing him shiver."

"He won't catch cold, will he?" Keith draped the towel around the bedraggled-looking dog. "Dad'll never let me keep him if he gets sick."

"We'll dry him, Keith," Sherry said. She stopped her mopping up long enough to be sure she had the boy's attention. "Keeping him isn't definite."

"I know. I know," he said impatiently. "*If* somebody owns him. Bet they don't." As if agreeing with his new master, the dog wriggled out from beneath the towel and licked Keith's nose. The boy hugged the wet pup and laughed gleefully.

Sherry sighed. She wished she hadn't gotten involved. Garrett Lock had an iron will and so, it appeared, did his son. Woe to anyone who got caught in the crossfire, she thought dolefully, plugging in a blow-dryer she recognized as Emily's. Sherry aimed it at the dog, rather than handing it to Keith, in case Rags objected.

He didn't, but settled on Keith's lap. If a dog was capable of smiling, this one did.

Nan stuck her head into the room once Keith had dried and fluffed most of the silky hair. "Oh, isn't he precious?" She stepped inside, closing the door behind her. "Sherry, I think he's a bichon frise. He hasn't been trimmed, but he's got the curled tail and the buff coloring."

"You mean he's not a mutt?" Sherry left the wet towels and tried to see something of pedigree in the animal sitting so contentedly on Keith's lap.

"I'm not saying he's a purebred. He could have mixed bloodlines. One of the secretaries in your dad's office has one." Nan ran her hands over the soft floppy ears.

"It's not a poodle mix?" Sherry couldn't exactly say when she'd started rooting for Keith's ownership of the little dog. But she realized she had. Chances of a dog with a highfalutin name like bichon frise being a stray were slim to none.

"Don't think so. Dorothy belongs to some statewide club of bichon owners. If you want to know more, give her a call."

Keith shut off the dryer. He hugged the little animal, the sparkle gone from his eyes. "Will the lady know if somebody's dog ran away?"

"She may," Nan said. "I believe her club has a registry."

Sherry tried discreetly signaling her mother to be quiet.

Nan was clearly puzzled by Sherry's signals a moment before understanding dawned. "Oh, Keith, honey. I didn't mean to imply this pup was dognapped or anything."

"Dognapped?" Keith's horror was evident in his voice.

"Thank you, Mother dear," Sherry muttered under her breath. "Give him something else to worry about, why don't you?" Sherry helped the boy up and turned him toward the door. "Keith, why don't you go show Rags to my dad?"

"You're gonna call that Dorothy person, aren't you?" Keith asked, eyes watery, lower lip quivering.

"No." Sherry held up her hand in the scout's-honor fashion. "Stay in here if you'd rather. I intended to ask Mom to rent Rags a room at the Campbell hotel for the night."

"For me, too?" Keith telegraphed Nan a hopeful look.

Sherry rushed to nix that proposal. She had a pretty vivid idea of what Garrett's reaction would be.

"I promise I won't be any trouble. I won't even eat breakfast."

Garrett showed up in the doorway in time to hear Keith. "Whoa. What's this about not eating breakfast, champ? Tomorrow's our morning for chocolate-chip pancakes. It's ritual on weekends," he told Sherry.

If Keith was torn, it was only for a moment. "Fix 'em for Sherry, Dad. I hafta stay here with

Rags. I don't want him to think I dumped him with strangers."

Judging by the way Garrett's brows drew together over the bridge of his nose, Sherry knew she hadn't underestimated his reaction one iota. Frankly she doubted Keith had only one night's stay in mind. "Is it halftime?" she asked. At Garrett's curt nod, she hustled her mother past him. "Mom and I will go pop a couple of bags of corn. I'll pour sodas all around." Never had two women beat a hastier retreat. They'd disappeared before Garrett could open his mouth.

Shortly afterward, a disgruntled man and his son followed them into the homey kitchen. The popcorn filled the air with an irresistible aroma that Sherry hoped would trigger an opportunity to sit around the table and talk convivially.

No such luck. Nolan, Emily and the kids returned just as the last kernels popped. Greetings weren't even complete when Nolan helped himself to the steaming bag and a stack of bowls. "We suffered through a terrible science-fiction flick and missed the first half of the ball game. C'mon, guys. Last one to the TV gets no popcorn."

Garrett, Mark and Keith watched him lope from the room. Garrett and Mark gathered soft drinks.

"I'm not a guy," Megan said as they followed Nolan. "But I like the Chiefs, too."

Left in the kitchen to await the second bag of

popcorn, Sherry endured Emily's grilling. "You rascal. Holding out on us, huh? Do I smell something cooking between our maid of honor and our best man?"

"Popcorn," Sherry said flippantly. Then spun and gaped. "*Best man?* When did Lock go from being handed a casual invitation to being best man?"

Emily took the bag from the microwave and dumped the contents in a bowl. Sliding it to the center of the table, she sat in the nearest chair. "Nolan's held off asking anyone from his department. He didn't want to step on toes. The other day, when Garrett helped on the house and we all had such a good time, Nolan asked him. He seemed genuinely touched, and agreed. Quit changing the subject." Emily idly picked up a piece of popcorn. "It's not too late to make it a double wedding."

"A double—?" Sherry swallowed a kernel whole. Nan reached over and pounded her on the back. "It's nothing like that, Em," Sherry choked out. She explained the meeting that had taken her to Garrett's tonight.

"Mm-hmm." Emily just smiled.

"Stop that, Em." Sherry flopped back in the chair, at once remembering Yvette. She straightened. "In fact, he had a date with Yvette tonight.

So *they're* more likely to take the plunge. She's declared him to be the love of her life."

Nan snorted. "Number what? She's in double digits when it comes to being in love, isn't she?"

"Even so, don't look for Lock and me to set off any rockets. He's my boss, for crying out loud."

Emily closed her eyes and cupped her hands around the popcorn bowl as if it were a crystal ball. "I see love in your stars. I feel it in the cosmic vibes."

Sherry laughed. "Get out hip boots, everyone. I hope you don't expect me to cross your palm with silver, Madame X."

"Okay, skeptic. But mark my words," Emily said smugly.

"Enough nonsense," chided Nan. "Sherry, what's going to happen about Keith and the dog? If he has to give Rags up, that boy will be heartbroken."

Sherry sobered immediately. "I wish it'd been a mutt. Then there'd be a better chance Rags hasn't got an owner. But if no one turns up, I can ask our complex owner to make an exception. Ron's a softie. I didn't tell Garrett and Keith, but Ron looked the other way when the kids who used to live in that house found a kitten."

"If Garrett relents and lets Keith spend the night tonight, on the way home you might introduce that idea gently. I can't decide if Garrett doesn't want to deal with a pet or if he's only concerned with breaking the rules."

Sherry gazed at her mother. "I'll attest to the fact that he's a stickler for rules. But if you convince him to let Keith stay here, I'll offer to talk to Ron."

"Deal." Nan stood. "Come help me tie satin ribbon around the rest of the favors. We can watch the game as we work. At the end of third quarter, I'll open the floodgates on the question of sleeping over. I think Mark and Megan will run with the ball from there, don't you?"

"Mom, I never realized you were so devious."

"Mothers have to be to survive kids. Just wait, you'll see."

Sherry shook her head. "Not me. Never." Yet even as the words left her lips, her head and her heart objected. She had to admit to suffering a stab of envy when Nolan, Emily, Megan and Mark had piled into the house tonight full of laughter.

Silly! It's just that old biological clock tick-tick-ticking. She bustled about cleaning up the kitchen.

"You're a regular Suzy Homemaker." Emily grinned, not the least deterred by the fact that Sherry was trying to ignore her.

At the pause between the third and fourth quarter, true to her word, Nan introduced the subject of Keith and Rags spending the night. As predicted, Megan and Mark jumped on the bandwagon. Poor Garrett didn't know what ran over him. Even Murphy barked his two cents' worth, waddled over, sniffed the pup thoroughly, then lapped Rags's face.

The group looked so right together that a bone-deep feeling of contentment mocked Sherry's earlier denial. No, she told herself, it was better—safer—to recognize the scene before her as a sham. She was Lock's subordinate; he'd never allow himself to get involved with a staff member.

Yet she continued to daydream and was surprised when everyone jumped up announcing that the game was over and the Chiefs had won.

"The Cowboys had three men out with injuries." Garrett made allowances.

"Traitor." Nolan poked Garrett in the ribs.

Doubling over, Garrett slapped Nolan's hands away.

"You try switching horses in midstream. I've been a Cowboys' fan all my life."

"You're lucky we're non-violent types," joked Sherry's dad. "In a lot of circles them's fightin' words."

Garrett's eyes lit on Sherry and he smiled indulgently. "Not all Campbells are nonviolent. Am I in danger of being murdered on the way home?"

"Not because of football ties. Keep heckling me and maybe yes." Sherry hadn't joked around in some time and realized it felt good. Being with her family felt good. When had she started spending so much time at work that she'd forsaken lazy evenings like these?

Garrett shook hands with Ben and Nolan, but his gaze remained on Sherry, who deftly tied a slippery ribbon around the last favor in the basket.

"Are you doing groom's cake, too?" she asked her mother. At Nan's nod, Sherry said, "Call me when you're planning to do it. I've wrapped enough groom's cake for friends' weddings I could cut those foil squares in my sleep."

"Always a bridesmaid, never a bride?" Nolan teased. "After the first of the year, guys, we're going to have to do some serious matchmaking for this lady."

"Not!" Sherry stood and punched her brother's arm.

Keith looked up from his seat on the floor between the two dogs. Dark eyes serious, he said into the sudden silence, "If I was older I'd marry her. She does neat things. Skates. Likes cool music, and she's really good at giving dogs baths."

For too long a time no one spoke. Nolan found his voice first. "All-important criteria for choosing a wife. Here, I picked Emily because she could cook." Mugging, he slung an arm around his sputtering fiancée's shoulders and nuzzled her ear.

After the laughter died, Garrett told Sherry they'd better leave. "I'll pick Keith up at ten tomorrow. And no dallying, son. I'm telling you right now, Rags stays here."

"Okay. But can I visit him every day until you know for sure he don't belong to nobody?"

"I won't promise, Keith. Next week the college starts budget meetings. I expect a lot of early mornings and late nights."

The boy seemed so distraught Sherry blurted without thinking, "If your dad doesn't mind, I'll bring you here to visit Rags."

"Really?" He perked right up. "Thanks!"

Garrett didn't say anything then. He did after they reached the car. "What are you trying to do, Sherilyn? Undermine me? Why give him false hope?"

"You're totally insensitive. He's lonely and he already loves that dog. There's a fifty-fifty chance no one will answer your ad."

"That'll be ten times worse. Who'd give him a home? I know you think I'm hardhearted. Not even I can take that fuzzy mop to the dog pound."

"What if I asked the complex owner to bend the rules? I know him pretty well."

"That's convenient. How well?" Garrett snapped, unable to disguise a thread of jealousy that he could actually hear in his voice.

Sherry heard it, too. "Ron Erickson is my dad's age. I went all through school with his twin sons. Anyway, what's it to you?"

"Nothing," Garrett muttered. "It's a better solution than your first one of asking Carla and the banker to give the dog a home," he said bitterly.

"If you have such negative feelings about your ex, why did you move here?"

Sighing, Garrett gripped the steering wheel tighter. When the silence dragged on, he explained Carla's belated interest in her son. "My lawyer said to play along. He thought she'd back off. I honestly don't know what I'll do if after all this time some judge gives her custody of Keith. She abandoned him when he was two. Doesn't that count?"

Sherry chewed at her lip. She'd counseled women who sobbed that same question in her office on numerous occasions. Over the years she'd gotten inured to the father's side of divorce issues. Oddly enough, she found herself in sympathy with Garrett. She didn't want to be. Every avenue she'd worked so hard to establish at the Hub assumed the woman—the mother—was virtually always the injured party. If Garrett's case was valid, how many other men shared his plight? Sherry refused to consider that her feelings might be biased. Garrett was probably one man in a million. And if he was such a great husband and dad… That spawned another question.

"Why haven't you remarried? I know it's not

for lack of prospects. I've seen women flock to your door."

"I...I..." he stammered. Although nearly six years had passed since his failure with Carla, Garrett still had trouble admitting he feared a repeat. He found it infinitely easier to let women think he preferred to devote his energies to work and to raising his son. Far safer than venturing his heart again.

"I'm sorry," Sherry mumbled. "I had no right to pry." Then tension was so thick she exhaled in relief on seeing they'd arrived back at the complex. Jumping out, she shut the door before he'd circled the bed of the pickup to assist her—something she noticed he did as a matter of course.

They walked in silence to his gate. Sherry would have hurried on to her place, but Garrett caught her hands, stalling her in the muted lamplight. "Don't rush off before I thank you. Maybe I didn't sound it, but I'm grateful you came along when you did. In Texas I had friends who were single parents. We shared war stories and lent each other a hand. Here, I'm on my own. And Keith..." Garrett swallowed hard and tightened his fingers around her hands. "It hurts me to see him unhappy. With budget talks starting next week, I'll have even less time to spend with him."

Sherry saw the shudder in his chest as he closed his eyes and released a pent-up breath. He'd just laid out another problem that she thought was a women's issue. She really had hidden her head in the sand. Impulsively she squeezed his hand. "I love kids, Garrett. And Keith's a fine bright boy. Why don't I collect him from day care? He and I can skate, rent videos or visit Rags. On the rare days I'm tied up with late meetings, I'm sure Mom would fill in. Just add our names to the authorized list."

Garrett, humbled and touched by her sincerity, searched for but didn't find subterfuge in the depths of her warm dark eyes.

"I...I don't quite know what to say. I've never had a sitter with a doctorate," he teased, freeing one hand to cup her cheek. The next second, without even knowing he was going to, he kissed her. It was a kiss born of gratitude, but his lips had barely connected with hers before it changed.

In shock, Sherry did nothing to break away. At least not at first. She rose on tiptoe, reveling in the weightless feeling that came with the unexpected kiss.

The squeal of tires out on the street jarred both of them into separating at the same time. Each tried to appear unaffected. Both breathed raggedly.

Sherry saw excuses building in his blue eyes. Preferring not to hear them, she whispered a husky goodbye and literally ran down the walkway to her town house.

Unsettled as she felt, she wasn't at all prepared for Yvette's verbal attack.

Pacing the entryway, an ugly twist to her mouth, Yvette shrieked, "Some friend! Where have you and Garrett been for three hours?"

"I…I…" Sherry got hold of her raw feelings and explained about the dog.

"Don't add lying to back stabbing! Keith wasn't even with you just now. I saw you kiss Garrett, Sherry." She crossed her arms and tapped a foot. "I want you to move out. Tomorrow isn't soon enough."

That sent a wave of anger through Sherry as nothing else had. "Me? I will not move. The lease is in my name. If anyone leaves it'll be you."

"Well, I don't have money for first and last months' rent. So we're at a stalemate. But don't think you'll get away with this. When I get through telling people what you've done, you won't have a single friend left." Snatching her purse, Yvette slammed out of the house.

Sherry stifled a cry with her fist. She stared at the door for a long time, hating the fact that a one-time friendship had ended so badly. Yet try as she might, she couldn't make herself feel bad about kissing Garrett Lock.

CHAPTER NINE

THE ENTIRE WEEKEND Sherry didn't catch sight of Garrett again. He called Saturday to ask her advice on wording the dog ad. She had reservations about it for Keith's sake. But in the end, she suggested also placing a notice in the neighborhood newspaper that was distributed free to homes near the school.

Yvette kept a low profile, too. Though Sherry was in and out running errands and doing laundry, their paths never crossed. Sherry doubted they'd salvage any part of the friendship that'd been forged when they were young. And it saddened her.

She also dwelt on the feelings that had developed between her and Garrett. After examining it from all angles, she'd come to the conclusion that the kiss had sprung from the tension of the moment. Nothing more.

Sherry was sure her assessment was correct when Garrett rushed into her office on Monday morning asking for—no, demanding—figures to take to his first budget exercise. She called them exercises because they were repetitive and raised everyone's blood pressure for weeks.

The way he barked at her, she decided any real or perceived emotions they'd shared had flown from his mind two seconds after parting—if those feelings had ever been more than a figment of her imagination. If anyone had even jokingly said a simple kiss would have such a profound effect on her, Sherry would have laughed outright. Since he'd certainly erased all memories of it, she'd show him she could be just as blasé.

"I saw your ad in Sunday's paper," she said by way of polite conversation. "I didn't expect it to run so quickly."

He glanced up blankly from a stack of reports Angel had handed him. "Ad?"

She could almost see his mind screech to a halt. "Lost and found. For Rags," she reminded him, leaning casually on the table where he was seated.

His eyes were level with a chunky gold-chain belt Sherry wore loosely looped around her hips. It circled a lime silk blouse that fell over the orangest orange skirt Garrett had ever seen. A floaty skirt reaching her knees on legs that were long and smooth and tanned. Garrett coughed, doing his best to refocus on the figures covering the pages now strewn over the tabletop.

"Well, did you get any calls on Sunday afternoon or evening?"

"Calls?" Garrett felt like a parrot. Some part of his brain functioned enough to know that. The rest was frozen in a purely male response linked to the vision shimmering before him.

"You think that by not talking about Rags the problem will disappear? I'm here to tell you it won't. Not that you'll care, but last night I phoned Ron and laid the groundwork for Keith to keep Rags in the town house. Ron hasn't agreed yet. But he hasn't said no, either. You're to give him a jingle if the pup's owner doesn't show up."

Garrett managed to assimilate every third word. Enough to get the drift. "No one called," he admitted gruffly. "Keith is flying in the clouds. I tried to tell him it's early to claim victory. He refuses to listen." Discussing his son served to take Garrett's mind off areas he had no business thinking about in the first place. Sherry was so cool today she couldn't have been as affected as he was by that kiss Friday night.

Even now he'd like to rattle her cage. See how cool she'd be if he got up, locked the door and announced that his thoughts ran toward the two of them staging an encore.

Bad idea. Garrett shrugged out of a suit jacket that suddenly made him sweat and snapped forward in his chair. Hoping to dismiss her with a roll of one shoulder and the appearance of dedication to the task at hand, he got out his pencil and set some purely meaningless figures down on the ever-present legal pad.

Sherry took the hint. "Guess I'd better quit bugging you. Any other information you need, just yell. I'm sorry we didn't finish our talk regarding the services we offer before you have to slice and dice our budget."

"Me, too," he grunted. And that was an understatement. There was much about Friday he'd like to play over. Ten percent he wouldn't trade, he thought reluctantly, swiveling to watch her leave the conference room.

Garrett tapped his pencil idly, wondering what Sherry liked to do on weekends. He wondered a lot of things about her. None pertained to work or, more specifically, to her department budget. After another five minutes or so of nonproductivity, Garrett stacked the papers one last time, picked them up and told Angel he was taking them back to his office. The look that young woman delivered him cut him down to size. She'd seen his interest in Sherry and made no pretense of liking it. That was okay. Garrett didn't care to have it flashing in neon, either. His interest was illogical. Insane. He met Angel's frigid gaze without flinching.

As Sherry worked in her office, Angel burst through the door, interrupting her dictation. Surprised, she faltered over a word and clicked off the handheld mike. She'd decided to provide Garrett with a list of the points she'd intended to make at the meeting they never had.

As Angel slapped the opened mail on the desk in front of Sherry, she said, "A yard or two more of that orange silk would have made a nice skirt." She hovered on the balls of her feet, scowling fiercely.

Sherry ran a hand through her gel-spiked hair. "Did I miss something? When I came in this morning, didn't you say, and I quote, 'Those are some hot threads, boss.'"

Angel widened her huge velvety eyes. "That was before."

"Before what?" Sherry rocked back in her desk chair to peer critically at the offending article.

"Before our top dog licked his lips as you strolled past like…like you were the feast at his last supper." Making a show of inspecting her glossy nails, she added, "And before I went for coffee and heard about your wild weekend. Guess it's not true what they say in country songs—that Texans have slow hands."

Once Sherry got her chin up off her knees, she folded her hands on her desk and asked Angel to sit. "Now then—exactly what did you hear and from whom?"

Angel plunked down in the chair. "Those blabber mouth clerks in accounting said your roommate caught you in a compromising spot with you know who." She shrugged. "They said some other stuff, too."

"Like what?" Sherry clasped her hands tighter. Yvette certainly hadn't wasted time spreading her dirt. The secretary to the accounting department chair was the best bet as to source. Lena Martin partied with Yvette's crowd and loved to gossip.

"If you deny it all, I'll hand their heads back on platters."

"That's a gruesome thought. No. We will not lower ourselves to their level. Nothing throws a monkey wrench into a rumor mill faster than no response."

"So it's true?" Angel climbed to her feet. "Men are no good. Haven't I taught you anything, boss?"

"Some men are good." Sherry's voice rose sharply. "You had two bad experiences, Angel. Now, you can choose to cloister yourself or you can venture into relationships more slowly, benefiting from wisdom gained."

"You've tumbled big time for the dude, huh?"

Sherry hoped her face wasn't as red as it was hot. "To work, Angel. We weren't discussing me."

"Yeah, but—"

Sherry cut in quickly. "What happened is nothing like they're trying to make out. Yvette has her nose out of joint. The rumors are a result of a tiff we had."

"Girlfriends like that you can do without. It'll be hard, but if you insist, I'll bite my tongue."

"I insist."

But as it turned out, quelling the rumors wasn't so simple. It didn't help that at ten minutes to five her phone rang and Garrett, in a dither, asked her to pick up Keith from his new day care.

Sherry glanced at her watch, then at the pile of dictation she'd barely managed to cut in half. Injecting enthusiasm into her voice, she said, "Sure. Did you clear me with the powers that be? I don't want to be accused of kidnapping."

"I did give them your name," he admitted, "at Keith's insistence. Would you believe I swore I wouldn't foist any more of my problems on you? I even called Carla, foolishly thinking she'd jump at the chance for extra time with him. She claims she wants to see more of him—but on her terms, I guess."

"That's too bad. So…will she give Rags a home if no one claims him?"

The line crackled in her ear with each breath he took. "No dice, huh?" she asked lightly.

"Not an option." Garrett didn't elaborate.

Reading between the lines, Sherry figured he and Carla must have had harsh words. She felt sorrier for Keith. After all her years of counseling women involved in broken relationships, she still naively hoped the adults could set differences aside when it came to doing what was best for their children.

"Our break is over," he said into the silence. "Are you positive you're all right with this? They sprang this late session on us without warning. I could skip out, but I get the feeling they're waiting to see if I do. Like this is a test."

"Probably. And the departments of the people who can't stay will suffer. Keith and I will get along fine. Don't worry. His bedtime is eight-thirty? Are there other rules I should know?"

"The only one I can think of is no dessert if he doesn't at least try everything on his plate. I suppose I should set more rules. Basically I'm pretty laid-back."

"For kids that's better than being uptight. Oh, one other thing—I assume Keith has a house key?"

"No. There hasn't been any reason for him to carry one. Look, I'm just downstairs in Frank's office. I'll run my key up to you. There's a spare in the kitchen junk drawer. If you two go anywhere, leave one under the front doormat for me in case the meeting breaks up early."

"Now that's original." She laughed. "First place burglars look, I hear."

"I don't have time to be creative. See you in a minute. And Sherilyn, thanks. I never had to call an agency sitter in Huntsville. I may have to consider it here." He hung up, but she held the receiver against her cheek for a moment, hoping to stretch the tingle of warmth that always accompanied the way he said her name.

Stupid. Dropping the receiver like a hot rock, she got busy locking away the student files that still needed counseling reports. She removed the tape from her machine, then carried it and the records she'd completed into the outer office to leave with Angel. She was still in the process of giving the secretary instructions when Garrett dashed through the door.

Sherry's heart flopped around inside her chest. She wished it would stop doing that every time he appeared.

Rushed though he was, Garrett took a minute to thank Angel for giving up her morning break to run copies of the data he'd needed from Sherry's department for today's meeting. Angel shrugged, but Sherry saw she was pleased. Kruger always made last-minute demands and never thanked anyone. Sherry's respect for Garrett climbed. Angel's self-esteem was higher than when she'd entered the program, but there was a long way to go. The verbal abuse she'd suffered at the hands of both husbands and her dad had taken its toll. The young woman didn't expect much from men and was rarely disappointed unfortunately.

Sherry tried to convey her appreciation in the ardent smile she sent him.

Smiling back, Garrett pulled a key ring from his pocket and fiddled with a key until he worked it free. When he'd entered the office, Sherry and Angel had been the only occupants. Three women staffers noticed him as they walked by the department, then hurried in, full of titters.

Sherry knew all three had designs on Garrett. She groaned inwardly, thinking he'd never get back to his meeting if they waylaid him.

Garrett glanced up and saw them bearing down on him just as the key popped free. He shoved it into Sherry's hand and was already in motion to leave by the time the three reached him. He straightened his tie, gave them a lopsided smile and a quick salute as he hastened toward the door. "I'm late for a budget meeting," he said, cutting off their requests. "I only stopped by to give my house key to Sherilyn."

Four pair of stupefied eyes swerved toward Sherry while Garrett blithely slipped out of the department, leaving her with the evidence dangling in her hand.

She'd kill him. Murder him with her bare hands. The censure in the ring of faces surrounding her was almost more than she could bear, and she attempted to exonerate herself with the truth. "I, ah, I'm babysitting his son while he's at the budget talks." Her feeble words fell on stiff backs and deaf ears. Her three colleagues took a hike.

"Babysitting?" Angel scowled blackly.

"It's the truth." Sherry spread her hands.

A sunny smile rearranged Angel's pretty features. "That's too hokey to be a lie. I believe you, boss."

One of Sherry's dark brows lifted slightly. "Yippee! A fourth of the rumors squelched."

"I see your point." Angel shut off her computer. "What was he thinking?"

"That he was late for his meeting," Sherry said wryly, realizing it was true. He'd be livid when he heard the gossip. And he'd never recall feeding it.

Angel snapped her fingers. "Go get the kid and parade him through campus. Take him to the cafeteria for supper. Introduce him around."

"The cafeteria? Oh, good plan. He'd get ptomaine poisoning, the dean would have me thrown in jail, then the rumors about me shacking up with Garrett wouldn't matter anymore."

"Okay, no cafeteria. How about the Haywire Hamburger?"

"Angel, you're a genius. I've always said they misnamed that place. They should have called it the Rumor Mill. Only…I so seldom go there, people might get the opposite idea. You know, that I was flaunting my *relationship* with Keith's dad." She made quote marks in the air.

"My kids love to eat there. We'd go with you, but it's too close to payday for me."

"I'll treat you. Keith's the same age as your oldest son. Please, Angel."

"You don't have to twist my arm. It'll take me about half an hour to pick them up from the sitter's and drive there."

"Done. It won't save my reputation entirely, but it's bound to help."

"Yeah. And when the man gets home, explain the facts of life on this campus."

Facts of life. The phrase played in Sherry's head over the course of the evening. A man like Garrett Lock probably *wrote* the facts of life. Wrote and tested. Sherry's mind kept drifting toward areas that were off-limits. Not really off-limits, but certainly dangerous. About the third time Angel had to draw her back from imagining exactly how it would feel to be in Garrett's arms, Sherry scrubbed the thoughts away. She concentrated on showing Keith a good time.

"That was a blast," he said as they climbed into Sherry's car after saying goodbye to Angel and her boisterous brood. "I'm glad you picked me up. Me'n Dad never do anything fun anymore."

"It's hard starting a new job, Keith."

"Yeah, I guess. I saved part of my hamburger for Rags. Can we take it to him?"

"Sure, sport. Then it's home to bed with no

stops." She reached over and ruffled his hair. "You don't have homework, do you?"

He leaned back, checking her out with a mischievous smile. "I got a book in my backpack that I'm s'pose to read 'fore I go to bed."

"Really? Why am I just hearing about this now, tiger?"

"'Cause I wanted to go eat burgers. And I wanna see Rags."

His honesty blew her lecture out of the water. "Fair enough." She smiled wryly. "I should have asked earlier about homework. Tomorrow I'll be smarter."

"You gonna pick me up tomorrow? Yay!"

"I'm only assuming your father has meetings all week. Before you get too excited, we'd better find out if he's made other plans."

"I guess you got more important stuff to do than hang out with a kid, huh?"

"Oh, no, Keith. But it's your dad's decision. He said he may call a professional sitter."

Keith's shoulders slumped. "Jason at my old day care said those sitters are meaner 'n' snakes. I like you 'cause you call me sport and tiger, and you're nice to dogs and you mess up my hair," he said shyly, slanting a glance through thick dark lashes.

Thrown once again by his candor, she didn't know how to respond. They'd already reached her parents' house, so she said nothing, just fell to brooding.

Emily noticed her moodiness and remarked on it after Nan had finished measuring Sherry for her maid-of-honor dress. "Something's bothering you, Sher. I know you feel I double-crossed you, falling for Nolan the way I did on the heels of announcing I'd never marry again. But…people change." She made a fist of her right hand and placed it over her heart. "Hearts change. I love him, Sherry. I'll spend a lifetime making him happy. I didn't ask him to pay the debt I owed my ex-in-laws. He insisted."

Sherry unfurled the cloth tape measure she'd been folding around her fingers and paced the sewing room, letting it whip like a flag in the wind. "I'm not blind, Em. I see how happy both of you are. Megan and Mark are thrilled, too." She paused, frowning. "Aren't you the teeniest bit afraid? What if things change again and your feelings for each other don't last?"

Emily studied her friend. "Are we still talking about Nolan and me, Sherry?" she asked softly.

Sherry's pacing grew more erratic. "I feel life as I know it slipping away. Keith…Rags… I'm getting too involved."

"Mmm. And with Keith's dad?"

"No." Sherry made a slicing movement with her hand.

Rising from the chair that sat in front of the sewing machine, Emily matched her steps to Sherry's. "I fought the attraction between Nolan and me. I had a hundred excuses why a relationship was a bad idea. Loving someone is risky. But what's the alternative? Spending a lifetime alone and lonely, that's what."

"I'm not lonely." Sherry recognized the falseness of the statement before the last word died away. "And if I am sometimes? I'll join groups and take more classes."

Emily gazed at her sadly. "How many hours a day can you stay on a treadmill?"

Unwilling to accept the truth of Emily's statement, Sherry bolted for the door. Once there, she waggled her left arm, pointing at her watch. "I have to get Keith home, Em. Eight-thirty's his bedtime. I have papers to grade and a test to set up before tomorrow."

"Stepping up the tempo, Sher?" Emily trailed her down the hall. "It's all right to let yourself like a man. Not all of them bite."

Sherry closed her ears and made a lot of unnecessary noise as she rounded Keith up. He didn't want to leave Rags. Getting out the door was a slow process, further impeded by Nan.

"We're barbecuing chicken tomorrow night," she said. "Why don't you bring Keith for dinner? That way he'll have all evening to spend with Rags."

It was on the tip of Sherry's tongue to refuse. But the boy's obvious delight had her mumbling acceptance. "If his dad has another late meeting," she qualified.

"If he doesn't," Emily piped up, "invite him, too. The more, the merrier."

Sherry knew exactly what had inspired Emily's invitation, and she had no intention of passing it on to Garrett.

Keith chattered like a parrot all the way home. "Can I check the answering machine?" he asked the minute Sherry opened the door. "I hafta see if anybody's claiming Rags."

"Shouldn't you let your dad handle that?" Sherry didn't want to be the one dealing with the boy's broken heart if an owner had called.

"Please," he begged.

"All right."

The phone rang as Keith reached for the machine. His face paled. "Maybe that's someone now."

Sherry grabbed for the phone on the third ring. "Or maybe it's your dad," she hissed. "Hello," she said, sounding out of breath. "Hello," she said a second time into the silence. Then she covered the mouthpiece. "It's your mom, Keith. She wants to talk to you. Here—take the phone."

"Hi, Mom," he said without exuberance. "That's Sherry. Dad's at a meeting. I don't know how late he'll be. Here." He extended the receiver to Sherry. "She wants to talk to you."

"Me?" Puzzled, Sherry put the receiver to her ear. "I'm the sitter, yes." She grimaced at the woman's frosty tone. "I think I can take a message," she said dryly, torn between telling Carla she had her Ph.D. or acting as if she was half a bubble off plumb—the airhead Carla judged her to be. In the end Sherry opted for coolly professional, knowing from experience that even after ex-wives remarried, they often felt proprietorial when it came to their ex-husbands. "You want Dean Lock to bring Keith to St. Louis this weekend? You'll expect him by 10:00 a.m. Saturday because you're planning a trip to the Mercantile Money Museum. I have that. I'll let him know to call you." Sherry turned away from Keith, who was saying "ick" and "yuck," so his mother wouldn't hear him. "The Magic House is more fun for kids Keith's age," Sherry found herself recommending. "Or the Huck Finn and Tom Sawyer cruises. I know Keith's been looking forward to seeing a stern-wheeler."

Sherry winced at the former Mrs. Lock's immediate putdown. "You're right, it isn't my place to make suggestions. Goodbye." Sherry started to slam the phone down, then thinking better of it, set it gently in the cradle.

"I don't wanna go to any stupid money museum," the boy muttered. "I'm gonna tell Dad I'd rather stay home and play with Rags."

"The museum isn't so bad, Keith. The history of money is interesting. And you get to see counterfeit currency."

"What's that?" He wrinkled his nose.

"I'll let your dad explain," Sherry told him. Eight was a little young to have much interest in money other than for spending. "See if there're any messages on the answering machine and then get ready for bed. If you hurry you can read me the book you brought from school."

"Dad bought me a book about Hercules. Will you read it after I finish mine, Sherry?"

Again she didn't know if she was overstepping her bounds. What if Garrett had bought the book specifically to read to his son himself? She mumbled something noncommittal.

They were both relieved to discover no messages except for one from Garrett, saying he thought he'd be home by ten. He sounded weary.

While Keith showered and put on his pajamas, Sherry wrote a lengthy note explaining Carla's call and left it on the counter.

Garrett got home early, it turned out. Keith was curled beside Sherry on his bed in the loft room when Garrett let himself in and called out a greeting. Keith had read all of his storybook from school and now Sherry was reading aloud.

"Upstairs, Dad. Sherry's almost done reading *Hercules*. Can she finish?"

Garrett reached Keith's room in time to see Sherry uncurl her legs and start to close the book. The scene presented such a cozy picture that first joy, then panic slammed through Garrett's stomach. His son, hair clean from a recent shower, looked sleepy and content as a cat, his head bobbing on Sherry's shoulder. And she resembled a vision he'd imagined too many times in years past when Keith was sick in bed and needed tending. That of a fairy godmom. Garrett had imagined having someone—a female someone—to share the parenting. He stopped at the threshold, not wanting to step inside and disrupt the scene.

Sherry couldn't decipher the strange look on Garrett's face. She must have been right about the book, she decided, scrambling up. "Why don't we ask your dad to read the end? Actually we just got to the action part. The guy stuff."

Garrett shrugged out of his suit jacket and stripped off the tie he'd loosened the minute he left the meeting. "Don't let me interrupt. I'm bushed. Think I'll go take a shower. Did anyone call about the dog?"

"Nope." Keith grinned happily.

"Oh, well." Garrett heaved a sigh. "I told them to run the ad a full week."

"I did take a message from your ex-wife," Sherry informed him. "I left it on the kitchen counter."

"Why didn't you let her talk to Keith?"

"She did. But she left the message with me. She wants you to call."

Keith yawned. "Mom wants me to go to some dorky money museum this weekend. I don't wanna."

Garrett slung his coat over his shoulder. "She canceled her last visitation."

"So?" Keith flopped back on his pillow. "If I go to St. Louis I won't see Rags for two whole days."

Sherry stood up, closing the book. "I'm sure you two need to talk this through." She handed Garrett the book and tried to slide past him out the door. "Oh, I have your key in my purse. I didn't leave it under the mat."

"I hate having to ask, but can you bail me out again tomorrow night? They set a meeting for three o'clock. I'm sure it'll run past five."

"Goody, goody." Keith hopped up and down on the bed. "Sherry's mom asked us to come over for a barbecue. Oh…you're 'vited, too, Dad."

"I am? What time?" He turned to Sherry with interest.

She shrugged. "Usually six-thirty. I doubt your meeting'll end by then."

"Don't sound so sorry."

She flushed. "I just know these deans. They talk every issue to death."

"You've got that right. Will you schedule some time for me in the morning? I need to know the fudge factors in your department supply budget and in the Hub's, before the others start that double-talk on me."

"You mean you'll go to bat for us? For the Hub?"

"Why wouldn't I? I believe in whole-life training."

"You do?" Sherry tripped over her tongue. "Then why are we always arguing?"

He grinned. "You tell me."

She narrowed her gaze. "Do the regents know how you feel?"

"I can't recall that they asked specifically."

"Well, whaddaya know." Sherry couldn't hide her smile as she stepped back into the room and waved to Keith. There was hope of salvaging the Hub, after all. "G'night, sport. See you tomorrow." To Garrett she said, "I'll clear my morning calendar. I don't have a class till one. Oh, and don't forget the message from your wife," she reminded him, all but skipping down the stairs.

Garrett stood on the top step and watched her

descent. Feeling the congenial warmth go with her, he called out impulsively, "Ex-wife. If it turns out I'm taking Keith to St. Louis this weekend, would you like to ride along?"

"G-go to St. Louis with you? Me? What for?" Turning, she gazed at him as if he'd lost his mind.

Her outspokenness stopped him momentarily. "This is your territory, doc. I sort of hoped you'd play tour guide. Show me the city."

"Oh, well, sure. I can do that, I guess."

"Good. I'll call Carla tonight and pin her down. Let you know tomorrow."

Sherry hummed happily on the way home. As she entered the town house, she was surrounded by the aroma of garlic.

Yvette scowled up from the sofa, where she watched TV. "My, aren't we cheerful. Did Garrett get home from his meeting?"

"How did you know he had a meeting?" Sherry turned her back on her housemate to close and lock the door.

"I have sources. Why didn't you say you were going to babysit the kid? It would have saved us fighting. Don't lock the dead bolt. Poor Garrett's probably starved. I'm taking him our second pan of lasagna." Her announcement was muffled as she disappeared into the kitchen and came out with the steaming casserole. She left with the dish before Sherry had recovered from her initial shock.

Sherry more or less expected Garrett to ship Yvette right back. As the night lengthened without any sign of her return, Sherry felt her earlier joy at being asked to go to St. Louis with him vanish. She drifted off to sleep so many times during her vigil that when Yvette finally did come in and Sherry heard the door close and the lock engage, she was too groggy from sleep to note the time. But it was late. Very late.

GARRETT DIDN'T MENTION his late-night visitor the next morning at their meeting. Neither did Sherry. Professionally, doggedly, she laid out the facts he'd requested.

"Thanks," he said, preparing to dash out of her office. "Now I'll be better able to defend our position on the Hub's value at the roundtable discussions."

When he left, to keep from feeling the loss of his presence, Sherry busied herself refiling student folders.

Garrett promptly stuck his head back in the room. "I couldn't reach Carla last night. She'd already gone to work this morning. I'll call her tonight."

Sherry yanked out another file drawer. "I may

have other plans." The lie tasted like ashes in her mouth.

Forced to deal with the disappointment he felt, Garrett said nothing for a moment. "I see." His tone said he didn't.

She lifted a shoulder negligently, still facing away from him.

He stared at the rigid set of her spine as empty seconds ticked by. Already late for a meeting in President Westerbrook's office, Garrett reined in his frustration. "I don't have time to discuss your sudden change of plans. It'll have to be later."

"Fine," Sherry snapped. But he didn't hear, as he'd already retreated.

Luckily she managed to avoid him for the rest of the day. He'd gone to his meeting when she closed the office. Actually she was late picking up Keith. As a result, they drove straight to her folks, where they were drawn into the barbecue preparations.

Immersed in her family's normal highspirited activities, Sherry finally succeeded in putting Garrett Lock out of her mind. Until she saw Emily stiffen and a funny expression cross her face. Sherry turned toward the house in time to see Garrett stroll into the backyard with Yvette clutching his arm.

Aware that Emily was watching her every reaction, Sherry injected pleasure she didn't feel into a passable greeting. And if she thought she could've got away with it, she'd have begged off staying to eat—say she was sick or something. Indeed, both Sherry's head and stomach hurt. Maybe she *was* coming down with the flu.

CHAPTER TEN

YVETTE MOLDED HERSELF to Garrett, at the same time ignoring Keith. Sherry wasn't the only one who noticed. Mark mentioned it, as did Emily. How Garrett could be so obtuse was beyond Sherry. While he didn't overtly flirt back, neither did he appear annoyed that Yvette monopolized him.

Visibly unhappy with his dad, Keith slipped off to play with Rags before he'd taken more than a few bites of dinner. Mark started to follow, but Sherry stalled him and requested a word alone with Keith. Mark slumped back in his seat.

When Sherry ran Keith to ground, he was sitting on the floor in the family room, arms wrapped around the stray pup he hoped to keep. "You okay, tiger? You barely tasted your food."

"Why did *she* have to come with Dad? I don't like her. She called Rags flea-bitten."

"Maybe Yvette was just joking around."

"She wasn't."

Sherry hunkered down and scratched the wiggly pup's ears. All three sat in silence. At last Keith spoke.

"Dad and me did okay in Texas. It's different since we moved. *He's* different."

"Different how?"

"I never had to visit mom. Just talk to her on the phone."

"Things happen in divorce that kids can't control, Keith. Fact is, you still have two parents. The separation is between them and had nothing to do with you. Before your mom remarried, maybe she wasn't in a position to have you visit. It doesn't mean your dad loves you less, Keith, because he's willing to share you with her now. Really, you're lucky to have such an understanding father."

Outside in the hall, Garrett, who'd managed to lose Yvette for the time being, heard Sherilyn and his son talking, and hesitated. Keith had been so withdrawn of late he was reluctant to interrupt their heart-to-heart. To hear Sherry Campbell sticking up for him stirred feelings that hadn't surfaced in a while. From the rumblings on campus, he wouldn't have thought she'd do that for him or any man.

Inside the room, Keith sighed and flung his arms around Sherry's neck. "I feel better. Do you think maybe your mom cooked extra chicken? I am sorta hungry."

Sherry tickled him until he giggled. "Cut

through the guest bedroom and slip out the sliding glass door. It'll get you to the grill faster." She got to her feet with him and pointed the way.

"Are you coming, too?"

She shook her head. "Think I'll toodle on home. I have a test to write up. You'll be going back with your dad."

"Oh. Okay." Looking more resigned than pleased, he shuffled out.

Impulsively Garrett stepped into the room. "I didn't mean to eavesdrop, but I heard what you told Keith. Thanks for backing me when you don't know my situation with Carla."

"Yeah, well, it's Keith who needs to hear any truths you're passing out."

Garrett flopped on the couch near where Sherry took a seat on the floor again. "The truth? I don't know what went wrong with my marriage." Moodily he described Carla's return to college at his request and her subsequent obsession with her career. "One day I came home to a note informing me she'd moved to St. Louis. She said she couldn't explain, but banking excited her— and our marriage was strangling her."

What Garrett didn't impart was that he'd gone through a long phase of self-blame, of thinking Carla had found him lacking as a man and that it therefore stood to reason other women would, too. It seemed easier to use Keith as an excuse for not getting involved. At some point, denying himself female companionship became habit.

Leaning forward, he clasped his hands between his knees. "Some of my colleagues claimed I let Keith fill an emotional void in my life. Maybe I did. I know I'm guilty of raking myself over the coals with what-ifs and should-haves. But the truth is…Carla left me to raise our son alone. Now I'm afraid, after all this time, her weaselly lawyer will make her out the heroine and me the bum. It happens to single dads all the time."

Sherry thought about the times her affidavits had helped make that very thing happen. "You're probably the exception," she murmured. "The divorced dads I meet are neglectful, abusive or deadbeats. Some are all three. A judge will look at your record. Maybe Carla won't want Keith full-time. From what he and you have said, she has a hard time following through on simple visitations."

"I have a letter from Carla's attorney that says I've had him to myself for six years and now it's her turn. As if our son's life is some sort of shuffleboard."

"Courts today are more apt to shuffle parents than the kids. They often ask the child what he or she wants. Keith isn't quite old enough to have his choice given full consideration. Twelve is the magic age. Still, his preference will carry weight."

"I hope it doesn't come to that. Would you like to be fought over like a bone?"

Sherry glanced away, then back at Garrett. She felt a tug-of-war inside her chest concerning her feelings for him. In advising him, she went against her number-one cardinal rule—kids belong with biological moms unless a woman's totally unfit. "Have you and Carla sat down and discussed what each of you believe is best for Keith? Without lawyers to muddy the waters?"

"When I got her first request six months ago, I tried to set up a meeting. Carla said no. Of course, she was deep in wedding plans. I called my lawyer. He said to send Keith to her wedding and that'd probably be the end of it."

"Do you like her husband?"

"No." An abashed grin lifted one corner of Garrett's mouth. "I hate the jerk's cologne."

"Now, that's petty."

"Yeah. But it beats calling him an out-and-out moron."

"Neither description earns you points in court. Strike that from the record," she said in a deep voice. "Witness conjecture."

They were both laughing at Sherry's rendition of a judge when Yvette burst into the room. "There you are." She threw herself down so close to Garrett she was practically sitting in his lap and sent a challenge to Sherry. "What's so funny?"

Sherry climbed nimbly to her feet, smoothing the pleats of the India-print skirt she'd worn to work. "An inside joke," she said, refusing to be cowed by Yvette's possessiveness. "I was on my way out when Garrett came in." She filtered out Yvette's image and focused on him. "I forgot to ask if you need me to pick Keith up from day care tomorrow."

"I can't impose. I'll call a sitting service. The joint deans have a six-thirty breakfast meeting in the morning."

"I don't mind taking him to school and picking him up," Sherry said. "I have no conflict tomorrow."

"I'll take the kid to school," Yvette butted in. "What time?"

"Eight." Garrett jerked toward her and frowned. "I'd rather Sherry took him, if anyone does. Involving too many people might confuse Keith."

"Okay." Yvette agreed with a smile. "I'll sleep in. You haven't forgotten the Conways' harvest party tomorrow night, have you, Garrett? I RSVP'd for us." She curled ring-clad fingers around his biceps.

Sherry failed an attempt to mask her surprise. And hurt. She'd been going to the Conways' harvest parties longer than Yvette. "Did Janice call with an invitation?"

"Yes, but this year's party is couples only. She knew you wouldn't have a date."

"I…" Sherry swallowed the remark she'd been about to make. Garrett would feel bad and definitely get Keith a sitter if she said she could *get* a date. For a minute she envisioned what they'd all do if she showed up at the Conways' with Keith in tow. Smiling at her private joke, she assured Garrett she'd drop Keith off in the morning and pick him up after school. "If he doesn't have homework and you don't mind, maybe we'll go play miniature golf. After that, we'll hit the virtual-reality arcade. It's really cool."

Yvette sniffed. "Sherry's such a kid. It's not my idea of fun. Is it yours, Garrett?"

"Yes, as a matter of fact. But, Sherry, don't feel you have to entertain Keith."

"I'm not. I'll enjoy it as much or more than he will."

Yvette got pouty then, so Sherry decided to leave. "I've gotta go. Touch base later."

"Wait, I'll walk you to your car." Garrett tried to peel Yvette off his arm, but she yanked him back down.

"For pity's sake, Garrett. Sherry's a modern woman. Don't insult her."

Garrett hovered in the half-upright position a moment. The blue eyes that sought Sherry's appeared unsure.

Those ingrained manners he'd mentioned, she thought. Why else would he offer to walk her to her car when he'd come with another woman? Assuring him she needed no escort, Sherry left. She stopped to tell her family and Keith goodbye, aching for the boy. If Garrett was in the market for a stepmom for his son, he could certainly make a better choice. But apparently men didn't select mates with any sort of logic. And Yvette had been searching for love all her life. In a stable relationship, maybe she'd settle down and be faithful to one man. It could happen.

Sherry could also meet space aliens on the drive home.

Somewhat melancholy and at loose ends when she got there, Sherry began cleaning the kitchen. She also rinsed out a blouse and finished the test for her advanced-psych class. Having exhausted herself mentally and physically, she fell asleep seconds after crawling into bed.

As a result, she missed hearing Yvette come in—wouldn't have known except that in the morning her bedroom door was shut. Last night it stood open.

Not wanting to risk another confrontation, Sherry decided to forgo coffee. Since Garrett said he had to leave early, maybe Keith would like to go out for breakfast. She packed her book bag and slipped out, relocking the door.

Garrett answered on the third ring of his door-bell. His shirt collar was flipped up and his tie was draped around his neck. Seeing Sherry, he snapped up a sleeve to check his watch.

"I'm early," she said. "I didn't think you'd want to leave Keith alone between the time you leave and when he's due at school."

"Not as a rule. Although I trust him not to get into trouble."

"I didn't mean he would on purpose. But accidents can happen. I don't mind if you give him my work and home numbers in case he needs help and can't reach you."

"I'm never far from my cell phone."

"Of course. I wasn't implying you're negligent."

His gaze swept lightly over her. Today she looked like a throwback to a flower child. A voluminous gold skirt skimmed the tops of her hiking boots. A rust-colored blouse hung loosely to her hips, gathered close to her waist by a rope with beaded ends. She left a scent of lilac in her wake as she stepped into the foyer, calmly laying out her plan for taking his son to breakfast. Something moved in Garrett's chest as he listened to her smoky morning voice. A hard-to-describe feeling. One that suggested there was a gaping hole in his life.

Garrett realized he must be staring at her as if he intended to lock her up and throw away the key. He grabbed hold of his tie with both hands to keep from grabbing her and kissing her lips. Garrett already knew how she tasted. Sweet. Very, very sweet. A tremor went through him. What was wrong with him? He wasn't usually attracted to women friends, colleagues or baby-sitters. Sherilyn Campbell fit the bill for all three.

Wiping suddenly clammy hands on his white shirtfront, Garrett loped to the foot of the stairs and bellowed for Keith. Equilibrium restored now that he was out of range of her perfume, he tossed Sherry an easy smile.

"Keith will like eating breakfast out. The lucky dog. I'm envious."

Sherry fought an overwhelming temptation to tell him to play hooky. She caught herself in the nick of time. *He's your boss, dummy!*

"You said you had a breakfast meeting, or I'd never have presumed to drop by so early."

"Breakfast to that crew is a box of jelly dough-nuts and three pots of leaded coffee."

"And you're a steak-and-grits man?"

"More like cold cereal. Or omelets if someone else is cooking."

"I love to cook. But it's no fun cooking for one." Suddenly she thought how that might sound and backpedaled. "Um, that's not an invitation." She ran nervous fingers up the strap of her shoulder purse and shifted from one foot to the other.

"Too bad. You missed seeing me lap up your lasagna like one of Pavlov's dogs." He screwed his face into a wry grin.

Her surprise at his admission turned into pleasure. "I didn't realize Yvette had told you I made the casserole."

"She didn't. The day Keith and I ate at Nolan's, Emily let the truth slip. She served a side dish of spaghetti. When I wolfed down my third helping, she informed me it was your recipe. Then went on to rave about your lasagna. I put two and two together. You can't have cooked for Nolan. Emily's praise of your cooking surprised him."

"Until he met Em, all Nolan did on weekends was work on his house. My mom cooks at our family gatherings. He's positive I never learned, even though I didn't set out to keep it a secret."

Keith appeared at the head of the stairs. His shirt wasn't tucked in, but his face was scrubbed and his hair combed. He carried sneakers and socks.

"Are you really taking me out for breakfast, Sherry? I heard you ask Dad. I hate grits. Mark went someplace that makes chocolate-chip pancakes. Can we go there?"

"Featherstone Café. Nolan and I used to badger my folks to stop there on weekends. I'd order strawberry waffles and Nolan would have chocolate-chip pancakes. Going there's okay by me,

Keith, if your dad'll let you have chocolate for breakfast."

Garrett gazed at Keith's beaming face, love filling his heart. As a result, his answer emerged sounding deep and a little scratchy. "Anything that brings a smile to your face is fine with me, son. If the food's as good as Sherry remembers, maybe the three of us can leave early for St. Louis on Saturday and stop there to eat."

Sherry's head came around fast. "Who three?" Did he mean Yvette? Probably. No, definitely. After seeing the two of them together last night and hearing about their plans to attend the Conways' harvest party, Sherry had to assume Yvette would naturally replace her as Lock's tour guide on the St. Louis trip.

Deftly tying his tie without a mirror, Garrett pinned Sherry with a look. "Do you have a problem with Saturday? I know last time it came up you sounded a bit vague. Listen, Carla wants Keith there by ten o'clock. If we're having breakfast first, we'll need to leave here by seven."

"You think Yvette can get up that early after partying tonight?"

Forehead creased, Garrett reached for his suit jacket, which hung over one of the newel posts. "I didn't ask Yvette. I asked you."

Sherry gnawed on her bottom lip as she contemplated both his exasperated stance and his words. "But you were together last night and the two of you are going to the Conways' tonight."

Retrieving his briefcase from the closet, Garrett checked his watch before rumpling his son's hair. "If I don't take off, I'll be late for the session. You live with Yvette," he said to Sherry. "You must know the woman doesn't take no for an answer. When she told me about the Conway bash, I thought everyone in town, including you, was going."

"That used to be the case. This couples-only qualifier is new. Look, I don't want to make you late for a budget meeting. I'll go to St. Louis unless you change your mind. Enjoy the harvest party. I'll have Keith home and in bed by eight-thirty."

"You're sure you're all right with this arrangement? If you want to get a date and go to this shindig, I'll be glad to bow out. I'm the Johnny-come-lately here. Those folks are your friends." He realized the minute the words were out that he didn't like the idea of her going with some nameless, faceless man. Hadn't Yvette said there'd be dancing by starlight?

Garrett wasn't the world's best dancer. Yet he had no difficulty imagining Sherry cutting a colorful swath across a dance floor. He conjured up a vision as she stood talking to his son. Scowling, he closed out the picture of her tripping lightly around a dance floor held tight to some man's chest.

From Garrett's scowl, Sherry could only conclude that he was still worried about imposing on her and keeping her from the party.

"Keith and I will have a ball at the virtual-reality arcade. Randy and Janice Conway have a daughter Keith's age. You need to meet other parents. Curtis Jensen's son is nine. He plays soccer—and I know that Keith played in Huntsville. The whole Jensen family's involved in mountain biking, too. They'll know how you can join these things."

"Soccer? Yeah, Dad! And I heard a kid talking at school. He said mountain biking at Lake of the Ozarks is the coolest. We should do that."

Garrett laughed. "Well, by all means, we need to get involved in something cool."

"Sherry," the boy said enthusiastically, "you can come, too. Your mom said the mountain bike in their garage belongs to you."

A denial lay trapped in her throat. Sherry wished Keith wouldn't be so quick to include her in his father's plans. Then Garrett felt he had to be polite. "Count the layers of dust covering that bike, tiger," she said. "I'm not only rusty at mountain biking, I'm corroded. Deal me out."

When Keith looked stricken, she felt compelled

to add, "Ask Mark and Nolan to go. I'll bet they'd love taking part in some father-son outings."

"That'd be okay. Wouldn't it, Dad?"

"Whoa. Aren't you two putting the cart before the horse? First I have to meet this Mr. Jensen and find out the particulars. It's not a done deal, son."

Sherry eyed Garrett with amusement. "Spoilsport. Don't you ever take risks?"

Garrett didn't respond because Keith asked him a question. "Dad, when will we know if I can keep Rags?"

He didn't want to deal with the matter of the dog, either. He felt buffeted between the two of them as they ganged up on him. "I have to go, Keith. We'll talk about the dog when I have time to sit down with you."

Sherry followed him to the door. "Coward," she murmured, stepping outside behind him.

"Yeah, yeah. You're loving every minute of me being on the hot seat, aren't you? I haven't had a single call about the dog. Plus, your mom phoned her friend Dorothy. She checked everyone in her bichon frise club and no one's lost a dog." Throwing a helpless glance back to where his son sat tying his shoes, Garrett muttered, "I suppose it wouldn't hurt if you asked Ron how firm he is on the Association rules. Since they allow families to buy and rent here, they should expect kids to want pets."

She tried not to smile at his reluctant concession. Didn't want to appear smug.

He saw in her eyes how much she wanted to. "Go ahead, crow. The mutt was kind of cute after you got him scrubbed. But don't tell Keith I said so, in case negotiations with Ron fall apart and I have to find another home for Rags."

Sherry propped a shoulder against the door frame. "You're pure caramel under that macho coating, Lock."

He made a face. "Leak that to the other deans and you can kiss funding for your pet project goodbye."

"They're blustering, right? They aren't really serious about closing the doors to the Hub, are they?"

"I'd say they are, yes." Garrett didn't see any way to soft-soap the truth.

His quiet answer jolted Sherry, though it shouldn't have come as any great surprise. She'd fought hard every year to save existing services. The women who desperately needed what the Hub provided would be the losers. And ultimately, so would the community.

Garrett strode the three steps back to lift her chin with the tip of one finger. "I haven't struck out yet. Trust me to save as much of the program as I can."

She hadn't expected his support and therefore

wasn't able to express her thanks. A nod was all she managed. It didn't help that her lungs felt squeezed by his proximity and her insides melted at his touch. Thank goodness he didn't linger long enough to figure out what held her tongue.

With a brisk, "See you later," he strode quickly through the gate.

As if her boots were glued to the porch, Sherry didn't move until she heard his truck roar to life. Keith, who'd been busy tucking in his shirt, joined her, forcing her to regroup.

Breakfast with Keith was delightful. For a child who was only eight years old, he had a wide variety of interests. On top of that, he had a stash of really dumb jokes that kept her laughing.

Something Sherry had never reckoned on was the number of college staff who ate at the Featherstone. True to their nosy natures, most dropped by her table for a variety of reasons, but really to meet Keith. Sherry could see the wheels turn in their small minds.

One of the flirtatious professors who'd hit on Garrett—in Sherry's presence—stopped at their table and gushed, "Is this charming child Nolan's soon-to-be son?"

Rarely catty, Sherry didn't know what made her introduce Garrett's son and then calmly go back to eating, instead of mentioning that she was kid-sitting. Sherry noted the jealous flare in Lynn Tabor's eyes before she whirled and swept out.

Hindsight being always better, an hour later Sherry wished she hadn't been so perverse. Especially when Angel recounted numerous new rumors flying around campus.

"Taking Keith to dinner with the kids and me explained why the big man gave you his house key," Angel lectured. "Showing up with him for breakfast at the staff hangout is like flaunting that you and Lock are having an affair."

"Get real, Angel. They're the same gossips who labeled me a man-hater before Lock came on board."

"Right. Which is why these juicy tidbits are so easily spread. They see this hot new jock dean thawing a formerly cold babe."

Sherry stowed her purse. She laughed, shaking her head.

"Boss, you are one naive lady. Kill these rumors now or they'll get uglier."

"After tonight I'm sure they'll die a natural death. Garrett is going to the Conways' harvest party with Yvette. Keith and I plan to hit the arcades."

Angel gazed down her pert nose and slapped the mail on Sherry's desk. "Why didn't you say so before I got all wound up?"

"It's therapeutic to let off steam. Now your

mind won't be stuck on silly rumors while you transcribe these three tapes and run 150 copies of this test."

Snatching them up, Angel crossed her eyes, stuck out her tongue and flounced out.

Sherry buckled down to a busy day. She only saw Garrett once, after he'd called and given her fifteen minutes to dig out old figures on the cost of the Hub's special tutorials. He ran by at noon to pick up the twelve copies. Angel had gone to lunch. Otherwise, Sherry wouldn't have seen him at all.

"Our meeting is getting pretty vocal," he announced, then dashed off without filling her in on particulars.

Again Sherry realized she was relieved it was Garrett in there close to the flames instead of Kruger. Or her, she admitted ruefully. But, boy, wouldn't she like to be a mouse in the corner when the others discovered Lock wasn't the team player they thought they'd hired to slash away at the Hub.

For a moment her thoughts were consumed with Garrett. The glint that came into his eyes when he faced a challenge. His rakish half smile when he won a point. His silky hair that her fingers itched to touch. *What prompted that?*

Angel's noisy return brought Sherry to her

senses. Although she couldn't recall what she'd been doing before Garrett walked in.

Shaken, she decided to grab a late lunch in the cafeteria. Judging by the way the few remaining occupants stopped talking when she entered the staff lounge carrying her bowl of soup, Sherry surmised she'd been the topic of conversation. Not wanting to be put in a defensive position, she left and found a quiet bench in the courtyard. From there she hurried off to class and after that, didn't have a minute to herself.

Angel's computer was off and the department silent by the time Sherry got back to her office to pick up her messages. One was from Ron, and she called him immediately. Good news—he'd convinced the Association to let Keith keep the dog.

"Yes!" Sherry waited until after she'd hung up to punch the air in victory. On the off chance she might catch Garrett at home or in his office, she dialed one after the other. As his home answering machine kicked in, she happened to glance at the clock.

"Yikes!" She scrambled to retrieve her purse. If the meeting was over, he and Yvette were probably at the Conway party. Rather than dwell on why that picture left a sour taste in her mouth, Sherry closed the office and rushed off to collect Keith.

Nolan Campbell touched Emily's arm and bent close to her ear to be heard above the band the Conways had hired. "Will you be okay on your own? I see Garrett and I want a word with him."

"Is there a problem with him serving as your best man?"

Nolan hesitated. "No. Maybe. I hope not." He angled across the patio, leaving his wife-to-be looking perplexed.

Garrett stood in the shadow of a giant oak tree, nursing the drink he'd accepted on arrival. Yvette wanted to dance. When he'd refused, she found another partner. That suited Garrett. He'd accomplished his goal in coming. Or rather, Sherry's goal. He'd met Randy Conway and decided his daughter was way too spoiled to make an appropriate friend for Keith. He and Curtis Jensen had hit it off. Garrett now possessed all of the facts needed to start Keith in soccer. Plus, he had a map to the mountain-biking trails.

Garrett glanced away from the dance floor as a tall form blocked his view. "Nolan." Straightening, Garrett offered his hand and a hearty smile.

"You jerk." Nolan crowded Garrett and avoided his hand. "If I was a fighter, I'd mop up the dance floor with you."

Garrett's fingers curled into his side. He glanced over his shoulder to see if Nolan's steely gaze was meant for someone else, but encountered only tree trunk. "Hold on, buddy." Garrett stepped forward, absorbing the other man's anger. "A blind man could see you're ticked off. But you have me at a disadvantage." Garrett spoke softly and distinctly.

Jostled by couples coming off the small dance floor, Nolan jerked a thumb toward the side yard lit only by moonlight. "A deaf man could hear the stories floating around campus, *buddy*." He dragged out the word, leaving no doubt he considered it false. "Let's take a walk."

Shrugging, Garrett dropped his unfinished soda into the nearest trash can. When they reached the moon-dappled yard, he turned and hooked his thumbs in his belt. "Suppose you enlighten me."

"In a word, Sherilyn," Nolan snapped.

Garrett waited. His shoulders tensed as his eyes traced the crowd. Was she here? Heart tripping faster, he searched for a glimpse of her impossibly short hair, listened for the sound of her throaty laughter.

Nothing. Of course—she'd taken Keith to the virtual-reality arcade. "Look, man." He spoke more sharply than he'd intended. "Sherilyn volunteered to take Keith tonight. I tried to get her to come to the party, instead of me. She and Yvette ganged up."

"I'm not talking about her time with Keith. At her age, I don't even have the right to question the hours she spends in your arms. But I think you should know that on our conservative campus it's her reputation being shredded, not yours."

"What are you talking about?" Garrett reared back.

"As if you didn't give her the key to your house in front of three of the biggest gossips on staff."

Garrett wiped at sweat that suddenly beaded his brow. "Is that what set you off? Our initial budget meeting ran late. I asked her to pick Keith up from day care. Well, I didn't ask. She offered, should the need arise. It did, suddenly. How *should* I have given her a key to my house? In a plain brown envelope by campus mail?"

"I suppose Sherry just happened by your place bright and early this morning, too?" Camp said curtly. "Early enough to take Keith to breakfast at the Featherstone."

"I can't say 'happened by' is accurate. She had it in her head before she came over. She said Keith shouldn't stay alone while I went to a breakfast meeting. Listen, I planned to call a babysitting service from the get-go. But this arrangement apparently suits her—and Keith. Frankly, I'm not sure it's anyone else's business. Including yours, *buddy*." Garrett thumped Nolan's chest twice with his forefinger.

"Sherry is family. You may get bored with the job and move on. She'll stay. In this town you don't live down gossip like having an affair with your boss."

"Should I take out a billboard saying we're not sleeping together?"

Nolan backed away from the fire in Garrett's eyes. "So…nothing's going on?"

"Nothing."

"Why?"

"Pardon me?" Garrett took an exaggerated whiff of Nolan's breath.

"I haven't even had a beer. Don't you find my sister attractive?"

"Yes, but—"

"But what? I never figured you'd believe that trash about her. She's no man-hater."

Garrett tipped his head and wiggled a finger in his ear. "Excuse me. First you threaten to tear me limb from limb for sleeping with your sister. Then you call me a jerk because I'm not. Which is it, pal?"

Nolan rammed both hands into his front pockets and gazed sheepishly at Garrett. "Guess I'm off base on both counts, huh?"

"Mm." Garrett's reply lodged in his throat as he remembered the heated kiss they'd shared. And the thoughts that kept him awake more nights than he cared to admit. Garrett chose not to tell Nolan just how attractive he did find his sister. Mostly because Garrett's feelings were muddled at best.

She was beautiful. Passionate about things she believed in. Easy to talk to. And his son thought the world of her. Beyond that, Garrett wasn't willing to venture. Except he knew he'd rather be with her and Keith tonight than at this dance with her roommate.

Nolan clapped Garrett on the back. "Glad we had this talk. Are you ready to go back and party?"

"I'm ready to go home. If you'll excuse me, I need to tell Yvette."

"She won't leave. Yvette parties till the cows come home."

Garrett shrugged. "We came in separate cars. If she chooses to stay, it's okay by me."

Which didn't stop Yvette from pitching a fit, trying to change his mind. Garrett stood firm, although embarrassed by the scene. As he told his host and hostess goodbye, they made him feel persona non grata. Garrett worried he might inadvertently have added to the lies circling campus. On the other hand, he'd convinced Nolan there was nothing going on between him and Sherilyn. As her brother and a respected member of the faculty, he'd probably set about successfully squelching rumors.

CHAPTER ELEVEN

ON THE DRIVE HOME Garrett had time to think more clearly. Was Sherry aware of the talk? he wondered. He'd lashed out at Nolan in a knee-jerk reaction, but Garrett knew how conservative college administrators could be—and how they reacted to news of divorce or hanky-panky involving staff. They got nervous. Very nervous. And that didn't even address his problems if Carla's lawyer got wind of slanderous gossip.

So what? This wasn't the eighteen-nineties. Both he and Sherry were single and past the age of consent.

Consent to what? Garrett snorted. A body would think something had happened between them. One kiss did not an affair make. But there were kisses…and *kisses*.

The smart thing to do was end all contact between them outside of work. Sherry hadn't seemed enthusiastic about going with him to St. Louis, anyway. It'd be a simple matter to say he'd changed his mind.

Except he hadn't. His son would be disappointed. Who was he kidding? *He* would be disappointed. Until this minute he hadn't realized how much he'd looked forward to Sherry's company on the return trip, after leaving Keith with Carla. Well, it couldn't be helped. As Nolan had so brutally pointed out, Sherry's reputation was on the line. Even conservative administrations looked the other way when male professors strayed. It might be the new millennium, but the double standard hadn't changed.

Parking in his designated spot, Garrett turned off the lights and yanked on the emergency brake. He ripped off his tie and, as he did, experienced a quiver low in his stomach at the memory of Sherry watching him tie it this morning. Her golden eyes had flowed over his chest. Garrett would bet money she didn't have a clue she'd done it or that he'd noticed.

He'd noticed all right. It was all he could do to keep his composure.

He shrugged out of his suit jacket, picked up his briefcase and slammed the car door with more force than necessary. At the gate his steps faltered. Warm light spilled from the windows of his home. In Texas, Keith had always stayed at the sitter's. The house had always been dark when he came home late. Who'd have thought a few lightbulbs would turn a man's guts inside out? Garrett pushed through the gate. If he'd suspected that, he'd have put a lamp on a timer.

The porch light, too, shone a welcoming beacon. Had Sherry left it on for him? Why were she and Keith home so early? He quickly checked his watch. Eleven. Not early at all. Where had the time gone? Although it had been after nine when he got to the party. The deans had hammered him all day and into the dinner hour, trying to wear him down and get him to pull the plug on the Hub. He'd trimmed so much fat from other beefy areas that he felt like the local butcher. Sherry would be pleased, he thought as he turned his key in the lock. He'd saved every one of her services.

Stepping inside, Garrett sucked in the scent of cinnamon and coffee. Another wave of nostalgia overtook his senses, one stretching back to the happy days of his youth. His dad, a writer, had worked at home. His mother always had a pot of coffee on, and she filled the house with the aroma of baked bread at least twice a week.

Until his stomach growled, Garrett had forgotten that he'd missed the barbecue portion of the party. All he'd had to eat since lunch was a handful of pretzels and half a soda. Bypassing the living room where the light was low, he headed for the kitchen, assuming that was where he'd find Sherry. The room was empty. He dropped his coat and case on a chair, staring at a coffee cake that sat cooling on the counter. Powdered sugar frosting still dripped onto the plate. He resisted swiping a finger through it for a taste and backtracked to the living room, calling Sherry's name softly as he went.

The minute he crossed under the arched doorway, Garrett saw why the house remained so still. She lay curled in the corner of his couch, feet bare, student papers floating unheeded from her lap to the floor. She'd fallen asleep.

A lump rose in his throat at the homey picture she presented. A half-full cup of coffee rested on a coaster. The lamp, though low, glinted off red and gold highlights in her sable hair. On a whim Garrett leaned down to see if the thick lashes that lay against her cheeks were a mix of colors, too. With her face shadowed by the sofa's winged back he wasn't able to tell. He did know that up close her skin reminded him of vanilla ice cream.

Twice he reached out to touch her cheek. Twice he drew back and watched the faint rise and fall of her chest. She slept, lips slightly parted. But no sound whispered through them. She looked like a waif, her face without makeup, hair feathered carelessly around it.

Garrett shifted on the balls of his feet. It felt as if unseen fingers clutched his windpipe, forcing his breath out in ragged spurts.

Sherry stirred. Her eyelids fluttered open.

Groggy with sleep, she sensed a presence. *An intruder?* Panic welled in her throat. Then she saw a dark shape looming over her. Rearing back, she screamed. She felt a textbook she'd been using earlier topple from her lap. Papers crunched under her feet as she tried to escape the hands reaching out to her—to clamp across her mouth. Her heart hammered wildly, deafeningly, in her ears. A second scream built. Fear tasted metallic on her tongue.

"Easy, easy." Garrett took his hand from her mouth and lifted her free of the books and papers scattered around her. "Don't scream," he said gruffly, tucking her face against his chest and her head beneath his chin. "It's me, Garrett. The last thing I wanted was to scare you. But you'll wake Keith." Smoothing a hand up and down Sherry's shuddering back, he slowly rocked from side to side.

She felt her heart drop from a gallop to a canter as she absorbed the heat pulsing through Garrett's shirtfront. A shirt that tickled her nose and crinkled crisply in her ear. She should say something to let him know he hadn't permanently warped her psyche. But lethargy seeped into her bones. She felt giddy and weightless, and closed her eyes again.

"Sherilyn? Are you all right?"

Nodding dumbly, Sherry wasn't even aware that

her arms were locked in a stranglehold around his neck. Because his worried questions beat rhythmically against her eardrums, she curved away from him with a sigh. "You scared me into next Juvember." Loosening her grip, she slid to her feet. "I'll live. You must wonder what kind of sitter falls asleep on the job. A burglar could have waltzed in and walked off with the silver."

A shaky laugh rumbled from Garrett's throat. "You're safe there. The silver went with Carla. As did any crystal, china and linens. Not that we had much. We were both struggling college students. Frankly, the pieces we received as wedding gifts looked out of place in our tiny apartment. I was just glad she left Keith's crib and chest of drawers." His thumbs scraped lightly over her jaw, while his gaze meandered lazily over her sleep-flushed features.

More conscious now, Sherry digested what he'd just said. Some of those wedding gifts must have come from *his* friends and family, and Carla took them all? When she'd counseled divorced wives who poured their hearts out in her office at the Hub, not once had she thought of an ex-husband's needs. Her focus had been on securing a workable household for the displaced mom and kids. Feeling guilty, Sherry stepped away from Garrett. She rubbed at goose bumps that rose on her bare arms.

"What's wrong? Did I hurt you when I yanked you off the couch?" He brushed her fingers aside and inspected her upper arms.

His warm breath skittered across her skin. Laughing nervously, she massaged away a shiver. "Garrett? Why did your lawyer let Carla take so much when you were the one left to provide a home for Keith?"

At the time of his divorce, he and Carla had shared a lawyer to cut costs. A lawyer *she'd* found. Too late, Garrett realized the man was her friend, not his. The one-sided disbursement of joint goods had been a sore point for a long time. One he never talked about. He couldn't think why he'd brought it up now. Garrett thought he'd finally evolved beyond the anger.

"We split six years ago. Maybe I don't have silver and maybe the furniture doesn't get dusted regularly. But I'd gladly stack up Keith's home against any you care to show me."

"I never meant… Garrett, I'm sorry." She closed the distance between them. "Your place has what a child needs most—love." Turning from him, she began to collect her papers and pile them neatly. "Keith and I had a blast at the arcade tonight. He's dead-eye Dick with the control stick. No Tiger Woods at golf, I'm afraid," she said, chuckling at the memory. "Did you have fun at the Conways'?" she asked lightly.

He knelt to help her. "I may as well tell you. I suppose you'll hear, anyway. Your brother gave me kind of a hard time. Then Yvette wanted me to stay longer and I left early. She's…not pleased."

"Oh, Yvette blows up and gets over it. But Nolan? He's normally so laid-back. What set him off?"

"I…" Garrett got very precise straightening the edges of a stack of tests. "Rumors concerning you and me," he growled. "On campus. Have you heard them?" Setting the papers aside, he paced to the fireplace and back, massaging his neck.

She turned aside to keep Garrett from seeing the hot flush climbing up her neck. "A little over a year ago Nolan was dumped by his fiancée, who made some cutting remarks in front of staff. The whole thing got blown out of proportion. It was headline news around campus until the next rumor hit the fan. I give the latest gossip a week— two at most—to run its course."

Garrett shifted a picture of Keith that sat on the mantel. "It's my fault. I should have called you into my office to give you my house key." He was on the verge of telling her about his decision to avoid contact with her outside of work when she glanced up from stuffing some of the papers into her book bag.

"Don't be so quick to take all the blame, Garrett. This morning Lynn Tabor stopped by our table at the restaurant. She confused Keith with Mark. I said he was your son. I just neglected to add that I was doing you a favor running Keith to school."

"Lynn Tabor." Garrett groaned. "So she assumes all women are like her? I've never met anyone who comes on so strong—except for Yvette. I've uninvited Lynn to my house twice. I've started keeping a list of excuses so I don't mess up and do something stupid like kill off my grandfather twice."

Sherry's eyes darkened sympathetically. "I know how Lynn is. She says vile things about people. She loves to stir the pot. Yet I deliberately let her think the worst. If I could take it all back, I would."

Garrett found himself growing angry at Lynn and those who listened and believed her lies. Lynn had probably fueled the first rumors he'd heard about Sherilyn. And Sherilyn had never acknowledged that the stories hurt her. But it didn't take a Rhodes scholar to see how vulnerable she was. Now he was glad he hadn't brushed her off. "You're right, Sherilyn. Campus rumors are short-lived. What do you say we don't let on we've heard them? Hey, join me for a cup of coffee and a slice of that cake some good fairy left in my kitchen. And I'll give you the best news you've heard all day."

A sunny smile brought a dimple to her cheek. "You saved the Hub?" Her shaky question vibrated with hope.

Garrett loved to see the eager anticipation flood her face and brighten her jewel eyes. He was tempted to drag out his response. But the breathless way she danced toward him, a bundle of nervous energy, had him reaching for her and blurting out the truth. "The budget committee didn't like leaving the Hub funding in, but I'm well within the parameters they set for total dollars. Outside of finalizing, it's a done deal."

Sherry threw her arms around his neck. Elated, she rained kisses on his face.

Tongue cloven to the roof of his mouth, Garrett could do little but grin like a fool. Encircling her with his arms was automatic. She made his head swim with the smell of lilacs and shampoo and something he'd begun to recognize as her special womanly scent. All his good intentions to keep a distance between them evaporated like smoke.

He kissed her back, at first matching her soft childlike pecks. Next came slower but as yet impersonal kisses between friends. Then, holding her head in both his hands, Garrett touched Sherry's lips with his tongue and kissed her the way a man kisses a woman he cares about. It'd been so long since he'd allowed himself to feel this way, the truth momentarily escaped him.

Sherry didn't realize she'd been waiting for a repeat performance of the last time they kissed until her fingers framed his face and she strained on tiptoe to feel his chest against her—didn't realize it until a fire ignited in her belly. It wasn't that she'd never kissed a man, as some on campus hinted. More that she'd never allowed herself to let go. With Garrett it was different. She couldn't hang on to a single solitary thought.

Time held no meaning until the grandfather clock standing at the foot of the stairs chimed twelve. Garrett broke away, dragging in ragged breaths as the sound clanged inside his head. His gaze left her swollen lips and smoky eyes to travel over her pale face, illuminated in the glow of the lamp. A lamp that also highlighted the wooden banister that led to the loft. A loft where Keith slept. Since the move, his son often fought bad dreams in the middle of the night.

What was he thinking? What if Keith—? Garrett catapulted away from Sherry, unable to even finish the thought.

"Garrett?" Her voice seemed to come from miles away as he stood in the middle of the room clenching and unclenching his fists.

Noticing his harshly set jaw, she felt heat blaze up her neck and sting her cheeks. Why didn't he say something? He was obviously drowning in remorse. What was the protocol in a situation like this? Should she laugh it off and leave? And then tomorrow morning return to business as usual? As she gathered books and papers, her hands shook noticeably.

All at once Garrett landed on a knee at her feet. "Don't look like that. Like we did something horribly wrong." He cleared his throat. "I just… If Keith… What I'm trying to say is…I don't make this a habit."

"If you think it's my normal modus operandi," she said hotly, "you're mistaken."

"I know that." He caught her fluttering hands and drew his thumbs back and forth across her knuckles.

She stared at his hands, remembering how she liked the feel of them on her skin. Not something she cared to have Keith see any more than his father did. They were friends, she and Keith. Sherry knew the boy was confused about his mother's sudden appearance in his life. Confused by her marriage to a man he didn't like. Keith was pretty vocal about not liking it when Yvette kissed his dad. What if…?

"Garrett." Her voice caught. "I'd never do anything to hurt Keith. This is my fault. I was deliriously happy that you'd saved the Hub. Things got out of hand."

Garrett absorbed her precise little statement. He felt like shaking her until she admitted the truth. But reason stole over him. Letting it go for the moment made sense. He acknowledged what they both knew—that Sherry had become Keith's rock. A liaison between himself and her was trouble looking for a place to happen.

"You're right." He cleared his throat. "You have my word this won't occur again. I hope you're not going to let one lapse on my part affect your relationship with Keith."

She shook her head, not trusting herself to speak.

"Good. So, now shall we have coffee and a slice of that cake?"

"I, ah…no. Have some if you'd like. Or save it for breakfast. It's late. I need to get home, Garrett."

Almost relieved—because he didn't know how he'd have managed to keep his composure as they sat knee to knee at his table—he escorted her to the door. "You'll still go to St. Louis on Saturday? Keith's counting on it."

She nodded. "But it'd be better not to spread the news around. There's no sense causing unnecessary talk."

"I agree." He said it easily, knowing he'd deal later with the lead sinker in his stomach. "I'd walk you home, except if Keith woke up to an empty house, he'd panic."

"No need to feel obliged. I am capable of looking after myself."

"When you care about someone's welfare, it's not an obligation."

Sherry had no comeback for that. She knew Garrett stood in the doorway and watched her walk all the way home. Twice she battled the urge to turn around and wave, but didn't trust herself not to run back and make a mockery of both their trite proper speeches.

Fighting raw emotion, she unlocked her door, stepped inside and tripped over an array of boxes. Then a sudden blaze of light made her blink in surprise.

Yvette crossed Sherry's line of vision and slammed a stack of Tupperware into one of the boxes. "Well, well, well." She circled Sherry, inspecting her flushed cheeks. "So Garrett left the party early for a quick roll in the hay with his so-called babysitter. Wait till everybody on campus hears that Ms. Goody Two-shoes has feet of clay, after all." She ended her tirade with a bitter laugh and called into the kitchen, "Lorraine, come here. This you won't want to miss."

Sherry bit back a groan when the flight attendant who lived a few doors down materialized in the archway. Sherry realized her cheeks were still red. There was nothing she could do to salvage that situation. Her only avenue was to divert attention from herself. "Care to tell me what's going on?"

"I'm moving in with Lorraine."

"Not with my Tupperware," Sherry said. "I sat through all those parties and shelled out my cash. You never went."

Lorraine smiled. "Because there weren't any men. Come on, Yvette. Let Sherry have her bowls. Neither of us cooks, anyway."

"I figure this stuff's community property." Yvette closed the lid to the box.

"For crying out loud," Sherry exploded. "This isn't a divorce." The minute she said it, Sherry felt a wrench. As if she heard the bonds of a friendship tearing. "Yvette, look at us. Are we going to let a man drive us to catfights?"

"Garrett's not a backstabber—you are, Ms. I'll-never-need-a-man. I, at least, don't pretend to be something I'm not. Let's go, Lorrie." Yvette latched on to the doorknob. "I'll pick up my stuff tomorrow after *she* goes to work."

Sherry stood amid the half-packed cartons for a long time after the two women left. Yvette's barb had hit its mark. Sherry took pride in doing for herself, not depending on a man. She'd taken basic courses in carpentry and auto mechanics. One of her strongest beliefs was that women should have the integrity not to change themselves for men or compromise their own principles. Was she guilty of that herself? She'd have to watch herself around Garrett Lock. She'd let a man she barely knew turn her inside out and upside down.

She went to bed vowing to keep him at arm's length from this day forward.

GOOD PLAN. And one that seemed to work, because it was as if Garrett went to work the next day having made the same vow. He took care not to single Sherry out in a department meeting where he discussed the budget.

She didn't know what arrangements he'd made for Keith, but Sherry didn't see Lock for the remainder of the week. Friday morning, Sherry remembered she hadn't told Garrett that Ron had okayed their keeping Rags. Rather than phone him, she dictated a crisp note. So crisp, Angel remarked on it when she brought the memo in to be signed.

"You and Macho Man had a fight, huh?" Angel stacked the incoming mail.

"I don't know what you mean," Sherry said tersely. "He's our boss. Kindly refer to him as Dean Lock. My superior is all he's ever been."

"Yeah, sure."

"Excuse me?" Sherry glowered at her.

"Nothing," Angel said. "Sheesh. I believe you, I believe you."

"Good. Then go out and squelch the gossip about us."

"No need. Everybody's talking about Trudy Morrison now."

"Trudy? That nice Trudy from English?"

"She's pregnant. No dad in sight."

Sherry schooled her features. She hated the way gossip streaked around their campus.

"You already knew," Angel accused her. "And you didn't tell me?"

"I didn't know. But if she is pregnant—which I doubt—it's her business."

"You're such a killjoy lately. Why don't you just go out with Macho Man and get it out of your system? Maybe you'd quit being a grouch."

"What?" Sherry dropped the microphone to her Dictaphone. It bounced twice before she regained possession of it.

Angel tossed her blond braid over one shoulder. "Oops. 'Scuse me, boss lady." She snatched up the correspondence Sherry had signed and ran. "I hear the telephone."

Sherry glanced at her call commander. Not a light blinked. Still, feeling more than a little embarrassed, she let Angel go. If it was that obvious she was frustrated, she simply had to hide it better—and that meant keeping her distance from Lock.

She might have stuck to her resolve if he hadn't

popped into her office at twelve, when Angel and both clerks were at lunch. Attached to the phone, Sherry watched him stride to her window and stand looking out over campus, his hands buried in the pockets of dry-cleaner-creased jeans.

Swallowing fast to rid herself of the pain that suddenly attacked her throat, Sherry abruptly terminated the call. "Dean Lock," she managed, "is something wrong?"

He turned slightly, light and shadows playing over his deeply scored cheeks, blue eyes almost indigo in the late-autumn sun. "I promised Keith we'd meet Nolan, Emily and the kids at the high-school football game tonight. President Westerbrook has invited all the deans to his house for cocktails. He's hosting an administrative contingent from Norway. They're here to set up a student-exchange program."

Sherry waited, certain he'd eventually get to the point.

He raked long fingers through already skewed hair. "I'd ask Nolan to pick Keith up from school, but he's not authorized. Not only that, I got your memorandum concerning Rags. When I leave Westerbrook's, I should go by an all-night market and buy dog food, a collar and a doggie bed, if they have such a thing."

When he gazed at her expectantly, Sherry cut through his roundabout speech and ventured a guess. "Would you like me to collect Keith from day care?"

"Would you?"

"You have to ask? Shall I take him to the game? Or would you rather we swung by a pet store?"

"Do you mind going to the game? I'd like to surprise him with the dog myself."

Sherry forgot her promise to be reserved. "I love football. And I hate going alone. So, Keith and I'll meet you back at your place about ten?"

"Good. Great." He grinned. "Keith has missed you, Sherilyn." He stopped short of saying he had, too.

"I've missed him." Her eyes lingered on Garrett, then she hurriedly glanced away.

"Look, this is stupid. You're still going with us to St. Louis tomorrow, aren't you?"

"Won't you need me to go by and check on Rags?"

"I'll call a dog walker so that someone stops by. Anyway, Keith's spending the weekend with Carla. I'll drive up Sunday afternoon again and pick him up."

Her heart beat a light tattoo. "I did promise you a tour of St. Louis."

"And breakfast at the Featherstone."

"Rain check? That'd be sure to cause talk."

"I'm inclined to say who cares? Logically, I

know you're right. Okay, we'll leave half an hour earlier and stop at a café on the outskirts of town."

"You're sure we won't be compromising our work relationship?"

"I am. And Sherilyn…I feel bad about Yvette moving out. Are you able to make the rent?"

"Yes." It was kind of him to ask.

He rocked forward on his boots. "What we do on our own time is nobody else's business." He looked fierce.

Her palms grew damp at the thought of what Garrett's statement suggested. "Agreed," she whispered. "I'd be happy to walk Rags and feed him if I get home from work before you do."

He dealt her a strange look. "Taking care of Rags is going to be Keith's responsibility."

"Definitely. But I'm offering to help if you get tied up here."

"Accepted. Now I'd better scram before the little pitchers with big ears get back."

Grinning, Sherry trailed him to the door. And she gave it her all to make sure Angel didn't see she was on pins and needles for the rest of the day. She left on time, making no mention to Angel about picking up Keith to go to the game.

Keith was thrilled to see her. They had a good time at the game. Or they did until Emily asked Sherry to drop by the next day for a fitting on her bridesmaid's dress.

"How about Sunday afternoon? I'm busy tomorrow."

"Working again? Sherry, when will you learn to say no?"

Sherry hadn't realized Keith was listening. He stuck his head around Mark. "Sherry's going to St. Louis tomorrow with Dad and me. I hafta stay through Sunday, but Dad's coming back home tomorrow night."

"Really?" Emily and Nolan chorused. Both studied her with exactly the same gleam in their eyes.

"No big deal," Sherry said as calmly as she could. "Keith's visiting his mom. Garrett asked if I'd give him a quick tour of St. Louis." She held her breath, glad when the home team made a touchdown that claimed Em and Nolan's attention. It ended the game and the crowd started to disperse. Cheers for the winners effectively cut off further talk. They'd parked in different lots, so they said goodbye at the gate.

Garrett was home with Rags and all his new paraphernalia when Sherry walked Keith to the door. Although Garrett invited her inside for coffee, she saw Yvette and Lorraine sauntering down the walkway, so she declined.

"I'll see you tomorrow," she murmured. "I don't want to intrude on your special night with Keith."

"Okay." Garrett didn't understand her refusal

and was disappointed. He named a time to leave in the morning, then wondered as he watched her disappear into the star-studded night if she really wanted to go to St. Louis with him, or if she felt obligated because he was her boss. Like he'd felt obligated to attend Westerbrook's gathering this evening.

Garrett tucked the notion away, planning to ask her pointblank the next morning.

A plan he immediately forgot when he found her waiting beside his truck first thing Saturday.

They enjoyed a leisurely breakfast at a truck stop on the freeway. Keith bubbled over with excitement. He talked constantly about Rags. But once they reached St. Louis, he fell silent. The change was so obviously connected to his visit with Carla that Sherry felt compelled to offer him some encouragement.

"I'll bet your mom has wonderful things planned for the two of you, tiger." Squeezing his shoulder, Sherry bolstered him with a big smile as Garrett drove past the Gateway Arch. "Look. There's a tram to the observation deck. You feel like you're up in the clouds. It's clear today, so you'll be able to see quite far."

Keith slumped lower in the seat. When they turned down a street of stately homes, the boy slid his sweaty hand into Sherry's. "Will you walk me to the door?" he asked her in a stage whisper.

"Oh, Keith." Sherry darted a quick glance at Garrett. "It's not my place. But I'll tell you what. If this good weather holds, Monday after school I'll take you skating in the park."

"Okay," he said. "Can Rags go, too?"

"Sure. Why not? You have a leash, I hope?"

"I got one," Garrett said, making a wide swing into a circular drive.

Sherry gazed at the manicured lawn and the huge columns supporting a pristine white structure. She couldn't help it—she whistled through her teeth.

Garrett laughed and so did Keith. Sherry kept her next thought to herself—that the place looked like a funeral home.

She waited in the truck, but couldn't help noticing Garrett's tense walk as he led his resistant child up the marble steps to the door. After what seemed to Sherry like a long time, a beautiful woman answered their knock. When Garrett gestured and the woman assumed a rigid stance, Sherry surmised she was viewing Carla. A blade twisted in her heart. Garrett's ex was gorgeous. He must feel a little bad about losing her. Trying to ignore that disconcerting thought, Sherry turned her gaze elsewhere.

She gave a start when she unexpectedly heard a sharp thump in the pickup's bed. A second later Garrett jerked open the driver's door. He landed in the seat with a whomp, and after two twists of the key, ground the gears.

"I could murder her," he snarled, backing out too fast. He jammed on the brakes and stopped abruptly at the street. "Something's come up at work again. Carla can't have Keith stay tonight, after all. In fact, she ordered me to pick him up no later than four." Looping his arms over the steering wheel, he sent Sherry an anxious look. "Do you mind staying in town for the whole day? It'll mean getting home late."

Sherry shook her head. "So that was Keith's suitcase you threw in back?" she asked insipidly.

"Yeah." He shrugged. "I have to admit Keith wasn't exactly heartbroken. So, what do you want to do?"

"You might be sorry you asked. I need a slip and shoes to go with my dress for the wedding. Since we're here for the duration with all these beautiful malls, you can take me shopping. I could use some help picking out a gift for Nolan and Emily, too."

"You're a good sport, Sherry. I had visions of you throwing a fit. That's what Carla would have done if the situation had been reversed."

Suddenly Sherry's outlook got a whole lot brighter. Garrett didn't sound like a man pining for his ex. Not even a little.

CHAPTER TWELVE

AUTUMN LEAVES had begun to drop from the trees and lay strewn about. Sherry loved to crunch them beneath her feet. The sun straggled through the trees, but there was a nip of fall in the air. "Are you ready for Halloween?" Sherry asked Garrett as they wandered along the pathways of Laumeier Sculpture Park, another pastime she enjoyed. It pleased her that he'd asked to see the work of artists on display there before they went on to the mall.

He caught a red-gold leaf that floated into his hand. Smiling, he tucked it behind Sherry's ear. "Keith's school sent a note home saying the room mothers host a small party on Friday. Will our complex get trick-or-treaters? Mark asked Keith to make the rounds with them in your folks' neighborhood. I'm not keen on them going alone. Figured I'd hang out in the background with a flashlight."

"We have very few kids show up in our area," she said, retrieving the brightly colored leaf and twirling it between her fingers.

He watched her kicking through leaves like a kid. Grasping the hand that didn't hold the leaf, Garrett toyed with the pearl ring on her finger. "Come with us. Nolan said your mom's making fresh doughnuts." He made it sound like the biggest incentive.

Sherry savored the feel of their joined hands, liking the sensation. "Dad makes cider every year, too. When we were kids the whole family fixed popcorn balls. I hope Emily and Nolan keep up the tradition in their home. This year Mom'll go all out for Mark and Megan. I predict she'll be in a blue funk after the wedding, when they finally move into Nolan's house."

Sherry stopped to stare at a bronze sculpture, but Garrett knew she was seeing a time gone by. "So, will you go?" he pressed, carrying her fingers to his lips.

She tried unsuccessfully to snatch her hand back. "I don't want to intrude."

"Sherilyn, it's your family. If anyone's intruding, it's Keith and me."

"Not true," she said. "You were invited. Although—" she grinned "—I could crash the party." She let him keep her hand, after all, and they swung their clasped hands jauntily as they found the next statue.

"The close-knit family you have is what I wanted for Keith. But my mom and dad retired to

Florida before I got married. Carla was raised in foster homes. And now," he said broodingly, "I've left the few roots I'd put down in Huntsville."

"So is this a permanent move?" Sherry asked, trying not to sound personally interested. "Some of the staff think you have your eye on a vice presidency at a more prestigious college, and Wellmont is just a stepping stone."

"Me, a VP?" A rumbling laugh shook Garrett's chest. "At Westerbrook's last night, someone introduced me as Wellmont's renegade dean."

"Probably Hadley from Accounting, right?" At his nod, she made a rude noise. "If brains were made of leather, he wouldn't have enough to saddle a flea."

Garrett laughed harder. "I'll second that. Are you sure you weren't born in Texas? You're full of country sayings."

"I listen to country music."

"You do? Something else we have in common."

The way he said something *else* in common chased hot and cold prickles up her spine. Here she thought they shared nothing more infatuation—which, according to her caseload of displaced wives, faded with the speed of light. The more time she spent around Garrett, the more she realized he possessed a sensitivity missing in other male acquaintances. For one thing, he really listened to a person.

Sherry imagined them being friends, as well as a couple. *A couple. Will you listen to that.* She stumbled to a stop and gazed across the park at nothing, shocked that she, of all people, contemplated such a thing. *Well, why not?*

Garrett leaned in front of her so he could look her in the eye. He traced the back of one finger down her pink cheek. "Before you hop a shooting star and zap another trillion light years away, how about lunch?"

"Sorry." She blushed, thankful he didn't probe her errant thoughts. "I, ah… Shall we eat at the mall? Then we'll be handy to buy the wedding gift and my shoes."

"I had something more clandestine in mind. Lunch on a lazy riverboat, maybe?"

"Cruises that serve food are overnighters. I've never done one, but I'm told visitors book well in advance. Day jaunts are narrated. If you'd rather do that than shop, you can drop me at the mall and pick me up later."

Garrett curbed his disappointment as he steered her toward his pickup with a hand at the small of her back. "I can't believe you've lived here all your life and have never gone on a dinner cruise. If Keith ever spends a weekend with Carla, you and I should go." Before he'd made his suggestion, Garrett hadn't realized how it'd sound. Sherry's sharp intake of breath told him clearly.

Her heart somersaulted in its rush to accelerate. She'd never gone on a dinner cruise because she'd never met anyone she cared to be confined with for a night of moonlight, champagne and romance. Not until now. Now her blood sang at the prospect. "I'd like that," was her only admission.

Garrett glanced away, barely trusting himself to nod. As if both shied from what was happening, they broached again the subject of grabbing sandwiches at the mall.

Right after they ate, Sherry led Garrett on a marathon shopping tour. He surprised her again by actively helping choose Emily and Nolan's wedding gift. And he never once griped about trekking from store to store. Eventually they found the perfect thing—a copper pot to sit on the vintage icebox Emily had refinished.

"You deserve a medal," Sherry said as he carried their packages to his truck. "I didn't hear a single complaint. But maybe you're in shock," she teased.

"It's been five years since I shopped with a woman," he mused. "I can't believe I'd forgotten how intense an experience it is. After my divorce, my mom decided to help me refurbish, and by the week's end my boots had holes in their soles. I tend to shop on a need-to-have basis and avoid malls like the plague."

"You mean your girlfriends never dragged you mall-hopping? That's un-American."

He held the passenger door open and gave her a hand up, debating whether or not to tell her that girlfriends had been scarcer than duck's teeth. He wouldn't want Sherry to get the idea he was weird or anything. On the other hand, if he insinuated he did things other than shop with his women friends, she would definitely get the wrong picture. So he smiled in a way he hoped said, *Don't ask me to kiss and tell,* and closed her car door solidly. They drove to collect Keith in companionable silence.

Sherry expected Keith to be elated after a day with his mom, and chatty. But the boy slid between Sherry and his father, crossed his arms and sat like a lump.

She finally broke the ice. "How was your trip to the Money Museum?"

Keith hiked a shoulder.

"That's no way to answer a lady, son," Garrett rebuked gently.

"Crawford 'splained too much. He thinks I'm dumb 'cause I don't care where money comes from."

Garrett's fingers tightened on the wheel. Crawford was a dolt, but Garrett knew from experience that if he said anything to Carla, she'd defend the banker to the nth degree. She'd twist things to make it all Garrett's fault. *He* didn't discipline Keith, or *he* spoiled the boy and let him run wild. Garrett had heard it before. To make matters worse, now Sherry was tossing him veiled glances, as if she expected him to do something about Crawford. Life had been so much simpler before Carla surfaced again.

Sherry decided Garrett wasn't going to get involved. "So, Keith," she said, "what about the phony money? Weren't the counterfeit bills cool?"

"They were okay. Crawford got super bummed out when I said they all looked alike."

Garrett scowled. "Where was your mother during all this?"

"She hadda go to the bank to make a big loan."

The muscles in Garrett's jaw flexed. Sherry marveled at his control. If it was up to her, she'd go back and have a talk with Carla. The more Sherry chewed on the reality, however, the more she saw that Garrett was caught between a rock and a hard place. He had Carla's attorney going for his jugular. Just now she held all the advantages. Sherry had witnessed the reverse enough times.

She tried her best to cheer Keith up. "Rags will love having you come home a day early, sport."

Keith's spirits perked immediately. "Go faster, Dad. I don't want Rags to think we left him."

"He'll be fine, Keith." Talk shifted to the dog

until they were about a block from home. Suddenly Garrett asked Keith, "Did your mom or Crawford give you a date for your next visit?"

"Mom's gonna call you before Halloween. Crawford doesn't approve of Halloween. I wanna go trick-or-treating with Mark. I don't gotta visit Mom, do I?"

"No. Not on Halloween. Crawford is—"

"Entitled to his opinion," Sherry inserted. She knew Garrett would regret badmouthing Keith's stepdad once he stopped to reconsider. "Hey, I thought of a place I think you'd like, Keith. Maybe sometime your mom can take you to see Mark Twain's boyhood home in Hannibal. It's fun climbing to the top of Cardiff Hill. And I love the tour of the Tom Sawyer caves. Are you familiar with Tom Sawyer and Huck Finn, Keith?"

"Yep. Dad read me the stories. Why don't *we* go? Huh, Dad?"

The possibility germinated. "Yeah. How about next weekend?" Garrett sought Sherry's eyes. "Maybe Sherry'll invite Mark." Garrett had a method to his madness. The boys could explore while he got to spend more time with Sherry.

"Are you asking me to go, too?" She wasn't sure if that was what Garrett meant.

"I'm asking."

Sherry's nerves tingled. "I...well, yes, then." They made plans before parting outside Garrett's gate.

THE TRIP TO HANNIBAL ended up being one of the most wonderful dates Sherry'd ever had. Even though she'd suggested the trip to cheer Keith up, it had all the earmarks of a date. Garrett was attentive. He teased, and flattered and bought her souvenirs.

The boys loved the caves where Tom Sawyer and Becky Thatcher had supposedly been lost. They were decidedly less enthusiastic about the museum.

Garrett had hoped the near-vertical hike up Cardiff Hill would wear the boys out so they'd fall asleep on the way home and he could ask Sherry out again. But the adults were the ones who yawned repeatedly. Keith and Mark sat in the backseat of Sherry's car, plotting how much loot they'd collect trick-or-treating the following Saturday.

CLOUDS MOVED IN as Halloween approached. Miraculously the rain held off. At the elder Campbells' home that night, after the trick-or-treaters returned with pillowcases full of candy, Ben Campbell struck a match to the leaves he'd spent the day raking into a big pile. In spite of thick smoke, the revelers scooted close to the fire to toast hot dogs and marshmallows. Megan, who claimed to be too old for trick-or-treating, told ghost stories guaranteed to spook the boys. An occasional adult was also seen glancing over a shoulder into the darkness beyond the fire.

Pilgrim, Nolan's yellow Lab, and the Campbells' old dog, Murphy, frolicked with Rags. All swiped tidbits of hotdog here and there if anyone's guard dropped.

When at last the fire died, the adults reluctantly called it a day.

Keith scrambled over and hugged Sherry around the neck. "This is the bestest Halloween I've ever had. I love you," he said, fighting a sleepy yawn.

Seated next to Sherry, Emily jabbed Nolan in the ribs.

Sherry saw a telling look pass between them. She also saw Garrett stiffen. Surely he didn't think she'd set out to win his son's affections on purpose. After all, he was the one who'd bugged her to come tonight. Frankly, she'd thought Garrett had been angling for more than friendship on their trip to Hannibal. Obviously not. She must be the only one experiencing wild, crazy dreams that tiptoed in at night to disrupt her sleep.

Emily snapped her fingers to jar Sherry from her trance. "I said, if you're free tomorrow night, could you meet with me? I have an appointment with a singer to choose songs for the wedding. Nolan says it's up to me. I'd like another opinion."

"Okay. Give me the address," Sherry said absently. "Is your church a drive from here?"

Emily gaped. "We're being married in Nolan's church. Y-your church," she stammered. "As a matter of fact, now it's Garrett and Keith's church, too."

Sherry felt sideswiped. She knew, of course, that Emily and the kids had been attending the family church. The church where her parents had exchanged wedding vows. Emily no longer had contact with her former in-laws or their church, so where else would she get married if not here? Still... Sherry didn't know why, but she'd always assumed she'd be the first Campbell of her generation to walk up that aisle. She acknowledged that it was a silly thought, considering her frequently stated assertions about marriage. And there wasn't even a groom in the offing!

Nan Campbell reached out to her suddenly pale daughter. "Sherry, are you ill? The hot dogs. Ben..." she said, helplessly imploring her husband.

"I'm fine." She would be—in a minute.

Nolan, blind to her feelings, teased her. "Not too late to make it a foursome, sis." He clapped Garrett on the back. "Two for the price of one. Ought to rock the hallowed halls of Wellmont, don't you think?"

Garrett surged to his feet. He ignored Nolan

and thanked Sherry's folks for including him and Keith in the festivities. Which wasn't to say that Nolan's shot in the dark hadn't set wheels grinding in Garrett's mind.

Keith fell asleep on the drive home, allowing Garrett far too much time to dwell on Nolan's remark. He understood how others might assume a relationship had developed between him and Sherilyn. He'd spent a lot of time with her lately.

Or had Nolan been goading his sister just for the sake of goading? Clearly marriage was the last thing on her mind. At his heavy handed hint, she'd looked like someone forced to eat a pickle.

That started Garrett wondering how Sherilyn saw him. Only as someone to help her thumb her nose at those on campus who whispered that she hated men?

All the signs said no.

Maybe she just wanted a short-term romance. If so, he'd been obtuse.

As he put Keith to bed, Garrett couldn't seem to shake the conviction that if he was smart, he'd forget about Sherry Campbell as anything but a colleague. But questions nagged him all night.

Next morning, Carla unwittingly offered Garrett opportunity to act. She called to request or, rather, demand that he bring Keith to St. Louis the second weekend in November. Crawford's daughter was coming to town, Carla said. And Crawford's daughter had a son Keith's age.

Crawford was a grandpa? Garrett hung up, mulling that over. He didn't know why he'd thought Crawford had been eternally single when he met Carla. Maybe because he was so strict with Keith. Shouldn't a grandfather be better attuned to kids?

Garrett climbed into the shower, trying to keep his mind focused on Crawford's relationship with Keith. Unfortunately last night's dream intruded. A dream of Sherry and him on a moonlit Mississippi riverboat cruise.

Would she go if he invited her? She ran hot and cold. But that time he'd suggested it, she actually sounded favorable.

It'd be a simple matter to phone and ask her. But dreaming of enticing Sherry into a romantic cruise was far easier than calling her and risking a no. While Keith ate breakfast, Garrett shut himself in his bedroom where he paced in front of the phone. He rehearsed his speech, yanked up the receiver, then dropped it back and sat down for a minute until his heart quit pounding like a jungle drum.

He reminded himself that good old Crawford hadn't let divorce deter him from pursuing another woman. That did it. Gut churning, head prepared for her refusal, Garrett dialed.

On her end, Sherry listened to his smooth invitation in disbelief. This was Garrett Lock, a man who just last night had turned seven shades of green at the mention of being involved with her.

Correction. That look—as if he'd sucked a lemon—came at the mention of *marriage*. What he proposed was a dinner cruise on the *Ozark Queen*. Moonlight, dinner and dancing. At least that was how it sounded.

Sherry feigned a fit of coughing and excused herself to get a drink of water. As she slugged it down, she practiced saying no. It wasn't working. *For goodness' sake, she was going to accept.*

She drew a damp palm over her throat. "Sorry. My toast went down wrong. Two weekends from now, you say?" She cleared her throat. "Um, my calendar is clear." Did that sound worldly enough?

"It is?" Garrett felt like a dope for doubting. "Fine. Good," he managed, clamping down on the ambivalent feelings still churning in his stomach.

Sherry twisted the phone cord around and around her finger. Now what? She wound the cord so tightly it cut off her circulation. Then she chastised herself for acting cowardly. Feeling the heat of embarrassment, she decided to fill the silence by asking a question.

She asked in her best counselor's voice, "How does Keith feel about spending two full days with Crawford?"

Garrett suffered a second stab of guilt. He couldn't very well admit that he hadn't informed his son yet. "About how you'd expect," he mumbled. "He hates leaving Rags."

"I'm sure my mom will dog-sit. Ah, um, I'd appreciate you not mentioning that I'm going with... that we're..."

"Hey, what do you take me for?" Garrett was impatient to get off the phone. All he could think was, What if there wasn't space on the boat after all this? "I, uh, hate to run, but I was just on my way out."

"Oh, sure. Bye then."

The minute Sherry disconnected, Garrett dived for the phone book. He didn't breathe again until the travel agent took his credit-card numbers to confirm passage.

"So that's that," he said aloud, after completing the transaction. He managed his first deep breath that didn't sound like air escaping a slow-punctured tire. He felt as if he'd just done something that would invite gossip. Which was stupid. They were both mature unattached adults, and he'd booked two rooms.

Midweek, Garrett received an administrative memo from the president's office stating that a contingent from campus had to go to Jefferson City on Wednesday, Thursday and Friday of the following week. The purpose: to protest legislative budget cuts. Garrett frowned at a list topped by Sherry's name. Was she drafted or had she volunteered? Jefferson City was a fair drive. The team wouldn't be back until late Friday night. Did it mean she'd had second thoughts about their weekend trip?

"THESE SILLY MARCHES in the capital don't accomplish anything," Sherry complained to Angel as she assembled material to keep her classes occupied for the three days she'd be gone. "All we do is spin our wheels."

"You didn't volunteer to go?"

"I'd sooner eat worms."

Angel tapped a finger on the memo that had come to Sherry in the form of a command. "I guess the big man delegated you, then, huh? I notice *he's* not on the list."

"Garrett?" Sherry flushed, realizing she'd almost said he wouldn't since they had plans for the weekend.

Angel gave her a speculative look as Sherry hefted her briefcase and bag.

Last to board the van, Sherry was surprised to see mostly deans and a vice provost already seated. Who had included her with the bigwigs and why?

Could it be Garrett? Maybe he'd gotten cold

feet about the weekend and figured if the committee returned late on Friday she'd opt out.

He didn't know her if he thought that. She always kept her commitments.

FRIDAY, WHEN SHE DRAGGED home at midnight, Garrett's house was dark. She'd accessed her office voice mail before boarding the van home. He'd left a cryptic message offering her a rain check. Oh, he sounded solicitous, but Sherry fancied she also heard a measure of relief in his voice. The jerk. Make her suffer with those pompous fools for three days, would he? All because *he* didn't have the guts to renege. Well, he could just tell her face-to-face. She fell into bed anticipating how floored he'd be to discover her, suitcase in hand, leaning against his pickup tomorrow.

If it killed her, she'd get up in time to do her hair and nails. A woman had her pride, after all. He'd never know she'd sprung for new clothes. She *had* entertained notions of making Dr. Lock's jaw drop with the slinky purple dress she'd purchased for the dinner cruise.

Sherry punched her pillow. She should have saved her money.

AT THE BREAK OF DAWN, Keith shuffled to the pickup ahead of Garrett. First to spot Sherry, he ran to her and enveloped her in a hug. "I heard

Dad tell your mom you went to Jefferson City. She's keeping Rags 'cause Dad's gonna ride on a boat this weekend." He hopped around and trampled on Sherry's toes. "I don't wanna visit Mom and Crawford. If you'n Dad are goin' on a boat, can I go, too? Please," he implored.

Garrett tossed two duffels into the back of the truck before laying a restraining hand on his exuberant son's head. His gaze skimmed Sherry's suitcase, then settled warmly on her face. "Welcome home. You look bright-eyed and bushy-tailed for having spent a week hassling our public servants."

Sherry searched for signs of displeasure in his eyes and saw none. The knots in her stomach unfurled. He did want her to go. Which meant he hadn't volunteered her, after all.

"Can I go, too? Can I, Dad? Can I?" Keith twirled under his father's hand, chanting his request like a mantra.

"Not this time, son. Hey, no long face. You're meeting Crawford's grandson. Your mom said Crawford bought tickets for all of you to see the Rams game."

Keith looked so terribly unhappy Sherry rushed to say, "Next week, if the weather's still good, how about if your dad and I take you someplace special?"

Her announcement piqued Keith and Garrett alike.

"Are you familiar with Precious Moments figurines?" When they both nodded, she boosted Keith into the pickup cab. Once they'd buckled in, she explained. "The artist has a chapel in Carthage. There's a park, gardens, a kid's castle. It's neat."

"A castle? Way cool! Can we go there, Dad?"

Garrett backed the truck out and pulled into the traffic. He waved to Lorraine, the flight attendant with whom Yvette now roomed. Sherry hadn't seen Yvette in more than a week. Odd... and disconcerting. They'd been friends so long. Lorraine had just climbed out of a cab. If she saw them, she didn't return the wave. Obviously the cold war continued.

Garrett didn't give it a second thought. "I've tentatively made other plans for next weekend, Keith. Nolan told me about the largest bass-fishing shop in the world. I have a hankering to buy a bass boat so Keith and I can do a little fishing," he told Sherry.

Keith clearly had a dilemma. "Me'n Dad love to fish," he said, appealing to Sherry with sorrowful eyes.

"No problem, sport. I know the shop he means. My dad and Nolan can get lost in it for days. Better take food and water," she teased.

"But the castle would be cool, too." Keith burrowed closer to Sherry's side. "It's fun when the three of us do stuff together. Ain't it, Dad?"

"Isn't," Garrett corrected softly. "And yes, I guess it is."

A gritty lump clogged Sherry's throat. The wistfulness in Keith's boyish voice and Garrett's deeper one forced her to examine some hard truths. She'd thought she had it all with her career and her independent life. She'd always said she didn't need love—and the things that usually went with it. Like marriage. She'd thought love was something you could control. Not long ago, Emily had tried to tell her that wasn't so; love had its own methods. She'd tuned Emily out.

Garrett gave up trying to sort out the series of dark looks on Sherry's face. She grew quieter and quieter the closer they got to St. Louis. After he'd walked Keith to Carla's door, he climbed back into the truck and sat drumming his fingers on the steering wheel. "Much as I'd like to go on the river cruise, it's your choice whether we go or not, Sherilyn."

She tensed. "I'm here, aren't I?" She hadn't meant to snap. It was just that confronting the way she felt—the way her *heart* felt—about Garrett Lock had sent her nerves into a tizzy.

"In body, maybe, but not in spirit."

Her eyebrows shot up. "If you've changed your mind, just say so."

Garrett patted his shirt pocket. "I bought *two* tickets."

"Would you feel less threatened if I paid for mine?"

He stopped drumming his fingers. "Me? I'm not. But you seem nervous as a goat on Astro turf," he said gruffly. More gently he added, "I've been looking forward to this."

"I understand the dinner cruise is considered quite romantic. Should be…fun."

He twisted the ignition key and the engine roared to life. "Yeah," he said.

Sherry couldn't be sure, but she thought she detected a tic near the corner of his left eye.

Garrett parked in the lot next to the docked boat. They continued to sit, watching the river eddy out of sight past the huge boat. Several couples and a family of five headed up the gangplank. The normalcy of the scene released them both. As Garrett climbed out and went to check them in, Sherry waited by the river.

"I'll just put our bags in our rooms," he said on rejoining her. "Meet me middeck near the paddle wheel. The captain said it's a must for first-timers."

"Sounds fine. Oh, you'll need my room key." She pulled it from the packet he'd handed her.

"Listen." Garrett cocked an ear as he took the key. "Is that a live band?"

She leafed through a brochure. "A three-piece jazz combo in the lounge. A dance band performs in the dining room tonight. If you'd rather hit the casinos, I'll be fine on my own."

"Bring that brochure. We'll go to the lounge and discuss options after we shove off. I wouldn't mind trying the slots, but if you're opposed to gambling, I'm okay with doing…whatever."

"I'm not a prude, Garrett. Some of us go into Kansas City for the jazz festival every year. We hit at least one river casino then."

"I like the jazz classics. I'm not much on the really experimental stuff."

"The oldies are my favorite, too." She hooked a thumb toward the lounge. "That kind. Hurry. I hate to miss that trumpet," she said, tapping a toe.

He grinned. Then unexpectedly he curved a finger and traced her chin with a knuckle. "Thanks for not begging off. I hoped you'd come."

She tilted her head, trapping his palm in the curve of her neck. "You might have said so. Bad communication causes most of the problems between men and women. I like honesty—things laid on the line."

He nodded, withdrew his hand, picked up the bags.

As he jogged off, Sherry gazed after him, paying scant heed to being jostled. An errant cloud drifted over the sun, blocking the warmth, and a breeze ruffled her short hair, chilling her bare arms. That was how fairies delivered premonitions, according to Grandmother Campbell. And premonitions never meant good news.

Donning a light jacket, Sherry scampered downstairs where she worked her way through a milling throng of people to wait, as Garrett had directed, near the stern. The engines gave a mighty rumble somewhere deep in the bowels of the boat. The paddle wheel rocked and shivered. Where was Garrett? He wanted to see this. Sherry didn't think he was going to make it in time.

He surprised her, slipping up behind her to encircle her waist with his arms just as the giant paddle slowly began to turn.

Those standing close to the wire cage, like Sherry, were sprayed. "Sorry," she gasped as she jumped back and landed on Garrett's toe. "I wasn't expecting a shower."

Laughing, he swiped at droplets dripping from her chin onto her blouse.

As the boat churned into the middle of the river, most of the bystanders left. Sherry hovered near the rail listening to the fading footsteps.

"Okay. So what's next, Doc?"

"Next on the agenda is a drink and checking

out the band that's bringing down the rafters in the lounge."

"Do boats have rafters?" Garrett asked, the beginnings of a smile teasing his lips.

"Beams, then," she said, dragging him up the steps. "Whatever. Are you always so technical?"

"No," he shouted, guiding her toward a table near the band. "Only when I know it's going to get a reaction."

"For that, you'd better buy me a soda."

Glad to have her joking and smiling again, Garrett snapped his fingers to attract a waiter and ordered two drinks.

They each had another before the band broke. Then they headed to the casino where they lost two rolls of quarters to the slots. Neither cared, because they'd become mellow. It was Sherry who pointed out that they should go back to their cabins and dress for dinner. Garrett would have been satisfied to stay and watch the expressions crossing her face when she won, lost or broke even.

Forty minutes later, when he got a load of Sherry's dress, Garrett was mighty glad he had listened to her suggestion. The confection she wore was slinky and showed her beautiful back. Tiny crystals sprinkled the flirty skirt, winking each time she moved. Sweat trickled down Garrett's wrists and pooled in the palms of his hands. His tongue felt oversize. "Nice dress," he managed to mumble when she tipped her head to one side and gazed at him oddly.

A sigh whispered through her. Shutting her cabin door, Sherry clasped one of his arms. She'd been afraid the dress was too much. Now she felt smug about her purchase. She'd wanted to make him stare. And she had.

Tiny lanterns glowed atop snowy tablecloths in the dining room. Each table, privately secluded among old treasure chests, added to the romantic ambiance. The salad was crisp and fresh, the fish grilled to perfection. The band played a mellow mix of old and new, and after dinner Garrett led Sherry to the dance floor.

If Garrett had to label the evening, he'd call the whole thing…romantic, he thought as they bumped cozily against each other while wandering slowly back to their rooms after dancing the night away. He took her key to open her door and recalled Sherry's warning that romance was what the cruise had been designed for. Funny, but right now that suited him.

As Sherry backed inside, he followed to bestow a good-night kiss.

Pleasantly serene, Sherry rose on tiptoe and nipped teasingly at his lips. Teasing stopped and serene fled when Garrett began kissing her the way she'd dreamed.

His kiss transported her to places she'd never

in her wildest dreams imagined visiting. She spiraled up and up and up until she thought she'd touch the clouds. As Garrett broke the kiss and held her close, Sherry Campbell quietly fell in love for the first time ever.

Wrapped tight in Garrett's strong arms, Sherry felt compelled to confess what was in her heart. "I love you, Garrett. And I love Keith. We'll be a family," she sighed. "A spring wedding, don't you think? March? Perfect for new beginnings."

Garrett's heart spilled over. Tonight he could believe in everlasting happiness. Tonight, with her, for the first time in a long while, he believed in love. Believed that having it all—not just a career but a wife, a home, a family—was possible.

CHAPTER THIRTEEN

A MARKED CHANGE in the drone of the paddle wheel woke Garrett. He sat on a small couch, a weight pressing against his chest. The lethargy in his limbs kept him from bounding up to check on the noise. A sleepy part of his brain, as yet disconnected from his body, seemed content to drift. *Drift.* He remembered boarding a stern-wheeler with Sherry. *Sherry.* Garrett's mind joined his body. It was impossible not to recall the most fantastic night he'd ever had, and the woman responsible for his happiness. He liked the warmth of her body curled against his. Garrett didn't want the day to intrude.

Sherry stirred and lifted her head from his chest. Dazed, she decided she'd slept in the same position too long. She had a kink in her neck and other aches. In an attempt to turn she hit a solid obstacle, and Garrett's morning voice rumbled under her ear like the fading echo of thunder.

"Easy, easy. Is this what I have to look forward to? You hogging the couch?"

Sherry smiled as she remembered the glorious

night she'd spent with the owner of that gravelly voice. "Are you always such a grouch in the morning?"

"Is it morning?" He'd hoped the night was still young.

She stilled and listened to a variety of muffled noises above and below the cabin. "We've turned and are headed back to St. Louis. The weekend is almost over."

Garrett pulled her close to meet a desperate kiss. His way of telling her that he'd delay the inevitable if he could. He wasn't good with the words even though he had no problem lecturing to a hundred students or arguing successfully in a room filled with peers. Emotional attachments were different. Harder. He couldn't seem to put his feelings into words. Carla had said so in her exit letter. Easing up on the kiss, Garrett worked to catch his breath and said with some difficulty, "It's light out. I have to go."

Sherry strained to reconnect. She scrambled off the couch as he stood up. Then she giggled. She couldn't help it. "Ah. Have I uncovered your deep dark secret? You're really Dr. Werewolf?"

She looked so adorable that Garrett hopped back to collect another kiss.

"You're too kissable, woman," he scolded, as she leaned in to steal another kiss. "Ordinarily I wouldn't complain, but if we leave this boat with me in my tux and you in that purple dress, I guarantee we'll be the talk of the town."

"Party pooper." She bounced back on the couch. "I expected a man who had a laughing pig on his desk to be more daring."

"Laughing pig?" he choked out. "Ah...the paperweight Keith bought me with his allowance. He said I looked too serious at work." He leaned over and nuzzled her neck. "You think I'm too serious?"

Sherry wound her arms around him and kissed him so hard, colored lightning flashed behind his eyes. Garrett reluctantly broke away.

"Meet you on deck for brunch in one hour." He ripped open the door and barreled out and into a couple who smirked when they saw his wrinkled shirt.

At the sound of the closing door, Sherry rose, hugged herself and spun around the room in pure jubilation. She never would have believed that love could create such a confusion of feelings. Weakness and strength. Danger and power.

She vacillated between purring like a kitten and roaring like a lioness.

Love. Who'd have thought Sherry Campbell, Ph.D., would ever fall so completely head-over-heels in love? Not one person who knew her, that was for sure.

After she showered and donned her oldest, most

comfortable pair of jeans and a faded sweatshirt, she actually peeked in the bathroom mirror to see if the difference she felt inside was visible. Only then did it dawn—her lips and only hers had used the L-word. Garrett had been remarkably silent. Sherry touched the cold glass, and a corresponding chill slithered up her arm.

Nonsense. Of course he felt what she felt. Love was probably old hat to Garrett. He'd been in love before and she hadn't. It didn't take an expert to understand that what they'd shared last night had been cataclysmic and earth-shattering. For him, too. She'd stake her life on it. But…maybe she was too confident.

She hit the light switch to obliterate her doubting image. Garrett would surely say something when they met for brunch.

He didn't. Though attentive, he avoided the topic of *them.* This, in spite of the fact that Sherry deliberately brought the conversation around to weddings. "It doesn't seem possible that Nolan and Emily are getting married in less than two weeks." Sighing, she gazed at Garrett over the rim of the sparkling orange drink she'd ordered to further enhance her romantic illusions.

"Yeah. Can you believe I've held the dean's job for almost three months?" Garrett glanced around for their waiter and signaled for a coffee refill.

Sherry blamed the weakness stealing over her

limbs on his clean soapy scent, which wafted across the table.

"Nice weddings take a long time to plan," she murmured. "Timing is important. Isn't it too bad Nolan and Emily's anniversary will always compete with the holidays?"

"It's their choice. Speaking of holidays, Keith gave me his Christmas list. And one almost as long for Rags. Can you believe it?"

Sherry set her glass down hard. "He wants a brother or sister most. He's very lonely, you know."

"Rags?" Garrett wagged his cup again at the tardy waiter who finally stopped to refill it. "If Keith asked you to soften me up so I'll buy him that kitten we saw at the pet store, the answer is unequivocally no. NO, in capital letters."

Sherry gave up. Not for a second did she think Garrett so obtuse that he didn't know she'd meant Keith wanted siblings. Nor was *she* dense. He was dodging the subject of marriage.

Well, she could be outwardly mature about that. If mountains hadn't moved for him as they had for her, why not be honest?

Because men played games. They liked to reel women out and reel them in again on a whim. She drained her drink and stood. Let him play someone else like a big-mouth bass. This fish was bailing out.

"Excuse me," she said right in the middle of his recounting Keith's Christmas list. "I'm sure you'll figure out what to buy Keith without my help. I'll see you when we dock. For some reason I didn't get a good sleep last night. I'm going to take a nap." And she walked off. Stalked was more like it.

Garrett puzzled over her little speech for so long his coffee grew cold in the cup. What did she mean, he'd figure out what to buy Keith without her? Had he been dreaming last night? Didn't Sherry say she loved his son? That they'd be a family?

Women. If he lived to be a hundred, he'd never understand them. So what if Sherry's kisses were the best he'd ever known. Neither he nor Keith needed another female running hot and cold, messing up their lives. It was better he'd found out now before Keith got too attached and ended up with his heart in shreds. As for Garrett, he'd been down that rocky road with Carla and had no wish to travel it again. Yet it hurt. Man, did it hurt.

Throwing some bills on the table, Garrett returned to his cabin. He packed his bag and, though his steps slowed as he passed Sherry's room, he continued on topside. Scant moments before the *Ozark Queen* cut her engines and let the current carry her to the dock, Sherry appeared on deck with her suitcase.

Garrett studied her from behind his dark glasses. She looked rested, he thought, a bit resentful about the sorrow that pinched his heart, but not, apparently, hers. He noticed something more, a cool pulling back, like she'd had second thoughts about last night and now couldn't wait to have the entire expedition over and done with.

Sherry deliberately distanced herself from Garrett. She detested tears, considered them a sign of weakness. Yet she had, in the solitude of her room, shed a few for him and for herself—for a loss she felt so keenly.

If Sherry hadn't seemed completely and icily unapproachable, Garrett might have tried to breech the gap yawning between them on the drive back to Carla's. But how?

He said nothing and, as a result, neither did Sherry.

Keith again waited on Carla's porch. As Garrett turned his truck into the circular lane, the boy tore down the walkway, waving madly, face ringed in smiles.

"Where is everyone?" Garrett asked, climbing out as Keith tossed his duffel into the pickup's bed and scrambled to claim his former seat in the middle.

"Crawford's at work. Mom took Georgette and Arnold to the airport."

"And left you all alone?"

"Don't yell at me. Georgette was plenty mad 'cause Crawford went to the bank hours ago and said he'd send Mom home. She just got here."

"I'm not blaming you, Keith. I don't understand what kind of bank demands they work on Sunday."

Keith scooted nearer Sherry. He peered at her somberly when she shifted away.

"Didn't you guys have fun neither?" he asked, his gaze darting between the two adults.

Garrett started the truck with a roar and jerked it into reverse.

Sherry mumbled something ambiguous as Garrett laid rubber all the way to the street.

Keith hunkered unhappily between them. Regardless of the fact that he announced several times during the drive that he wanted to stop and eat, his dad continued on in moody silence.

Sherry rallied once and asked Keith who'd won in the Rams game.

"We didn't get to go. 'Stead, Crawford helped Arnold with his stupid old coin collection."

"What?" Garrett took his eyes off the highway. "What did he and your mom do with you?"

"Nothin'. Crawford told Mom if I was gonna live there, I hadda learn to occupy myself." He picked nervously at his fingers. "I don't gotta live there, do I?"

"Not if I can help it," Garrett replied grimly.

"Tomorrow I'll have a talk with your mother." Garrett glanced at Sherry, wishing she'd say something to quell the anxiety circling like a flock of buzzards in his stomach.

Her eyes were closed—in a pretext of sleep. He could tell she was pretending. Worry gripped him more tightly. Would a judge recognize Carla and Crawford's supervision of Keith as lackadaisical? Or—considering how much overtime Garrett worked—was his care of Keith any less neglectful?

Custody was Sherry's turf. Garrett would give a lot for her advice. She didn't offer any. And once they arrived at the complex, she collected her bag and left, her goodbye and thanks a shade warmer than frosty.

"What'd you do to Sherry?" Keith demanded before he and Garrett reached their home.

"What makes you think I'm responsible for her bad temper?"

"You always argued with Mom. She said so. And she left. Now I'll bet Sherry's gonna go away, too."

"I rarely argued with your mother. And I'm not responsible for what Sherry does or doesn't do," Garrett yelled as Keith slammed inside and tore upstairs. He exhaled noisily. "Do you want to go get Rags tonight?" he shouted from the foot of the stairs. "If so, straighten up and fly right."

Minutes ticked by before Keith's sullen pinched face again appeared at the top of the stairs. "I want my dog, but I don't wanna talk to you."

Garrett's stomach bottomed out as he slowly dropped his suitcase. "I'm sorry your mother left us, son. And it's time I tried to answer questions you have."

Keith wouldn't look directly at his father.

Garrett sat on a step and patted the carpet beside him. Without waiting for Keith to join him, he said, "The divorce wasn't my idea, son. I gave your mom everything I knew how to give." He clenched a fist over his heart. "Love wasn't enough to make her happy. Sometimes it isn't, and that's nobody's fault. Not mine. Not yours."

Keith crept down the stairs and slid wiry arms around Garrett's neck. "Sherry's not like that, Dad. Her heart is this big. Bigger." He threw his arms as wide as he could. "She loves kids and dogs and other stuff. Love'd make her plenty happy, I bet."

Garrett closed his eyes and dropped his chin to his chest. He couldn't meet the hope shining in his son's eyes.

An hour later they had Rags home. Keith was lying on the floor watching TV, his dog curled at his side. Garrett sorted through the mail. There was a letter from Carla's attorney. He ripped it open and read it fast. Then stunned, he read it through more slowly. It contained a lot of legalese, but the gist was a warning for Garrett not to try to rush into a marriage with a virtual stranger for appearance's sake.

The letter fell to his lap. Carla's lawyer had obviously learned via Keith that there was something going on between him and Sherry. Or Carla had suggested as much. Wouldn't they love to drag Sherry's name through the mud? Wasn't it fortunate, then, that she'd cooled off when she had? Folding the letter, Garrett returned it to its envelope. He walked over and stuffed it in his desk with the other correspondence belonging to his case.

"Keith," he said, "tomorrow, I'm hiring someone to look after the house and you. What Sherry needs is for us to do our thing and give her space to do hers."

"No, it's not what she needs." Keith jackknifed into a sitting position. He enfolded Rags in his arms as he glared at Garrett.

Garrett steeled himself to ignore his son's misery. He wondered if there was a way to back out of buying this town house. But he couldn't really afford to lose the earnest money. "Is what I said clear, Keith? After tomorrow there won't be any need for you to call and bother Sherry."

Keith snapped off the TV and ran upstairs. "Sherry doesn't think I'm a bother. When I get

big, me'n Rags are gonna live alone. Aren't we,
Rags?"

Garrett gazed after the pup scrambling to keep
up with the boy. He considered finding a parent-
child counselor. It would help if Carla went, too.
But she'd refused to consider a marriage counselor. And when did he have time? This job kept
him so busy he barely saw Keith now. "Remember—you aren't big yet," he called sternly just
before Keith's bedroom door slammed.

Next morning Garrett counted on the boy's
anger having blown over.

But Keith remained mute. After dropping him
off at school, Garrett called Westerbrook's office
and explained he'd be late. "I'm stopping by a domestic employment agency. I can't keep imposing
on Dr. Campbell."

Westerbrook coughed. "Wise decision, my boy.
In fact I'd planned to have a talk with you today.
Yesterday Sheldon March's wife said somebody
saw you, Keith and Sherilyn putting suitcases in
your truck. I'm sure it was perfectly innocent, but
talk of that nature causes big trouble on campus."

Garrett was so knocked off his pins he couldn't
think of anything to say.

"You understand the position, I'm sure. Faculty
would never accept it, what with Sherry reporting
to you. They'd dump her as department chair."

"But she's tenured."

"Tenure won't protect her in an elected post. Why belabor a dead issue, eh? All I'm saying is that it's good you've come to your senses and are hiring a sitter. I'll be happy to pass on the reason you're late to the budget committee today. Very happy."

Garrett clutched the receiver to his chest after Westerbrook clicked off the line. The tattletale had to be Yvette's new roommate—the flight attendant—what was her name again? Listening to Westerbrook's warning, Garrett was doubly glad now, for Sherry's sake, that she'd abandoned their deepening relationship. Although he already missed her. When they were together he'd foolishly believed marriage was possible.

With his lousy track record, he should have known better.

ANGEL POUNCED on Sherry the instant she set foot in the department. Hustling her into her private office, the secretary shut the door. "Wait'll you hear the scuttlebutt flying around campus this morning. People are saying you spent the weekend with Dean Lock." Angel laughed uproariously.

Sherry plopped her briefcase on the desk and gazed at Angel with dark-ringed eyes. "I did. I'm a fool, Angel." Sherry walked to the window, leaned a shoulder on the frame and gazed at a row of leafless trees. "I let him break my heart. Compared to that, a few nasty rumors are painless."

"That rat! I'll poison his coffee."

Sherry almost smiled. "I said it before and I'll say it again, no man is worth leaving your kids in foster care while you do hard time, Angel. I walked into this with my eyes open. I'll take my licks on campus. Only...will you run interference between Garrett and me for a few days?"

"You got it, boss. I won't poison his coffee. Just make him wish I had."

"No." Sherry shook her head as she pushed away from the window. "Once I get past seeing him at Nolan and Em's wedding, our only contact will be professional. I can handle that. Remember I told you to think of a lost love as you would a death? I need time to grieve, then I'll be good as new again."

It wasn't until after Angel left quietly without comment that Sherry wondered if her secretary bought into any of this—if she and the others Sherry counseled believed time healed all wounds. Sherry had to believe it, or she wouldn't make it through the day.

But get through it she did. She avoided Garrett before, during and after school on Monday and Tuesday. By Wednesday, she'd begun to breathe easier. Then as she left her one-o'clock class, she glimpsed him hurrying toward his car. Her heart squeezed. Had something happened to Keith? Several seconds passed while she debated chasing after him to ask.

Fortunately a student stopped her, seeking her advice about a topic for a paper, and kept her from making a big mistake. She cared a great deal for Keith Lock. More than she had any right to. Sherry knew Garrett had hired a sitter. Everyone on campus and in the complex knew about the plump grandmotherly woman Garrett had retained to take Sherry's place. Admittedly Sherry missed the time she'd spent with Keith. She missed laughing and talking with Garrett, too.

Her admission might have eased some of Garrett's guilt when, for the second day in a row, he was called to school because his son had picked fights on the playground.

"Is something going on in Keith's life we should know about?" the soft-spoken principal asked Garrett in the private meeting she'd requested.

He clasped his hands between his knees and tapped his thumbs together. "Keith is angry with me. I thought he'd get over it in a day or two, but he hasn't."

"Who is Sherry? According to our records, your ex-wife's name is Carla."

Unprepared for the question, Garrett straightened sharply.

The principal removed her glasses. "Keith

didn't mention you when I questioned why he'd flown into a rage. He said he missed doing things with Sherry."

Garrett ran a damp palm over his mouth and chin. "Sherry picked Keith up from day care on a temporary basis until I could hire a full-time sitter."

"Ah. A high-school girl." The woman smiled. "Maybe you could arrange for her to ease out of his life gradually. I gather they skated, played miniature golf and watched videos. Rainy as it's been, he'll soon forget the sporting activities. But perhaps she'd continue the movies once a month or so."

"Sherry isn't a high-school girl. She's a colleague of mine. A professor with a busy schedule."

"But if she's as nice as Keith claims, I'm sure she'd make time to help."

Garrett stood. "He'll see Sherry at her brother's wedding next weekend. Thank you for your time and advice, Mrs. McKay. I'll give it serious thought."

"Keith is a sweet boy. Oh, and, Dr. Lock, normally I don't involve myself in situations with noncustodial parents. But yesterday, I had a call from your ex-wife's lawyer. He beat about the bush in lawyerly fashion. The upshot is I gather she wants Keith to live with her permanently. If she's said as much to Keith, this may be another reason he's acting out."

Cold dread wrapped around Garrett's windpipe, choking off his breath. When he wheezed a few times, the principal stepped to her sideboard and poured him a glass of water. "I assumed you knew. I'm sorry this came as a shock."

"I knew. I thought if I cooperated…" Garrett broke off helplessly.

The principal sat again and laced her hands. "You know, don't you, that Keith's change in classroom behavior will give them a tremendous lever?"

Garrett nodded. "I do. Again, my thanks for the advance warning." He left her office this time without being called back. The boy Garrett collected from the time-out room had torn jeans and an eye beginning to turn interesting shades of purple. And he puffed up belligerently, acting contrite only when it became clear his dad wasn't going to rake him over the coals. Still, he didn't apologize for his behavior.

Twice after Keith had gone to sleep that night Garrett lifted the phone and tried to muster the nerve to call Sherry. He'd given his new sitter the night off, but not even that helped. Garrett turned in after midnight, the phone untouched.

THE MIDDLE OF the next week, Carla called him at work. "I talked to Keith last night. He says he can't come to St. Louis Saturday because of a wedding. Anyone I know?"

"A history professor from my campus. Nolan Campbell."

"Campbell? Any relation to your so-called babysitter?"

Garrett didn't like the smirk in Carla's voice. "Nolan is Sherry's brother. But I have a full-time sitter now. I assumed Keith would tell you."

"He did. So things didn't work out with you and Ms. Campbell, hmm?"

"Dr. Campbell," he lashed out. "And there was nothing to work out. I'm busy, Carla. Why the sudden inquisition about my love life? What's really on your mind?"

"The only interest I have in your love life is how it affects my son."

"I could point out that your interest comes about eight years late. But I'll let my lawyer do that in court. Isn't that what all this is leading up to? A custody battle?"

"We don't have our case built yet, Garrett. You'll be the first to know when we do. I just don't understand why Keith turned down a chance to visit us to go to the wedding of a man he can't know well at all. Is this your doing?"

"Keith pals around with Nolan's stepson, Mark. Did you ever think Keith might be more excited about visiting if you didn't run off to work every time he shows up?"

"My work. That's always been a thorn in your side, hasn't it, Garrett?"

"Not your work, Carla," Garrett said quietly. "Only your obsession with it to the exclusion of everything else in your life, including your son. I'm not turning Keith against you. You're doing a fine job of it yourself."

"Oh, yes. As if you spend every waking minute with him. Keith has a room full of toys and books here. And Crawford spends quality time with him. Don't try to insinuate I'm a bad parent because I work to help provide a better life. Anyway, for your information, Keith said his class has a parent-child outing to the St. Louis Children's Music concert on the Wednesday after Thanksgiving. He asked me to go. Not you, Garrett. Me!"

She couldn't have hurt Garrett more if she'd cut out his heart with a dull knife. Keith hadn't said one word about the outing. But Garrett would be skewered and roasted on a spit before he let Carla know that. "I suggested it," he lied. "Despite what you think, I'm not trying to prevent you from building a relationship with our son." He paused. "Don't let him down on this, Carla."

"I won't. And since you have him for Thanksgiving, I'm including him in our Christmas plans with Crawford's children."

A protest rose to Garrett's lips, but he let it die. Carla would love to have him contest the original custody decree. It said Keith would spend alternate holidays with each parent. If he spent Thanksgiving with Garrett, Carla was supposed to get him for Christmas. That was the agreement in theory; in practice, Garrett had always had him full-time.

"Okay. I'll see that we have our tree early. Spell out the dates you want him and forward them to me by email. I hate to cut you short, Carla, but I'm late for a meeting."

If he'd surprised her with his generosity, Carla didn't let on. She hung up immediately. Garrett battled the billowing anger that he seemed unable to quell. Just as fast, he plunged into a loneliness the likes of which he'd never felt before. Not even when Carla had walked out. The thought of spending Christmas without Keith—he couldn't even imagine the void. Christmas was a time for families. He didn't know what people who had no one did over the holiday season. He slid into a depression he couldn't seem to shake.

Garrett kept waiting for Keith to tell him about his invitation to Carla. The boy ignored his father and said nothing. Keith played with Rags and remained aloof and distant. Garrett actually looked forward to Nolan and Emily's wedding.

"Where's our present?" Keith spoke to his dad

for the first time in weeks after climbing into the pickup to go to the big event.

"Sherry and I went together on a gift. She took it to wrap."

"Oh. I saw her leave, but she didn't have nothin'. She sure looked pretty, though. Did you see her when she went by our house?"

"No. I must've been getting dressed. Maybe she already took the gift to Nolan's house. A lot of people prefer to not mess with gifts at the reception."

"You been to a lot of weddings?"

"Enough. There's a lot of standing around. We'll know a few people, and I'll introduce you to my colleagues and their families so you won't be totally bored."

"That's okay. Me'n Mark are handing out groom's cake at the reception. We got a special place to stand and everything."

"Oh." Garrett had assumed they'd be together. He hadn't given any thought to being alone. But alone he was from the minute they stepped inside the church. Keith had rushed off with Mark. And Garrett felt the isolation deep in his bones.

He'd no more than glanced over the crowd when he noticed Sherry flitting from huddle to huddle, a vision in rust and gold satin. Garrett couldn't take his eyes off her. He even found the sprig of white flowers nestled in her short, gold-tipped dark hair enchanting.

A punch of jealousy ripped his joy away when Sherry rose on tiptoe and kissed two beefy guys who'd just arrived. His stomach didn't settle until she turned to speak with a leathery-skinned woman walking between the men. The woman chewed a huge wad of gum.

Garrett heard Camp greet the gum-chewer by name. Maizie. She and Sherry seemed to be the focus of a gaggle of strangers—well, strangers to Garrett in that they weren't from the college community. Two elderly women converged on Sherry. The three shrieked and hugged. Doris and Vi, Sherry called them. A man with a booming voice and a swagger plowed into the center of the group. Someone near Garrett whispered that the loudmouth and his wife had flown in from Philadelphia specifically for the wedding. It finally fell into place for Garrett. These were people Nolan, Emily and Sherry had met on their summer trek.

Garrett lost track of Sherry momentarily. The next time he spotted her, she and Megan were laughing with a stocky female who walked with a slight limp.

"There's Gina," exclaimed Mark. "Everybody we met on the wagon train came to see Mom and Nolan get married. Even that witch Brittany." He pointed to a young woman with shoulder-length blond hair. "Hey, Brit brought a boyfriend, and they both look normal. Cool, huh?"

It was nice, but Garrett had no clue why Brittany shouldn't look normal. Then she turned and Garrett realized he had seen her before—with Sherry at their first fateful meeting. The blonde had done nothing but scream even before Sherry hit him. To say he'd made a bad impression with his scruffy appearance was putting it mildly.

Feeling disassociated from the mainstream of the party, Garrett made his way to the vestibule. Once there, Sherry's dad steered him toward a woman handing out boutonnieres. He thought he might snag a word with Sherry when, as attendants, they witnessed the signing of the marriage certificate. But she barely acknowledged him. She, Emily and Megan took off immediately—to dress the bride, they said.

Retreating, Garrett slapped the nervous groom on the back. "Nolan, old son, you look far too relaxed for a man about to meet his doom."

"I'm counting the hours until the honeymoon. All this folderol is for Emily." Nolan waved a hand. "Her first wedding was a disaster. I want to wipe the memory of it from her mind. Most women dream of wearing veils and yards of white lace. I couldn't care less about any of those trappings. But I'll jump through all the hoops because I love her."

Garrett thought about his first wedding as he pocketed the ring. He and Carla had stood before a justice of the peace. Her wedding to Crawford had been a huge white-tie affair.

As he trailed Nolan into the main sanctuary, Garrett remembered the dreamy glow on Sherry's face when she talked of having a spring wedding. A perfect time for new beginnings, she'd said. Funny, he hadn't pegged her as the type to get all misty-eyed about marriage. Showed how little he knew about women. How little he knew about Sherilyn Campbell. And now it was just as well, he lamented.

The music signaled the start of the ceremony, and Garrett took his place beside the groom. The organist struck chords to announce the arrival of the maid of honor. Turning, Garrett watched Sherry drop rose petals along a creamy satin runner. He knew the moment the bride appeared, only because the crowd surged to their feet. However, he missed Emily's entire walk. Garrett's mind's eye placed Sherry in that dress of white froth. And imagined her floating toward him—to accept his ring on her finger.

Garrett tried to focus on the unity candle that sat on a table atop the dais. At the rehearsal, kept brief so everyone could celebrate Thanksgiving in their own homes, Garrett had learned that Nolan and Emily would light the unity candle with tapers placed on either side of it. The candle's inner glow signified the undying flame of love. As the minister opened his Bible and began, "Dearly Beloved..." Garrett shifted so he could keep his gaze on Sherilyn.

Emily's voice rose clearly and distinctly for all to hear as she promised to love, honor and cherish Nolan until death.

Garrett rallied long enough to press the rings into Nolan's profusely sweating hand. Ah—so the cool professor wasn't so cool, after all. Which was further evidenced as he twice tangled up his promise to Emily. But Nolan redeemed himself. His voice dropped, he took Emily's face between his shaking hands and recited a poem that spoke eloquently of his everlasting love for her.

Sherry had tears streaking silently down her cheeks. And Megan, who'd lit the candelabrum, scrubbed at hers. Garrett blinked rapidly, his eyes still on Sherilyn. Love might have eluded him; however, every word Nolan spoke applied to the feelings that squeezed unmercifully at Garrett's heart.

Anyone could see how the best man and the maid of honor pined for one another, Nolan thought to himself. So did Emily. And Sherry's parents. Mark, Megan and even Keith noticed it. Not Sherry. She didn't once glance toward Garrett. And he was a man in denial.

Yvette Miller missed the looks, or chose to ignore them. At the huge reception where people laughed, ate and toasted the happy couple, she was never far from Garrett's side. Her friends made a big to-do when Yvette caught the bouquet Emily threw straight at Sherry.

Most of the byplay escaped Garrett. He held his breath, waiting to see what Sherilyn would do when she caught the bride's bouquet. He wanted her to have it. He remembered how she'd fondled the fated rose he'd brought her… It seemed so long ago.

Then Yvette picked the posies right out of midair. Garrett blinked. He felt sad and upset for Sherry. It was at that moment he realized how deeply he loved her. Now, when a relationship between them assured her removal from the department that was so important to her. Now, when it could interfere with his retaining custody of Keith.

During the cutting of the cake, Garrett decided it'd be best for everyone concerned to completely sever ties with Sherry. So he smiled at Yvette when she flirted, even though his heart wasn't in it.

"My car's in the shop, Garrett. I rode in with a friend who couldn't stay for the reception." Yvette stepped in front of Garrett, cutting off his view of Sherilyn.

"You need a lift home?" he asked politely.

Yvette tapped his chest with the white bouquet. "You offering to take me for a ride, big guy?"

Garrett regretted his offer at once, but saw no way to extract himself. "Yes," he mumbled, his eyes drawn to Keith and Mark who ran pell-mell toward him.

"Dad." Keith bounced up and down. "Mark and Megan are gonna stay all night with Sherry. Nolan's mom and dad have lotsa company, and Nolan and Emily are going on a honeymoon for the weekend. Sherry's gonna pop popcorn and show videos. I'm invited! Can we go now and get my sleeping bag?"

Garrett sensed Yvette's sudden interest in his proposed childless state. She was really pretty obvious. He might have consciously decided to forget Sherry; that didn't mean he was interested in a night of meaningless sex.

"No, Keith." Garrett didn't try to qualify his refusal. He just knew he wanted Keith as a buffer.

Yvette snuggled close. "What would it hurt, Garrett?"

"A ride home doesn't entitle you to interfere in decisions regarding my son."

Something flickered in Yvette's green eyes, but she kept hold of Garrett's arm.

"I wanna go with Sherry," Keith whined. "Why can't I? She said to bring Rags."

Never once in all of Keith's young life had Garrett ever fallen back on the lame excuse, "Because I said so." He did now, adding, "Lower your voice, Keith. Stop making a scene in front of my friends and colleagues."

Not only didn't Keith lower his voice, he threw a doozy of a fit.

Garrett added to the scene by half dragging the wailing child out of the reception. It was an awkward retreat, particularly as Yvette clung stubbornly to Garrett's left arm and he was left-handed. All eyes in the room registered the struggle he had opening the door. He muttered under his breath.

From the sidelines, Sherry listened to Keith's hiccuping sobs. Everyone who remained in the hall heard the boy sob her name and heard Garrett tell him to hush. If any of their colleagues still believed rumors linking her and the new dean, he'd effectively squelched them. Squelched them, and at the same time delivered her a slap in the face. At least, that was how it felt within a heart that still yearned for him. It hurt so badly Sherry actually thought about quitting her job and moving far, far away.

CHAPTER FOURTEEN

THE LONG THANKSGIVING weekend and the disaster at the wedding reception were minor blips in Garrett's mind as he struggled with the monumental task facing the budget committee on their return to campus. The order—cut another hundred thousand dollars from the academic budget before the state legislature convened in January.

For once Garrett didn't mind that Keith was still sulking. It meant the house was quiet at night except for the click of his calculator. He went home exhausted by the battering he took from other committee members during tense meetings. Again they wanted to slice the Hub completely. Its cost didn't justify the narrow population it served, they said. Garrett didn't know why he stayed awake at night trying to devise ways to save the program. When he'd asked for legitimate areas to cut, instead, Sherry hadn't turned in one concrete suggestion. Didn't she realize something had to give?

Between his discouragement at the incessant rain pounding the daylights out of Missouri and Sherilyn's stubborn unwillingness to give him data to work with, Garrett was left brooding over his figures for the third day in a row. He was exhausted; no one knew how tempted he was to chuck everything and just give up. He didn't expect Sherry to beg for her program, but he needed her expertise. Her fire. She avoided him on all levels. The tic below one eye reminded Garrett that he was partly to blame. He should never have crossed the invisible line from professional to personal. Never with a woman below him in his chain of command. Remembering her passionate face as she worked with those hardened students, he massaged the ache in the back of his neck, shuffled the stack of departmental budgets and began punching in numbers again. He'd already met with three program chairs. They'd hacked unneeded extras. Garrett wanted Sherry to come forward on her own. On day ten, he sent her a memo demanding they meet the following afternoon.

Next morning when he received an email from Carla spelling out the whole of Keith's school vacation for her custodial visit, Garrett was so bleary-eyed he had to check the dates on the calendar twice. He could hardly believe her request. As anger warred with loneliness and anxiety, he stared at the wall behind his computer screen for a full ten minutes and contemplated how far he'd get if he took Keith and ran.

Carla was wrenching Keith away from him,

and there wasn't a thing he could do about it. She didn't need to go to court again. The old decree, put together when he'd bent over backward to be fair, gave her alternate holidays and all summer vacations.

Thunder shook the corner window in Garrett's office. Lightning separated the sky, and he felt as if it had torn through his heart. The phone rang three times before he picked it up with a shaking hand.

"Dean Lock? This is Angel. Dr. Campbell forgot she'd agreed to accompany one of our students to her appointment at the Center for Families in Transition this afternoon. Maria Black's husband blew into town unexpectedly. He's making waves. Demanding to see Maria's little girl. Dr. Campbell said if you can stall the committee today, she'll dig out anything you need and bring it tomorrow. You understand, I'm sure. Armando Black is a total jerk."

Garrett drummed his fingers on his desktop. "Is that part of Dr. Campbell's job? Involving herself in a student's divorce?"

Angel's voice took on a bitter edge. "Speaking from experience, I say thank goodness someone like her is willing to go beyond her job. Otherwise, unless a person has a lot of money, no one advocates for kids and ex-wives."

She struck a nerve in Garrett that was too raw.

He felt like one of the walking wounded just now. "Oh, I'm sure Maria's lawyer cut her a sweet deal. Tell Dr. Campbell that if she wants to save the Hub, she'll make this meeting with me today. I'll wait." He heard the department secretary scoop in a deep breath.

"I'm sorry, Dean. She left already. With the weather and all, I guess she didn't want to chance making Maria late. That'd be points for Armando."

He picked up a ruler and snapped it in half. "When do you expect her back?"

"Tomorrow morning," Angel said in a small voice.

"Fine. Leave a message on her home answering machine. Never mind, I'll do what I have to do with the Hub, and I'm sure Dr. Campbell will figure it out." He slid a finger over the disconnect button rather than ruin Angel's hearing by slamming down the receiver as he was tempted to do.

In a black mood that matched the clouds rolling across campus, Garrett selected a felt pen and slashed through Sherry's pet counseling program. According to several members on the budget committee, all Dr. Campbell did in those counseling sessions was teach divorced women how to give men the shaft. Even the indigent had court-appointed lawyers. Too many shysters. Here was a line item—the Hub passed out literature telling women how to get free legal assistance. Free shysters. Without a twinge of remorse, Garrett x'd through the entire amount. And so he progressed, service by service. The retyped budget for the Hub that came up on his computer spreadsheet looked markedly different from Sherilyn's original. He printed it, ran a copy and shoved it under her office door right before he dashed out into the rain and splashed through the puddles to his truck. There weren't a lot of cars left in the staff lot. He hadn't been home on time one night in two weeks.

Sitting through traffic light after traffic light, watching his windshield wipers struggle to combat the steady downpour, did nothing to improve Garrett's mood. And because his babysitter had needed this week off to be with her daughter who'd had emergency surgery, Garrett still had to drive to Keith's temporary day care in water nearly up to his hubcaps.

Once he finally reached the facility, he realized he wasn't the only late parent. But he *was* the only father. From the lack of wedding rings on the harried-looking women hustling by, Garrett deduced that at this center there were roughly ten times more single moms than dads. Near the door, Garrett saw the umbrella of the mother who'd just passed him with two children turn inside out. He rushed out to lend her a hand.

"Thanks, but I can handle this myself," she said, raking him with bitter eyes. And indeed, she ripped the umbrella he'd taken from her out of his hand and proceeded to bundle her two little ones and their diaper bags into the car, leaving Garrett standing in the rain. "If I waited around for a man's help," she muttered, climbing into the driver's seat, "I'd either drown or grow mold."

Garrett winced as she slammed her door. He turned up his coat collar, hunched his shoulders against the rain and covered the distance to the building again, where he saw Keith peering anxiously outside.

"Where've you been, Dad?" The boy shrugged into his slicker. "I hate it when I have to wait with all the babies. C'mon. I wanna go home." It took Keith two tries to shut the passenger door of the pickup. "Brr," he said. "Can we have stew for supper?"

Surprised by his son's sudden talkativeness, Garrett agreed. "How about if I build a fire in the fireplace and we eat off TV trays for a change?"

"Don't you have to work tonight?"

Garrett shook his head—although he'd begun to have a twinge or two of guilt at how he'd slashed Sherry's budget to ribbons. On the other hand, Keith seemed guardedly happy over the prospect of their eating together. What was done was done. "Do you have homework, son?"

"Nope. We practiced for our holiday program all day. Oh—don't forget to sign my permission slip to take the bus to St. Louis tomorrow, or else I can't go."

Garrett felt the truck's rear wheels hydroplane in a puddle. He slowed to correct his course, saving his frown until they'd stopped at the next intersection. "I forgot—the St. Louis Children's Music concert. Keith, surely the school officials won't let you go in this weather."

"Uh-huh, my teacher said."

"Did you remind your mother? Is she definitely meeting you?"

"Yep. Just her and not Crawford. It's gonna be so cool. We get to see Frosty the Snowman and everything. He's not real, but that's okay. I wish I didn't hafta visit Mom and Crawford over Christmas break. Crawford's kids and grandkids are gonna be there." The young voice quavered, and he scooted closer to Garrett.

A stab of loneliness interfered with Garrett's ability to breathe. He ruffled his son's rain-damp hair, not trusting himself to speak. He swallowed a painful lump and then another, but discovered they severely limited his end of the conversation for the remainder of the drive home.

Rags met them at the door with hearty barks. The dog walker had stopped by at lunch, so the poor dog had been confined all afternoon. "Take him out, Keith," Garrett said. "But wipe his feet well before you bring him inside again. Cleaning muddy prints from the carpet isn't my favorite chore."

"Okay. Can I check the answering machine first? It's blinking." It was a habit he'd gotten into after they'd advertised for the dog's owner.

"Go ahead." Garrett stripped off his topcoat. Keith liked to listen to the sales pitches and donation requests that came in during the course of a day. Garrett was happy to leave the task to his son. "I'll go make sure we have a couple of cans of stew." He paused in the act of hanging up his coat as he heard his ex-wife's voice filter into the room.

"Keith, it turns out I can't go to that concert tomorrow. Sorry, but the head of our branch called a department meeting. I'm so close to a promotion I don't dare not attend. But you're grown-up enough to understand. We'll have two weeks together at Christmas. There goes my phone, I've got a client. Bye, honey."

Garrett didn't need to see Keith's face to feel his disappointment. It emanated from the slumped shoulders and the dejected way he hung his head. But what could Garrett say that wouldn't reveal the anger he felt toward Carla at this moment? He passed a shaking hand over his own eyes. How many times did this make now that she'd let Keith down? Too many!

"Dad?" Keith's voice wobbled and his eyes shone overbright. "Can you go tomorrow? There's room on the bus. My teacher said so right before she told us to bring our permission slips."

Garrett wanted to say yes more than he wanted to breathe, but today's decree from Westerbrook scheduled budget meetings back-to-back tomorrow. "Son, I can't. I'd like to, but it's too short notice. If I'd known, I could have planned ahead and—"

"That's okay." Keith cut him off, sank down on his knees and gathered his moppy dog in his arms. "When I walk Rags, I'll go ask Sherry. I bet she'd like the concert. She loves music."

Garrett thought how furious Sherry was going to be in the morning when she got a load of what he'd done to the Hub. He actually looked forward to doing battle with her. Maybe now she'd give him some helpful suggestions. Any response, even a full-scale eruption, would be more satisfying than her recent passive-aggressive reactions.

"I'd rather you didn't call Sherry."

"Why?" There was a stubborn edge to the single word.

"Because." Garrett knew he sounded no less stubborn. "I said don't, and that's final." The frustrated wave of his hand brought Keith's attention to the renewed rattle of raindrops on the living-room windows. "I wouldn't be surprised if they canceled the trip, Keith."

"They won't. And everybody'll have a mom there but me."

Garrett recalled the first time he'd had to attend a couples function alone, after Carla walked out. He knew the desperation Keith must be feeling. Garrett's heart wrenched for his son. He considered asking Emily if she could spare time to go with Keith. Just as quickly he discarded the idea. Only yesterday Camp told him Emily was steeped in the final stages of their book. An editor had requested sample chapters before the wedding.

Garrett closed his eyes and ran down the list of other women he knew. A pathetically short list. "Maybe Yvette's free, Keith." If Garrett sounded hesitant, it was because he *was* hesitant. Yvette Miller didn't need much encouragement to hang around. Garrett hated to give her any. But neither did he like seeing Keith distraught.

"I don't like her." Jumping up, Keith dumped Rags off his lap. "I don't care what you say, I'm gonna ask Sherry."

"No, son, you are not." Garrett caught Keith by the arm as he raced for the door. He held the boy firmly even though he tried to tear free. "If you persist in this nonsense, Keith, I will not sign your permission form. And if you choose not to

ask Yvette, I'm afraid you'll have to resign yourself to being on your own."

"That's not fair." Keith stomped his foot. Tears
furrowed his cheeks. Rags, sensing something
had upset his favorite human, began to whine.

"Life isn't fair, Keith. Now what's it going to
be?"

In their short test of wills, Keith lost. Shrugging, he dug the form out of his jeans pocket. "I
really, really wanna go to the concert," he whispered.

"All right. I'm not doing this to be mean." Garrett took the paper, pulled out his pen and scribbled his name. "Now, let's eat. How about biscuits
to go with our stew?"

"I'm not hungry," Keith mumbled. "May I be
excused?"

Garrett studied his son a lengthy moment. But
he was reluctant to heap one humiliation on another. Pride was important. He inclined his head
slightly, allowing Keith to save face. "If you work
up an appetite walking Rags, there'll be plenty
to eat."

Keith nodded. After stuffing the permission
slip in his book bag, he carried his reluctant pet
into the stormy night.

They didn't stay out long. Garrett heard the
door slam again as the smell of stew began to per-
meate the house. He sighed, listening to Keith's

footsteps march upstairs. Then he turned back to the eight-o'clock news. The Mississippi and the Missouri rivers were both rising. Garrett doubted the concert was going to be an issue tomorrow. Even though the bridge that crossed into the city was high above the river, the roads that led there ran through lowlands.

Keith finished wiping Rags's feet, opened his bedroom door and shoved the pup inside. He closed the door softly and tiptoed into his dad's bedroom. Quietly he lifted the phone and dialed Sherry's number, which he'd carefully committed to memory.

She answered on the first ring. The weather had been so ghastly she'd come straight home after dropping Maria Black off at a shelter following their trying session with a counselor who didn't see through Armando's phony charm.

"Keith? What a surprise. Is everything all right? You're not stranded at day care, are you?" Sherry knew that Garrett might well have been tied up in a late budget session. She realized with a guilty pang that she hadn't done anything to make his time at these meetings easier. And she was worried. They'd already cut funding once, yet the newspapers were filled with rumors of massive legislative cutbacks.

"My mom called, Sherry. She can't go to the concert in St. Louis with my class tomorrow. Will you go? As my friend?" His whispery voice held a trace of recent tears.

Pain wrapped spiky fingers around Sherry's heart, stealing her voice for a minute.

"That's okay," he said in a bleak voice. "I didn't figure you could. Dad can't, either, 'cause it's last minute. I thought maybe…" He dissolved in sniffles.

"Wait." It was impossible not to respond to the anguish in his voice. "I only teach one class tomorrow, and my students are pretty caught up. I still have two days of personal leave coming," she muttered, thinking out loud as she paced the length of the phone cord. Frankly, the way Garrett had withdrawn so completely after the boat trip, she was shocked he'd let Keith ask her. Then she had a dark thought. Perhaps Garrett didn't know.

"Is your dad still at work, Keith?" Sherry more than half expected the boy to grudgingly admit that Garrett was.

"He's home. He picked me up at day care." Keith gave a brief explanation of the sitter's dilemma.

Sherry's heart began to thud loudly. Maybe Garrett had had a change of heart. If he approved of her going with Keith tomorrow, how could she refuse? "I'd be honored to go as your friend, tiger. When and where should I meet you? Are the moms carpooling?"

In a happier, more hopeful tone, Keith laid out details.

"A school bus? Two buses? Ah." Sherry cringed inwardly thinking of the two-hour trip to St. Louis crammed on a bus of boisterous third-graders. However, by the time he'd described the concert in an unmistakably excited voice, she hung up feeling some enthusiasm herself. She smiled softly, her heart lighter for bringing joy to Keith. Undoubtedly Garrett would be relieved, too. Really, if truth be known, Sherry was glad she didn't have to drive, considering the weather predictions.

She watched the local news as she prepared soup. But her thoughts kept wandering down the street to Garrett and Keith. Hard as it was, Garrett seemed to cope with Carla's on-again, off-again involvement in Keith's life.

Sherry sat down at the kitchen table with her steaming bowl of vegetable soup, realizing she'd come home angered by divorce after the emotional meeting at the Center for Families in Transition. Divorce didn't close the door on a couple's problems. Hearing the terrible things Armando and Maria screamed at each other, Sherry found herself wondering if they'd ever been in love. In contrast, Garrett's dealings with his ex-wife appeared quite reasonable. Perhaps the principles of the Hub were remiss. Only one-half of a separated couple was recognized when, in fact, where children were involved, the two halves of a couple remained emotionally connected for years.

Sherry laid down her spoon. Excitement began to sing in her blood as she turned over the possibilities in her mind. Whole-life counseling should include men, as well as women. Too bad she had to wait until next week to present this brainstorm to Garrett. What would a few extra days matter? Tomorrow belonged to Keith. He saw her as someone he could count on. She would not shortchange him for the sake of her job or anything else.

Sherry snapped off the television and went to phone Angel. Technically personal days were supposed to be requested in advance and required the signature of the immediate supervisor. Since Garrett was Sherry's immediate supervisor and since he knew the trip with Keith necessitated her taking time off work, he obviously planned to approve her paperwork after the fact.

"Angel," she said, speaking to the department secretary's home answering machine, "I won't be in tomorrow. Please cancel my nine-o'clock class. Tell them to read two chapters ahead and prepare for Monday's quiz. Oh, and don't worry about me. It's not an emergency. Have Garrett sign my leave request and send it on to personnel. His ex copped out on Keith again at the eleventh hour. I'm filling in for her on the third-grader trip to a Christmas concert in St. Louis. Call me if you get home soon. Otherwise, see you bright and early Monday."

Garrett invaded Sherry's dreams that night. At first she lay awake listening to the steady drumming of rain on the roof, trying her level best to be practical and not to read anything personal into his allowing her back in Keith's life. But as the rain slackened, images of Garrett—how it would feel to curl up next to him every night—whisked her off on a tangent. His kisses had been tender. Giving. He had felt what she'd felt. She'd seen it in his eyes when Nolan recited that poem at the wedding. So why had he backed off? Fear, maybe? Because he'd had one failed marriage?

One clear thought transcended all others. Keith's phone call tonight represented a major capitulation for Garrett. Keith was the most important person in Garrett's life. That call spelled a definite softening in his feelings for her. Otherwise Garrett wouldn't have let Keith ask her to be his pro-tem parent.

Things would work out between them. This was a start.

Snuggling under her comforter, Sherry yawned and gave fleeting thought to getting up and calling him. Wind gusted outside and whistled around the corner of her bedroom window. She burrowed deeper and decided to phone him while she cooked breakfast.

Sherry woke up with a start and registered the fact that even though her bedside clock said 5:00 a.m., it was much later. Too much light filtered into her room. She turned on the lamp and lunged for her watch. "Oh, no! It's after nine!" The power must have been knocked out sometime during the night. And Keith said the buses were to leave his school at ten.

Flying to the window, Sherry was relieved to see that the rain had let up, even though low black clouds shrouded bare-limbed trees and wind buffeted the evergreen bushes. She let the curtain drop and ran to her closet; she chose boots, black tights and a wool skirt that hung to midcalf. And layers on top. A T-shirt topped by a cardigan that had a collar to fold out over the neck of her raincoat. For good measure, she slung a wool scarf around her neck.

Once dressed, she hurried into the kitchen to fix instant oatmeal. As she poured steaming water over the oats, she tried calling Garrett's house. No answer. Well, she could only hope he'd made Keith dress sensibly. On afterthought she dialed his direct line at the office. After the fifth ring she gave up. Obviously he knew her well enough to trust her to be there for Keith.

The buses were loading when Sherry drove through the school gates. She saw Keith pacing the walkway looking anxious. He didn't see her, and it took her several minutes to find an empty parking space.

"Hi, sport. Sorry I'm late," she apologized as she ran up to him all out of breath.

"Sherry, you came. I knew you would. I knew it." The boy propelled himself into her arms, nearly knocking her off the curb.

Regaining her balance, she hugged him, laughed and ruffled his hair.

A serene-faced woman disconnected herself from a group of rowdy students. "Professor Campbell. I'm Keith's principal. I'm so glad you could make this outing. We've had a number of parents cancel. Keith has mentioned you many times. Frankly, I wasn't sure his father would follow my advice to wean Keith from you slowly."

Sherry glanced up and into dark assessing eyes. "You and Garrett discussed me?" The words "wean Keith from you slowly" spattered goose bumps up her spine.

"In a manner of speaking." The principal's gaze slid away to the two yellow buses. "No matter. You're a lifesaver. Our rules say a minimum of one adult per ten students on a field trip. Counting you, we barely made the quota on our second bus."

Sherry's stomach gave a little lurch. Thirty eight- and nine-year-olds were a lot for three adults to oversee.

The principal noticed Sherry's quick glance at the dark sky and reached over to pat her hand. "I've called the weather bureau at least six times already. They assure me that with the velocity of the wind in another hour, the next front will be Indiana's problem, not ours."

The oatmeal lumped in Sherry's stomach flattened a bit. She smiled down into Keith's eyes and slid an arm around his jean-jacketed shoulders. "So what are we waiting for, tiger? Let's get this show on the road."

His ear-to-ear grin was all the validation and reward Sherry needed for braving several hours on a bus with a load of noisy kids. Because they'd boarded late, the two of them worked their way to the back. Sherry's heart swelled every time Keith paused to introduce her to friends, his hand firmly ensconced in hers.

GARRETT HAD STAYED UP half the night suffering guilt over the hatchet job he'd done on Sherry's program. He'd let his anger at Carla spill over into his work—something he hadn't done in years. About midnight, he'd admitted he'd been angry at Sherry, too. Angry, mixed-up—and in love with her. It wasn't her fault things had moved so fast. They needed to talk. Needed to desperately. His heart cracked and crumbled at his feet every time he passed her on campus and she deliberately crossed the street to avoid him.

He would have taken the first step toward communicating this morning. She'd told him that a lack of communication was at the root of most relationship problems. But he had to get to the campus before she did. In the middle of the night, he'd decided to go down fighting for every service Sherry's department offered. Luckily he had a master key that fit all the offices. He'd retrieve the copy he'd shoved under her door and she'd never be the wiser. He figured she hadn't stopped by her office last night; if she'd found the budget, she would've been pounding on his door regardless of the hour.

Garrett felt like a man given a pardon. This evening, he'd start mending fences. It might be good to see if Nan Campbell would watch Keith while he took Sherry to dinner, then plied her with soft music and good food. That was about the best medicine he could think of to begin healing ills. A good way to say *I'm sorry.*

He pulled back a sleeve and glanced at his watch as he parked. Late though he was after dropping Keith at school, he hoped he'd beaten Sherry to the campus. He also hoped they'd cancel the trip to the concert. He'd explained to Keith at great length this morning that they were going to get some things straight with Carla. That was another decision he'd made in the middle of the night—if the lawyers couldn't hammer out an agreement that was fair to Keith in the custody issue between him and Carla, he'd go before a judge and plead his case.

Immediately after he'd collected the budget mistake from Sherry's office floor, he planned to call Carla and let her know he wasn't having any more of her jerking Keith around like a puppet on a string. Maybe they'd make progress if he couched it in terms she understood—such as telling her that if Keith was a client, she'd never cancel an appointment at the last minute. He wasn't trying to keep her from seeing their son, but Keith deserved better than she'd given so far.

It started to spit rain before Garrett had reached the outside steps. He frowned at the low-riding clouds. Keith's principal had been on the phone with the weather bureau when he'd gone into the school this morning. She'd said they predicted the storm would blow over Missouri. So much for predictions, he thought sourly as he took the steps two at a time to avoid the rain that now pelted faster.

He shook droplets off his winter wool jacket, wishing now that he'd insisted Keith at least take his raincoat. Although, when would they be out in the weather? Only to walk from the bus to the concert hall and back to the bus again. Kids didn't melt, he reminded himself.

"Good," he grunted with satisfaction. He was first in. There were no lights on in the department yet. Garrett flipped on the lights as he made his way down the hall. He dropped his briefcase on his desk. It contained a newly revised version of the budget that he'd pored over until four in the morning. His portion of the cut was a mere twelve thousand dollars. He wasn't going to let the seven other deans force him to accept more.

At midnight, he'd recalled the claims he'd made at the time of his interview—a budget always had fat to trim. Sherry's program provided the community with a much-needed service, and he wouldn't let committee members run roughshod over him because he happened to be new. They wanted to cut the Hub completely. He wouldn't let them. Sherry trusted him to save it, and save it he would.

After booting up his computer, Garrett hurried down the hall and unlocked Sherry's office door. The report lay where he'd hoped it would. He felt his shoulders relax even as he picked it up, backed out again and closed the door. Then he turned and ran smack into Angel.

"Are you here to sign Dr. Campbell's personal-leave form?" she asked, eyeing the packet of papers in his hand.

"L-leave?" he stammered, creasing the budget sheets in half so Angel wouldn't be able to see what he'd done.

She set her purse on the desk and pulled a blank form out of a cubbyhole. "Just sign the bottom line and I'll fill in the rest. Oh…what should I list as the reason for her absence?"

Garrett gaped at her, then at the paper she'd thrust into his hand along with a pen. "Reason? The truth, of course. Why is she taking the day off?" He half expected Angel to say Sherilyn was accompanying Maria Black to court or something.

Angel crossed her arms and gave him a look that said he must be dense. "Really, Dean Lock. With those gossips in Personnel, you can't want to say she's escorting your son on a field trip."

"She's what?" Garrett dropped the pen. He tried to make sense of Angel's announcement as he searched for the pen. "How? Why…?" he finally managed.

Angel narrowed her eyes, studying him down the length of her nose. "In a message she left on my answering machine at home, she said you knew. She said your ex bowed out and she's replacing her."

"Keith," he growled. "That little monster. I told him not to call her. He must've done it, anyway. That explains why he was so cheerful this morning."

"Does this mean you won't sign Dr. Campbell's leave request?" Angel gave Garrett the evil eye. "No offense, Dean, but you're such a dunce. She really loves your kid—and you, although why is beyond me. No, it's not," she corrected with a wave of her hand. "Women are saps when it comes to picking men."

Garrett was about to protest that Sherry wasn't a sap and, anyway, it was none of Angel's business when the telephone rang. As she reached for it, he scribbled his name on the form and left it for her to handle, deciding it was safer to bail out than get into a discussion that threatened to become far too personal.

At his office door he heard his own telephone. Turning to his secretary, Garrett muttered, "If that's Westerbrook or one of the other committee members, say I have to redo my proposal and I'm going to be late for the meeting."

The woman's cry of alarm halted his steps. Glancing over his shoulder, Garrett saw terror and sorrow and pity cross her face. "In Danville," she said, voice erupting in fits and spurts. "The school bus your son is on skidded off the road and into the Loutre River. The principal is calling all the parents to come to the school and wait for further news."

Garrett watched her hang up the phone as if another man resided inside his skin and had received the awful news. "Keith," he said brokenly, remembering the excited child he'd dropped off at school a little more than an hour ago. "And Sherry," he whispered, thankful somewhere deep in his heart that she'd cared enough for Keith to be there on such short notice. What if he lost them both?

Ashen-lipped, he instructed, "Tell Westerbrook." Then, fearing his knees wouldn't obey the need to get him to Keith's school in one piece, Garrett tore out of the office like a man possessed.

CHAPTER FIFTEEN

THE BUS DRIVER was a round jolly woman of inde-
terminate age. The teacher was so young Sherry
doubted the ink on her certificate had dried yet.
But the kids loved her, and they listened when
she told them to sit and be quiet. Even if it was
beyond the capacity of eight- and nine-year-olds
to stay quiet long. Fifteen minutes into the drive,
the bus pulsed noisily again with their laughter
and excited squeals. Another mother, who accompanied her delicate-looking daughter, glanced at
Sherry, grimaced and pretended to plug her ears.

Attempting to bring order to chaos, the teacher
clapped her hands. "Let's practice the songs we're
doing in our upcoming holiday show. Soft voices,"
she said.

Keith scooted closer to Sherry. "Our program's
on the Friday before Christmas. Will you come?"

"Didn't you invite your mom?"

He leaned his curly head on her shoulder. "Only
Dad. Mom never has time."

It was said with a careless shrug, but Sherry

picked up on his pain. "Remind me when we get home, sport. I'll check my calendar."

"You will? Cool." He sat forward, eyes bright as he joined the other singers.

He had a nice voice. Clear. Pure. Sherry sat back and smiled. Two songs later, she wondered if Garrett knew that his son had a gift for pitch and tone. He must, she decided, losing herself in thoughts of Garrett. Maybe fathers didn't get worked up over things that weren't athletic. She liked to think Garrett would.

The bus slowed to a crawl. Sherry craned her neck to see out the window, which was clouded with condensation. Reaching across Keith, she rubbed a spot clear. It was darker out than when they'd started. She felt a ripple of unease overtake the singers. The bus driver and the teacher appeared deep in conversation. The urgency of their body language communicated itself to Sherry. "Keith," she murmured, leaning close to his ear, "I'm going to the front of the bus for a minute. You stay right here."

He nodded and slid into the chorus of "Rudolph, the Red-nosed Reindeer."

Lurching down the narrow aisle, Sherry determined that their bus had stopped behind the other one. Through the front window, she saw that the highway ahead was underwater.

"Problems?" She dropped into an empty seat

behind the teacher. In answer, the radio crackled and a disembodied voice, presumably from the lead bus, queried whether they should go on or turn back. "Turning here won't be easy," a woman said.

"Your call," advised Mary, the apple-cheeked driver. "Must be raining harder upriver than the forecasters thought. Never seen the Loutre River this high. How deep do you think it is?"

The lead driver didn't respond. Instead, the big yellow bus crept forward. Sherry held her breath as inch by inch the tires churned, soon to be swallowed by swirling, muddy water. As if sensing something amiss, the children let their voices trail off thinly, and silence fell over the interior. Someone began to whimper. The other mother on board, Erica Hanover, tried to console the crying youngster.

Sherry hadn't realized she'd been holding her breath until the companion bus emerged on higher ground beyond the point where water covered the road.

"Well, now. That wasn't so bad," boomed the driver's cheery voice. "This old storm will probably blow out before we head home. Hang on to your seats, kiddos, we're gonna give Lucy Belle here a little bath." The kids all giggled as the woman thrust the bus in gear and lovingly patted the dash.

Sherry made her way back to Keith. She felt the bus skid and cried out in surprise as her thigh smacked a metal seat rim. It hurt, and she almost landed in the lap of a sweet-faced girl whose pigtails wrapped her small head like a crown. "Excuse me," Sherry gasped. Suddenly she was tossed in the opposite direction and fell to her knees. As children began to scream, she crawled uphill to reach Keith. The bus pitched and rolled as she sat down hard and rubbed at a rip in her tights.

Cries of panic escalated. The sound bounced off the ceiling as the bus whirled dizzily. Occupants were tossed first one way, then another. Unsure what was happening, Sherry gripped Keith with one hand and with the other, tried to shield two boys on the opposite side of the aisle. A sheet of water splattered the hole she'd rubbed on the glass earlier. Immediately afterward, the window was slapped by a series of tree branches. With a sick sinking weakness that threatened to bring up the small amount of oatmeal she'd consumed for breakfast, Sherry realized they were no longer on the road.

"Find something solid and hang on, kids!" she shouted. "Stay in your seats and don't let go. We'll ride this out." The bus bucked and shuddered and spun for what seemed an endless amount of time. Sherry had difficulty maintaining a positive face.

She fancied that her whole life passed in a blur. Memories, good, bad and in between skittered through her head. Regrets—yes. She was never going to see her children graduate from Wellmont. Never going to get married so she could *have* kids, even.

And Garrett—he'd be left forever alone because she'd failed to protect the boy he'd entrusted into her care. She met Keith's frightened blue eyes and pinched white face, and vowed if there was any possible way to save him and these other children, she'd use her last breath to do so. For the moment, though, she sheltered as many small bodies as she was physically able to collect. The bumps and shrieks from other parts of the bus told of an appalling lack of adult shelters.

A terrible scrape and screech of metal brought renewed terror to the occupants, prompting wild screams. Then, mercifully, the buffeting stopped and the bus rocked gently as though cradled by invisible arms.

Sherry straightened and put aside Keith and the others who'd clustered in her arms. "Miss Briggs," she called to the teacher above the din, "what is it? Shh, children. Don't anyone move. We're caught on something, I think."

"Looks like we've run aground. No, we're hung up on a tree, maybe," yelled the driver. "The river's raging, but I see land off to the left."

"Does the radio work?" Sherry asked, hope overtaking apprehension. She again ordered the kids in her immediate vicinity to remain seated. Slowly, carefully, she moved forward, checking and attending to injuries as best she could, always wiping away tears. Erica Hanover shook like a leaf, but she tried to calm those closest to her.

After trying several radio frequencies, the white-lipped driver got a faint response. She sliced a hand through the air to quiet the crying. "The other bus reported the accident. All we have to do is sit tight and wait for rescue." She unbuckled the first-aid kit and sucked in a breath when the bus rocked precariously. Taking out a medicated swab, she rolled up her pant leg and wiped a trail of blood that ran down her leg. "Leg might be broken," she muttered, passing Sherry the kit.

Sherry glanced out through the miraculously unbroken glass and into the greedy, sucking floodwater doing its level best to dislodge them from their perch. The young teacher appeared to be in shock. Unless she snapped out of it, that left Sherry, a shaky Erica and a crippled driver to see to the transfer of thirty crying kids, some of them injured. As if things weren't already about as bad as they could get, Keith suddenly launched himself against her thighs and dropped an unexpected bombshell.

"This is all my fault! 'Cause I was bad. Dad

said I couldn't ask you to come—and I did. I sneaked into his room and used his phone. Now he'll be mad."

Sherry's heart had just settled a bit. Keith's declaration sent it skittering again. *Garrett didn't know she'd come with Keith. He hadn't had a change of heart. And if by some chance Angel didn't get her message, no one knew where she was.*

None of which mattered now. Nor did it have any direct bearing on how she felt about Garrett and Keith. She loved them. It was simple, really. Love had always seemed so complicated. It wasn't at all. A studied calm invaded her body as she patted Keith's head. "Honey, I promise your dad won't be mad." She smiled into his teary face. "Trust me," she said. "I want everyone to sit as still as mice. Keith, why don't you and Miss Briggs start another Christmas song?"

Keith brushed a lock of hair from a thin cut that bloodied his forehead and, along with his teacher, sang "Silent Night." At first in a high quavery voice, then growing stronger as the other children joined in.

Sherry shucked off her cardigan and wrapped it around a thin girl who'd begun to shake. She used her scarf to make a sling for a boy whose arm she feared was broken. The teacher rallied and worked the other side of the aisle. She, a gray-faced Erica and Sherry took care of the hurt and the frightened. All thirty kids were gut-wrenchingly scared. So was Sherry.

GARRETT WHEELED into the elementary school parking lot behind a van he knew belonged to the family of one of Keith's classmates. The guy stopped in a bus-loading zone and jumped out. So did Garrett. The woman behind him did the same. Garrett raced into the office in time to hear the principal say the accident had happened about thirty-five minutes east of the city.

"A thirty-five minute drive on a good day," she said. "With this unexpected flash flooding, driving conditions are anything but ideal."

"Has anyone been in contact with the bus driver?" Garrett asked.

"Our other driver. She apparently crossed a low spot in the highway, but when Mary's bus reached the middle of the crossing, a wall of water came out of nowhere and broadsided her bus. Both Montgomery and Warren counties have dispatched rescue crews. News is sketchy, but we must be patient."

Garrett glanced around at the worried faces of the other parents. "Why are we waiting here?" He started elbowing his way to the door.

The principal held up a hand. "Don't do anything foolish, Dr. Lock. The police and volunteer rescue teams are gathering. Rushing up there will only overload highways already devastated by this freak storm."

"Those are our kids," Garrett said emotionally. "How can we sit on our duffs when extra hands may help?"

"Let's go, then," chimed in another man. "My wife planned to go on this trip, but she woke up with the flu. My daughter's alone."

"I have four-wheel drive," announced a father who'd just come in. Most of the men who were present charged out and piled into his vehicle. No one spoke much on the drive. The storm that was supposed to pass over lashed them with dark fury. Garrett conjured up happy visions of Keith and Sherry as if doing so would keep them safe from harm. When they slowed at a railroad track, he remembered Carla. He dragged out his cell phone and placed a call to the bank, only to be informed by someone with a bored voice that both Carla and Crawford were in meetings and had left word they couldn't be disturbed.

Garrett felt unwarranted anger crowd out his good sense. "Tell Carla," he snapped, "that the son she'd promised to be with today is in a school bus trapped in the middle of some river." The man seated on his left supplied the name, which Garrett added before he signed off.

"When the rescue teams reach them," the man

said, "they'll transport any injured kids to St. Louis."

Garrett didn't want to think about injuries. But of course it was a possibility. He paused, admitting how glad he was that Sherry was there to look out for Keith.

When they reached the area, which police had cordoned off, and saw the roughly tumbling debris-filled river that had jumped its banks, Garrett realized injuries were more than a possibility. A shed bobbed past, followed by a car that cartwheeled out of sight around a bend in the out-of-control tributary. His hands shook and his blood froze.

The men jumped from the vehicle and waded toward the rescuers clustered near a boat. Two men dressed in hip waders and yellow raincoats wrestled a small aluminum boat onto a flatbed truck. Two others were unloading motorized rubber rafts from another truck.

"Any updates?" Garrett demanded. "We all have kids on that bus."

One of the men, a grandfatherly type, looked up. "When we got downstream in this boat—" he tapped the aluminum hull "—we saw the bus hung up on a tree growing out of a sandbar. The kids were singing Christmas carols. Beat all I ever seen. The current's dicey. Near impossible to get this baby close. One of the moms, a spunky little gal, busted out a side window and rigged a rope slide from inside. We got maybe twenty kids and a skinny teacher out. Water's icy, though, and some of 'em were cut and bruised. Top of that, a few hit floating debris. Each batch we hauled ashore, rescue vehicles carted 'em off to various hospitals."

"So you got everyone out?" The fear gripping Garrett's stomach uncoiled in a rush.

"Nope. Weren't that lucky. The bus broke loose and shot downriver about a hundred yards. She went under up to the bottom of the windows. Appears to be lodged on a boulder sticking out of a shoal. Still has the spunky mom, a pretty hysterical mom, an injured driver and mebbe ten kids on board. Problem is, the shoal sits smack in the middle of a big eddy. Tossed this puppy around like so much flotsam. They're gonna try rubber rafts. Maybe they'll roll easier with the swells. Don't know what the crew up there'll do if that fails."

The man who'd given Garrett the lift waded close to the two rescuers. "Any way you have names of the kids already taken off the bus?"

The old fellow rubbed his bald pate. "Me'n Joe are headed upriver to get a lady and her cat hanging on a roof. See that gent?" He pointed to a young man working a base radio attached to a Red Cross vehicle. "He can probably give the hospitals a jingle and get names. The kids were already tagged for their field trip, which helped."

Garrett thanked the men. Then the worried dads converged on the man with the radio. After a suspenseful ten minutes, they pored over the list of rescued children. When Garrett read Keith's name, there was no describing the relief he felt. But where was Sherry's? He ran down the scribbled names more slowly. Her name wasn't there.

"Could there be someone who didn't get reported?" he asked the radioman. Garrett held his breath.

"Nope. The hospitals know who they admitted."

"Is it possible someone didn't need admitting? I mean, if she wasn't injured?"

The volunteer on the radio shook his head. "They were all wet and banged up. Even if they were only treated in Emergency, the hospital logged a name."

Garrett's heart plummeted. Did that mean Sherry was still on board? The first man had said a spunky mom, a hysterical one and the bus driver were the only adults left. Of course, he'd have no way of knowing Sherry wasn't some kid's mom. It'd be like her to stay if she thought she could help. Somehow Garrett knew she wasn't the hysterical woman—and that left the "spunky" one. His heart swelled with pride, although he didn't have a right. She was a treasure, and he'd been a fool.

The owner of the four-wheel-drive vehicle touched Garrett's shoulder. "My daughter, Phillip's girl, and Henry's son are on the list. We're driving on up to St. Louis. Since Keith's there, too, I imagine you'll want to ride along."

Garrett was torn. Keith must be frightened and he could be hurt. Garrett had a burning need to go with the men and check his son's fingers and toes as he had done at birth. But if Sherry was still stuck with the other kids, she might need him more. Keith, at least, was safe and in the hands of medical personnel.

"A lady I care about hasn't been accounted for. Would you find Keith there and tell him I'll be along as soon as I can?"

"I will. But what about transportation, Lock?"

"I'll catch a ride on one of the rescue rigs. Either that, or on the other bus. Looks as if they plan to wait out the rescue here."

"Well, good luck. You better believe I won't be so quick to sign one of those permission slips the next time."

"You and me both." Swamped by second thoughts, Garrett nevertheless jogged over to where two men were getting ready to launch one of the motorized rubber boats. "I think my lady is stranded on that bus. You have room for me?" Until he so possessively claimed Sherry, Garrett hadn't realized it was precisely how he felt about her. *His lady.* Now, if he could just be granted the opportunity to tell her, maybe everything would be right with his world again. He *would* get the opportunity. He refused to think otherwise.

The boatmen took one look at Garrett's determined face and made room. "Lose the vest and tie, buddy," said one. "Hope you're not the queasy type. That ol' bus is on mighty shaky ground. She could topple anytime."

"No," said Garrett, as if by force of his will it would stay afloat.

When they docked downstream, he saw that the situation was worse than he'd imagined. The bus, clinging to the shoal by who knew what, rocked and teetered in the gusty wind.

"We're trying to snag the front end with a grappling hook to hold the bus in place," announced a very wet policeman, one of a small force on the riverbank. "The current's too swift. Keeps tossing it back at us. We're worried about sending boats in. Afraid the force of the river will smack them against the bus and push her off that shoal."

"You know who's on board yet?" Garrett could see outlines through the foggy windows, but not clearly enough to make out anyone in particular.

"Three women and about ten kids. Bus driver probably has a fractured leg. She refuses to bail out until all the kids are safe. One lady has a cool head. Sent the injured kids out with the first teams. The ones who're left are in better shape. Sorta. The other adult is frantic. Her kid refused to jump earlier. She wouldn't leave the little girl."

"Better shape, but scared witless." Garrett heard sobbing even as faraway as they were. "Can I borrow that?" He pointed to a bullhorn another man was holding.

"Sure." The man handed it over.

"Sherry! Sherilyn, it's Garrett. If you're on the bus, signal me, please."

Sherry's breath bunched and her throat closed. The tears she'd held at bay up to now gathered behind her eyelids. *Why was he here? Didn't he know Keith had gotten out?* She wanted to shout but was afraid to in case the noise dislodged the bus. Carefully she edged to the open window and waved at the group of rescue workers. Was it her imagination or had the water risen? Why couldn't she remember if it'd come to the rim of the window before? She felt a jiggle and heard a sickening groan. The bus rocked wildly. Sherry stopped waving. She held her breath and waited for the bus to break loose and be at the mercy of the torrential river again. Luckily it held.

From the minute he saw her wave, a cold purpose replaced Garrett's fear. "Look, if you can't shoot that grapple out to the bus, why not swim it out?"

"Are you nuts?" A fireman shook his head.

"The eddy's too fierce. It'd suck a man down. Unless you're a Navy Seal?" His voice filled with hope.

"An experienced hiker is all." Garrett paced the shore, feeling inept and frustrated by the rampaging water. He watched in silence as yet another attempt to launch the grappling hook fell short. It sank like a rock in the massive whirlpool. Retrieving it was no easy task. It kept catching on weeds.

"Look, we can't just stand here and watch them sink, too. How about if I lash a rope around my waist so you can pull me back? Once I reach the eddy, shoot the grapple. I'll find it and hook it to the bus."

"Might work, but it's pretty risky." Two men consulted for a minute. "You'd have to stay clear, yet be close enough to reach the hook. Need to connect it to the front axle. Otherwise, tension from the winch will rip hunks out of the bus."

The rescue-team organizer shook his head. "It's too chancy. That bus could go at any time and the weight'd crush anyone in the vicinity. I can't be responsible for sending you or any other man on such a dangerous task."

"Then I'll be responsible." Garrett stripped off his watch, his jacket and his shirt. He snatched the bullhorn again. "Sherry, honey, I'm swimming out to attach the hook to the bus. If anything happens to me—" his voice faded, then grew stronger "—be there for Keith." Dropping the horn, he looped a rope through his belt and took the plunge. The shock of the cold water almost did him in. He made it to the eddy by sheer force of will and discovered that another rescuer had followed.

Sherry steepled her fingers over her mouth to keep from crying out. Blood thundered in her ears. What Garrett had said sounded like a declaration of love. But maybe she'd read too much into it. People said and did things under duress they wouldn't ordinarily. "Erica...kids," she whispered through her tears. "Let's sing a happy song for those men out there."

And they did. They sang "Santa Claus is Coming to Town." The warbling voices reached Garrett's ears. He focused every ounce of his energy, imagining Christmas with Sherilyn, Keith and Rags. He conjured up a crackling fire in the grate and saw Sherry and Keith smile as they opened gifts. His partner signaled for the grapple. It sailed through the air, landing five feet from Garrett. It took both men to lift it. Three times they tried to connect with the axle. Three times the bus shifted and groaned, and the current drove them away.

"Won't work," shouted the second man.

"One more try," begged Garrett.

A last-ditch effort. Despite their shivering, they

hooked the grapple to a front fender. Weakly they signaled for those on shore to reel them in.

That crew didn't waste any time. While Garrett and the second man were hauled back, others launched two motorized rubber rafts. Their attempt to rescue the remaining kids as they had the others failed. The rafts were too unstable to hover long enough for Sherry and Erica to slide kids down a rope. After four tries, they only managed to transfer two girls into the arms of the frantic boatmen.

Blood flow restored to his chilled limbs thanks to thermal blankets, Garrett paced the shore. "If Sherry slid kids down the rope to a man stationed in the water," he said, "they might get wet, but that guy could pass them out to the boats. I'm game," he added.

"Yeah," said his wet pal. "Alternate boats. Work a round-robin deal, bringing kids ashore two at a time before they get hypothermia."

"What about you?" demanded the team leader. "You'll freeze."

"I'm all ears if you've got a better plan," Garrett said, steely-voiced.

A newcomer sloshed up. "I have two wetsuits in my four-by-four. If the swimmers wear them, they could stay in the river longer and with less danger."

"Nelson, what took you so long getting through

the brush?" said the coordinator. "We only have one volunteer for this crazy scheme. Do we have two?"

Several hands shot up. The chief tagged a young fireman.

Garrett donned the clammy wetsuit and boarded the first of the small boats. About eight feet from the bus, he slid into the freezing water and let it carry him over to the bus. Pumped on adrenaline, he ignored the wind and rain. Rescue efforts went smoothly until his partner handed off the last child and they were left with the three adults—none of whom fit through the window they'd been using as an escape hatch. And the driver had a possible broken leg. The only way the adults could possibly get out would be if they opened the bus door. And the minute they did that, the bus would fill with water, upsetting its tenuous balance.

Precious time ticked away while both boats made a trip to shore and back again. Garrett's teeth clattered. He felt what little body heat he'd conserved slipping away. The first of the yellow rafts was a stone's throw away when Garrett heard a giant rending, like the sound of a train squealing into a station. It didn't take a genius to figure out that the hook, which held by a single prong, had bent the fender out of shape.

Garrett's heart slammed in his chest. To get

this close and then not rescue the woman he loved was unthinkable.

"You ladies get out the door fast and swim toward us," the other rescuer yelled.

"Garrett." Sherry's white face appeared at the window. A window through which water now sloshed over and into the bus. "Mary Jones, our driver, is hurt, and Erica Hanover can't swim."

Garrett heard fright nibbling away at Sherry's courage. "Hang tough a little longer, babe," he said through lips barely able to form the words. "The minute the door opens, shove Mary out. I'll get her into the first boat. My pal will catch Erica. You shoot right behind her. Swim away from the bus as hard as you can and tread water. I'll come back for you." He waited for an answer, not positive he had the strength left to pull any of it off. "Sherry?"

"Y-yes," she answered. "I'm getting rid of my skirt and boots." She didn't tell him she thought she might have broken a rib when she'd heaved the last sturdy boy out the window. Garrett's skin looked blue. He didn't need extra stress.

"Okay. Ladies, prepare for a shock. The river's like the Arctic." Even as he said it, the rain turned to sleet. "When we count to three, open the door."

As if they'd choreographed the scene a hundred times, Sherry followed his instructions. Mary first. Garrett got her in a fireman's hold.

His buddy picked up Erica and swam for the second rubber boat. All might have gone like clockwork if Garrett had been able to boost Mary Jones into the craft as planned. The woman, still fully clothed, simply weighed too much for his tired muscles.

The men in the craft worked diligently to lift her. It proved impossible. In the end, they sped away holding her fast to the side. Garrett had heard Sherry hit the water seconds behind Erica but didn't see where she'd gone while he struggled with the injured driver. As he frantically searched the water around a third craft, a flimsy motorboat he hadn't seen before, a louder noise claimed his sluggish attention. A horrendous screech, a huge sucking sound followed by a loud pop. Garrett saw a fender, severed from the body of the bus, sail through the air over his head. He automatically ducked under the water.

As though from a distance, he heard warning cries from the boat. In spite of the fact that his arms had grown heavy, he surfaced and spotted Sherry's head bobbing in the water. He was so overjoyed to see her he ignored the hiss of the grappling hook that, when freed, snaked the length of the rope. He saw it strike Sherilyn's shoulder.

She and the hook sank without a sound.

Garrett bellowed like a bull as the river sucked

her down. A red splash of blood arced across Sherry's white T-shirt moments before she slipped from his limited view. Fighting off the hands reaching to haul him into the small motorboat, Garrett lunged over to where he'd last seen Sherry. But he hadn't allowed for the widening whirlpool now gobbling up the bus. Each breath he took burned like fire as he dove below the murky brown water.

The men on the boat kept yelling at him to give up. "Come on!" they shouted. "It's too late for the woman. Save yourself!"

They all urged him to stop except for the man who'd helped Garrett rescue the kids. He stripped off a down jacket and dived in again. He forcefully boosted Garrett over the side into the aluminum craft and discovered that Garrett's fingers were twisted into the fabric of the woman's soggy T-shirt. A second rescuer went over the side to assist his teammate.

Several pair of hands worked to pry Garrett's fingers loose. "Let go," growled a ragged voice. "Trust Johnson and Stroud to get your wife into the boat."

Wife! She wasn't, Garrett's fuzzy brain responded. But he loved her and he couldn't let go. He clung even after the other two men rolled her in. They motored to shore as they had done with the bus driver.

The boat struggled to land with its heavy load.

Three more men hit the water to help. Finally, one hauled out a knife and cut Garrett loose from the woman he held in a viselike grip.

Garrett grinned like a fool when at last they tumbled a sodden Sherry into his arms. His joy fled the minute he saw her face—ghostly white and still as death. In spite of first aid rendered on the spot, the jagged cut that ran from Sherry's shoulder to midway down her spine continued to ooze blood.

Medics loaded them into ambulances. They worked to staunch the flow of Sherry's blood while trying to bring up her temperature. And Garrett's.

The sleet, pelting down now in fine white crystals, slicked the roadways and made the drive to the hospital interminable and treacherous.

Garrett huddled under a thermal blanket, shivering in spite of the hot fluids the medics forced him to drink. He doubted he'd ever be warm again. Sherilyn hadn't moved. It wasn't fair. She'd saved the children. How could fate then turn and steal her away? How would he face Keith? What could he possibly say to a kid who, against his father's expressed edict, had innocently talked her into coming on this death trip?

The medic thrust another steaming cup of hot boullion into Garrett's red hands. "Her vitals are weak. But she's exhibiting a strong will to live.

Talk to her. We aren't sure an unconscious person can hear. Some researchers believe they can."

Garrett scooted closer. "I love you," he said softly. "Keith loves you. Help me out here, lady. Don't you dare let go." He bent over and kissed her icy lips.

The female medic who checked the electrodes connected to Sherry's chest smiled at Garrett. "Keep saying what you're saying. Her pulse is getting stronger."

So he kept up a litany of love-talk, at which he'd always been terrible. At long last the medical vehicle pulled beneath the portico of one of St. Louis's finest hospitals. Then trauma teams whisked Sherry in one direction and him in another.

By the time technicians had checked and released Garrett, who had no lingering ill effects, he'd wearied of asking questions about Sherry and getting no answers. He might be a hero, and the nursing staff all claimed he was, but one thing he wasn't—official kin to Sherilyn Campbell. That cold hard fact precluded his getting any information whatsoever. After he'd produced ID, a nurse led him to Keith. She claimed they were inundated with TV cameras and reporters and had to be careful who they let in to see the victims.

Keith hugged his dad and asked tearfully, "Have you seen Sherry?"

"She's here. But they'll only tell her family how she is, son."

"Then call Nolan or Sherry's mom and dad. Are…are you mad 'cause I asked her when you said I shouldn't?"

"I'm not mad, Keith. Still, there'll be consequences for disobeying."

"Okay. But, Dad, if she's hurt bad it's my fault."

"No. She came because she loves you, Keith. We'll find out how she is." Garrett picked up the phone and dialed Sherry's folks. They couldn't believe she'd been in the wreck that headlined local news. "We're coming to St. Louis," Nan said. "We're leaving now."

"No one will tell me a thing," he complained.

"Tell them you're her fiancé," Nan suggested. "That worked for me when we were in college and Ben suffered a football injury."

Garrett coughed and sat down to steady his legs.

"Well, for pity's sake, Garrett, I know you love her. And last night in a dream, I saw her standing at the altar of our church in a wedding gown. It wasn't coincidence that the groom looked a lot like you."

"That'd be a long shot, Nan. Right now I just want her well."

"Long shot? Nolan told Ben you and Sherry

were both AWOL from campus today. He and Emily wondered if you two had eloped."

"A grapple struck her. I'm really worried," he confessed in a thin voice.

"Have faith, Garrett. We'll be there in an hour and get you in to see her."

Word on Sherry's condition came sooner and from a surprising source. Carla and Crawford popped into Keith's room unannounced.

"Keith!" they exclaimed. "We were told you were fine. But your leg?"

"Sherry handed me down the rope. I fell and hit something in the water. A big rock, maybe. Sherry's the one hurt bad." Tears trickled down his pale cheeks. "They won't tell Dad nothin'."

Carla and her husband glanced at Garrett. "We just saw her—in Emergency," Carla said. "She asked about you and Keith. They'd just sewn her up apparently. She was fine enough to give me a lecture about parental responsibility."

Carla sat beside Keith and held his hand. Her eyes filled with tears, and Crawford gripped her shoulder. "You've no idea what hearing about this did to me. Learning that neither Garrett nor the hospital could reach me really shook me up. Garrett, Keith—I've decided not to pursue full custody. My lifestyle didn't allow for motherhood eight years ago and if anything, demands on my time are even greater now. You're part of me, Keith. I don't want to lose touch again, but I have to face facts. All I can ever be is a part-time mother." She sobbed quietly. "I want you to visit us whenever possible. And Garrett—" she faced him "—you've done a fabulous job of raising our son."

Keith gave a whoop, then said with more decorum, "You're okay, too, Mom."

Crawford started to speak, but the door opened and a nurse wheeled Sherry in. "Keith," she gasped. "Your leg? They just told me you'd been admitted."

"Yes," the nurse said dryly. "Dr. Campbell should be in her own room, but she refused to go until we brought her by to see this young man and his father. It's against the rules, you know."

Garrett sprang from his chair and rushed to her side.

Keith sat up in spite of his elevated leg. "My broke leg don't hurt, Sherry. You saved me and all the other kids. You were right, too. Dad's not mad that I invited you."

"Keith." Garrett wagged a finger.

"Well—" the boy looked contrite "—he said I have to lose privileges 'cause I went behind his back. But...he didn't sound all *that* mad."

Carla lobbed a gaze between her son and Sherry. "Has anyone told you, Dr. Campbell, that you'd make a good mother? And wife," she said pointedly to her ex.

Sherry gaped at the woman. "I, uh, know people who wouldn't agree." Was she so transparent that Carla saw right through her half-baked attempt to hide her love for Garrett and Keith?

Crawford, the emotionless banker, certainly did. "A client of mine—the doctor who examined Garrett—said he drove them nuts asking about you, Ms. Campbell. Perhaps Garrett'll give us some time alone with Keith while he makes sure you're settled in your room."

"Dr. Lock can stop by 302—briefly," said the nurse who was already backing Sherry's wheelchair out the door. "I figure we have fifteen minutes max to get her into bed before that painkiller kicks in and sends her nighty-night."

"She's looking pretty rocky," Garrett said hesitantly. "Maybe I shouldn't go."

"Do…please." Sherry held up a beseeching hand, then let it fall quickly to her lap. "Unless you'd rather not." Her lashes fluttered down to cover her eyes.

Garrett thought she looked terribly pale, although she had more color than she'd had during the drive to the hospital.

Carla nudged Garrett forward. "Quit looking like a lovesick calf caught in a hailstorm and go get her."

His lips curled in a sheepish grin. "That noticeable, huh?"

"Yeah," Crawford, Keith and Carla all said together.

Garrett frowned at his son. "You're eight years old. What do you know about lovesick looks?"

"I'm almost nine. I watch TV. And you've looked that way since you and Sherry had a fight. Me'n Rags love Sherry, too, so don't blow this, huh, Dad?"

"We did not fight," Garrett said huffily, hitching up jeans dried stiff from the silt in the river. What a way to look when a man went to propose to the woman he loved. But then, from that first stormy night they'd met in Kansas, nothing about his relationship with Sherilyn Campbell had been exactly normal.

He entered Sherry's room as the nurse slipped out. "Talk fast," Sherry muttered, her speech slightly slurred.

Garrett gazed at her sweet face. Her short spiky hair made a two-toned splash against the pillow. He remembered how silky it'd felt against his palms that night on the *Ozark Queen*. Afraid of hurting her, he touched the back of her hand—not the one sprouting the IV.

Her smile was off-kilter. Garrett wondered if he'd already lost her to the sedative. But she crooked her finger at him, then patted a spot on her bed.

He sat carefully. "We have a lot to talk about, you and I. Earlier I thought I'd lost you." His voice broke. Nipping in a sharp breath, he attempted to laugh. "Takes getting kicked in the head to show some guy what a fool he's been."

Sherry covered his hand with her smaller one. "You were kicked in the head? By whom? When?"

"Figuratively speaking," he said gruffly, threading their fingers and bringing hers to his lips. "You've given me no reason to believe you still consider March a perfect time for new beginnings," he murmured, "but…well, I love you. Will you marry me?"

How she responded so quickly for someone in her shape, Sherry would never know. She lunged forward, flung her arms around Garrett's neck and smothered his lips with a kiss aimed at cutting off any objections he might have raised.

"I take it that means yes," he gasped when they were forced apart to breathe.

"It'd better," chorused Nan and Ben Campbell from the open doorway. "The doctor downstairs said he'd ordered strict bed rest for Sherry. I got the feeling," said Ben dryly, "that the old duffer had something far less strenuous in mind."

Sherry slid back into bed, a silly smile flitting along her lips. "What lousy timing. A marriage proposal at last, and I can't stay awake. But I'm holding you to this, Lock." With that, her lashes drifted down and she was fast asleep.

EPILOGUE

THE CITY HOSTED a parade to honor the hero and heroine who'd kept the local school-bus accident from going down in the annals of history as a tragedy. The parade was front-page news.

As a rule, parades made dull stories. So did averted tragedies. What Sherry Campbell and Garrett Lock provided was better, as far as the reporters were concerned. A love story. The whole world, they soon discovered, loved a love story. At least, the people of Columbia did.

Because the couple had decided on a spring wedding, Garrett and Sherry had reporters dogging them for four months. Also wedding consultants, jewelers, caterers, florists and photographers. Merchants weren't trying to *sell* them services; shop owners begged to *give* them every aspect of a fairytale wedding.

"Shall we elope?" Garrett suggested hopefully. He and Sherry had just sneaked out the back door of the plastic surgeon's who'd conducted a final exam on her now-healed shoulder.

"Are you serious?" Sherry asked as they piled into the back of her father's van.

By pre-arrangement, Ben and Nan Campbell had brought Keith, Megan and Mark along. The whole group was headed to a celebration dinner hosted by Nolan and Emily because an editor was interested in their manuscript, *Who Really Settled the West?*

Garrett hooked one arm around his son's shoulders and tucked Sherry into the crook of the other. "Well, eloping's starting to sound good...."

"But if you 'loped," Keith said, his bright smile fading, "my class—all the kids you helped off the bus—they wouldn't get to be ushers or hand out groom's cake like me and Mark did at Camp and Emily's wedding."

"True," Sherry said. "The kids are looking forward to taking part in our wedding."

"Mom promised I could buy my first pair of high heels to wear when I light your candles," Megan wailed.

"If you eloped," Nan gasped, "that beautiful gown Yvette talked her merchandiser into giving Sherry would go to waste."

"True," Sherry agreed. "But Yvette's apology for starting those rumors means more to me than any gown."

"Speaking of rumors..." Ben smiled at them both in the rearview mirror. "I hear all this publicity has set your board of regents on their ears. In the entire history of Wellmont, they've never let spouses work together in the same department—until now."

Sherry batted her eyes at Garrett. "Sheldon March made it very clear that while I may have helped a few kids out of the bus, you, my love, are the real hero. And since you saved my life, Garrett, he strongly implied I should never oppose you on budget matters again."

Garrett started to snort indignantly, then reared back and favored his soon-to-be-bride with a steely blue gaze worthy of a Texan. "Sheldon's right, little lady, and don't you forget it."

Sherry sputtered. "I was kidding!"

"Me, too." Garrett leaned over and kissed her. Once. Twice. The third time she melted against him with a sigh.

"Those kisses, Lock. That's how you got me to make the Hub co-ed." She held out her left hand and studied the engagement ring Garrett had placed there the day after he proposed—when she was still in the hospital. "Remember how much Angel hated the idea? She called me a traitor and threatened to wax the floor with your butt. Um, Angel changed her tune," she said for the benefit of the others. "After Garrett advertised our new counseling services and twenty divorced and single dads signed up the first day."

"Is that why Angel agreed to be one of your bridesmaids?" he asked.

"Probably. So there's another reason we can't elope."

"I'm tasting defeat, but refresh my memory on why else we shouldn't do it," Garrett muttered.

"To show whatever jerk left that article on my desk about failed second marriages that we're going to beat the odds."

"You'll succeed if you two stay away from water. Bad history there," Nan Campbell put in. "Better add something in your vows about keeping your feet on terra firma."

"Can't," Sherry said. "The owner of the *Ozark Queen* saw our picture in the paper and he offered us the boat for a week."

"Does that 'clude me?" Keith piped up.

Garrett vividly recalled the last trip. Silver moonlight dancing off the water. Sherry's slinky purple dress—and everything that occurred thereafter.

Her thoughts similar, Sherry straightened Garrett's tie.

"Uh…cough…cough…uh," he wheezed.

"Yippee! Dad said yes! I can go. Those are the noises he makes when he wants to say no, but ends up saying yes."

"Not this time, Keith." Garrett's voice was strangled. "Honeymoons are strictly a party for two. You and Rags will stay with Mark, Megan and Pilgrim. But I promise, son. One day soon Sherry and I will take you on a river boat. It'll be our first trip as a family."

Keith bounced happily up and down. "Then I'll be like Mark. I'll have it all."

Mark made a face. "Not quite. You still won't have a dorky sister."

"Oh." Garrett tweaked Sherry's nose. "I think Professor Campbell and I might be willing to try and correct that oversight."

Her lips curved in a satisfied smile. "If that's a challenge, Dr. Lock…I accept."

* * * * *

REQUEST YOUR FREE BOOKS!
2 FREE WHOLESOME ROMANCE NOVELS IN LARGER PRINT
PLUS 2 FREE MYSTERY GIFTS

✻✻✻✻✻✻✻✻✻✻✻✻✻✻✻✻✻✻✻✻✻✻✻✻✻

HEARTWARMING™
❋❋❋❋❋❋❋❋❋❋❋❋❋❋❋❋❋❋❋❋❋❋❋❋❋

Wholesome, tender romances

YES! Please send me 2 FREE Harlequin® Heartwarming Larger Print novels and my 2 FREE mystery gifts (gifts worth about $10). After receiving them, if I don't wish to receive any more books, I can return the shipping statement marked "cancel." If I don't cancel, I will receive 4 brand-new larger-print novels every month and be billed just $4.74 per book in the U.S. or $5.74 per book in Canada. That's a savings of at least 21% off the cover price. It's quite a bargain! Shipping and handling is just 50¢ per book in the U.S. and 75¢ per book in Canada.* I understand that accepting the 2 free books and gifts places me under no obligation to buy anything. I can always return a shipment and cancel at any time. Even if I never buy another book, the two free books and gifts are mine to keep forever.

161/361 IDN FVXV

Name _____ (PLEASE PRINT) _____

Address _____ Apt. # _____

City _____ State/Prov. _____ Zip/Postal Code _____

Signature (if under 18, a parent or guardian must sign)

Mail to the **Harlequin® Reader Service:**
IN U.S.A.: P.O. Box 1867, Buffalo, NY 14240-1867
IN CANADA: P.O. Box 609, Fort Erie, Ontario L2A 5X3

* Terms and prices subject to change without notice. Prices do not include applicable taxes. Sales tax applicable in N.Y. Canadian residents will be charged applicable taxes. Offer not valid in Quebec. This offer is limited to one order per household. Not valid for current subscribers to Harlequin Hearwarming larger-print books. All orders subject to credit approval. Credit or debit balances in a customer's account(s) may be offset by any other outstanding balance owed by or to the customer. Please allow 4 to 6 weeks for delivery. Offer available while quantities last.

Your Privacy—The Harlequin® Reader Service is committed to protecting your privacy. Our Privacy Policy is available online at www.ReaderService.com or upon request from the Harlequin Reader Service.

We make a portion of our mailing list available to reputable third parties that offer products we believe may interest you. If you prefer that we not exchange your name with third parties, or if you wish to clarify or modify your communication preferences, please visit us at www.ReaderService.com/consumerschoice or write to us at Harlequin Reader Service Preference Service, P.O. Box 9062, Buffalo, NY 14269. Include your complete name and address.

HWDIR13

LARGER-PRINT BOOKS!

GET 2 FREE LARGER-PRINT NOVELS PLUS 2 FREE MYSTERY GIFTS

Love Inspired®

Larger-print novels are now available...

LILPDIR13

ReaderService.com

Manage your account online!

- Review your order history
- Manage your payments
- Update your address

*We've designed
the Harlequin® Reader Service
website just for you.*

Enjoy all the features!

- Reader excerpts from any series
- Respond to mailings and
  special monthly offers
- Discover new series available to you
- Browse the Bonus Bucks catalog
- Share your feedback

Visit us at:

ReaderService.com

RS13